When Wolves Breathe

KIRSTEN GALE

For those who stood beside me when the words flowed
and when they refused to come at all.
To my family and friends—old and new—
your love, patience, belief, and quiet encouragement
carried me through more than you know.
This story exists because you did.

Trigger Warnings

Wolves who do not respect personal boundaries
Blood. Not metaphorical.
Psychological manipulation presented with confidence
Unreliable narrators who insist they're the reasonable one

Childhood trauma that did not stay in childhood
Sharp objects used in ways HR would not approve of
Adults making catastrophic decisions
Nursery rhymes that have taken a dark turn
Abandoned buildings with deeply questionable energy
Breathing that signals danger, not romance
Grief that festers
Obsession disguised as devotion
Law enforcement that may or may not be helpful
Familial bonds under extreme pressure
Emotional damage, artfully arranged
Situations where someone absolutely should not have gone in there

Reader discretion is advised.
If you prefer tidy endings and stable minds, this may not be the forest for you.

PROLOGUE

The cold concrete of the Bandon warehouse felt unforgiving against my frail, shivering body huddled beneath a tattered blanket soaked with the dampness of the Coquille River. The chains bit into my ankles, sharp and unyielding, their weight a constant reminder of my captivity. My breaths came rapid and shallow, each one a struggle against the heavy, moldy air. My eyes, wide and restless, darted across the shadows, searching for threats I felt but couldn't see. The warehouse had a pulse—a low hum of danger that thrummed in the walls, in the damp air, and in the creaks of the old beams overhead.

I whispered, "Humpty Dumpty sat on a wall," my voice fragile and fragmented, barely holding my shattering mind together. The rhyme echoed off the moss-covered walls, lost to the dampness before reaching anyone who might have cared. It had become my daily ritual, that childish chant—a comforting thread I held onto as the world around me dissolved into chaos. I recited it each morning—or at least I thought it was morning, since no light penetrated the boarded-up windows. Time felt like a ghost there, slipping away like the current of a river.

My mind unraveled, and hallucinations began to emerge. Outside, I saw wolves prowling the dunes, their eyes shining like the glassy river surface under the moon. A child's face appeared in the shadows of my thoughts, her lips whispering inaudibly. My heart ached as I held the frayed cloth, its faded fibers the only remnant of a stolen life. I struggled to recall her name, but it slipped away, lost in the fog of years chained by abuse. The cloth was my anchor, yet it wasn't enough to bring me back.

The faint hum of a boat's engine echoed through the tunnel into my concrete cell, accompanied by muffled voices that made my heartbeat quicken. Over time, I had come to recognize that the low drone was a sign of his coming. I focused my gaze, straining through the darkness as a tall, broad-shouldered figure entered, limping with uneven steps like a wounded animal. He muttered, "Baa, baa, black sheep," his words looping as if in a twisted prayer, a routine as familiar as my own chants. He checked my chains, tugging them just enough to make me wince. For a moment, my eyes flickered with recognition—perhaps—but that feeling was lost amid the chaos of my thoughts.

Using a bloody nail, I etched a wolf's paw print into the wall, my hands trembling. "Wolves... they took everything," I whispered, my voice faint. It was another ritual—marking the passing of days or nights—with those rough carvings. The wall was filled with them, a jagged map of my fear and defiance.

He paused, gloved finger tracing the new paw print, his silence forming a silent pact—a secret I couldn't grasp. His cold eyes, like the depths of the river, fixed on my sunken face, unreadable. Then he casually tossed a protein bar onto the ground, the wrapper crinkling softly. I quickly grabbed it, my movements frantic, and sank against the wall. I hurriedly tore open the wrapper and ate small bites, savoring each crumb while my stomach churned with hunger and fear. Uncertain of when he might return with more, I rationed it carefully, stopping before it was finished.

He gave my chains a slow, deliberate tug that sent a jolt of pain through my legs, then slammed the door shut as he slunk back into the depths of the tunnel. The boat's hum faded, leaving only an eerie stillness. Then, a wolf's howl cut through the darkness, sharp and chilling, before falling silent—it had to be my imagination, more like hallucinations. The air became heavier, pressing against my chest, as if the warehouse itself lost its breath. I curled tighter under the damp blanket, my eyes scanning the shadows, waiting for the next sound, the next threat, the next piece of my mind to slip away.

1
Alexis

G ranite pressed into my palm, its unforgiving chill seeping into my skin and settling deep in my bones, echoing the ache splitting through my chest. If not for the three men standing beside me—steady, watchful—I would have crumpled where I stood, folding into myself and sobbing until the world blurred away. Fortunately, I told myself I was more composed than I had been in the past two years during our visit to this solemn place.

Asher pulled me up by my arm, then wrapped his arms around me, holding me close with his comforting warmth. I watched his face as tears rolled down, mixing with the light rain. He looked away from the words on the headstone, then offered a small smile before bending to kiss me softly. He tasted of salt and peppermint.

"You guys are a bunch of softies," Cooper said, breaking the silence as he threw his arms around Tanner and Asher's shoulders, pulling us into a tight huddle. I had grown to love this about him—he would call us soft, yet he was the biggest of all.

"Come on, man, you reek," Tanner proclaimed as he tried to pull away, which only made Cooper squeeze us tighter—if that was even possible.

Cooper sniffed his armpit and laughed. "Woo, that is rough. Sorry guys, I didn't have time to shower after going to the gym."

"You know they have showers at the gym, right?" Asher said, effectively breaking us out.

Tanner took a small journal from his pocket, ripped out a page, and placed it next to Sadie's name as he wiped the moisture from his face onto the sleeve of his jacket. This was his third poem for her since she was taken from us, and each one had become longer and more polished. Considering his success in his advanced language arts classes, this was no surprise.

"Tan, why don't you put it in here?" Cooper said as he produced a metal-framed picture he had painted of all of us. Off to the side, he had another slot for Tanner's poems to slide into. The frame had two stakes, and he pushed it into the ground above her headstone. "I made it in art class, and water won't get inside."

Yep...the biggest softy.

Tanner was crying hard now. "Thanks, Coop." He slid the poem inside.

We were silent as we stared at the painted picture. He had captured our likeness very well, but with a depth of longing I couldn't describe.

"Wow," I breathed. "You've improved so much, Coop." My chest tightened. A fleeting thought about what life could have been like if Sadie had been in our lives crossed my mind. We wouldn't be in this creepy graveyard.

"Thanks. I couldn't have done it without all of you."

That was likely true. We all relied on each other over the past few years. If I could choose, I'd still be hiding under the rock I willingly pulled myself under during the first six months of college, but that was a losing battle with these three, especially Asher.

It was still there. The ache, the memories, and no matter how much time went by, the pain would still be there.

Tanner kissed his gloved fingertips, then placed them on Sadie's painted form. "Let's go. Mom and Dad are waiting for us."

Gold Beach always seemed colder to us when we returned from college. Each year that passed meant we spent less time visiting. Austin had the warmth we needed in ways beyond just the weather.

I held Asher's hand tightly, warm in mine, as we silently walked through the graveyard, the only sound being the crunch of our feet on the crisp December grass.

"Have you both found out if you got into the internship program yet?" Tanner asked, kicking a rock down the hill.

Asher and I exchanged a quick glance and shared a small smile. He squeezed my hand tighter. "We did. Found out last night before our flight. We got into the summer program."

Cooper slapped us both on the back, which made me stumble, and I was thankful I didn't like heels. "Sorry, Lex. I'm just so proud of you two. You'll both make such great advocates."

The last three years have been both incredible and challenging. After Sadie and Luke's deaths, returning to high school in Gold Beach became overwhelming for me. Despite being regarded as a hero for defeating Nathan and a corrupt detective, I was still subject to whispers and stares whenever I went into town. I ended up staying with the Finn's and earned my GED while becoming a recluse. Asher needed time to recover as well and decided to turn down Princeton, citing that it was more his father's dream than it was his. So, we didn't waste time; both Asher and I began taking online college courses before deciding that the Four Blind Mice would move east to Texas for college.

We passed under the arches at the entrance to the cemetery, where we saw Keith and Tami waiting for us in their cherry red Cadillac Escalade.

The sky bled streaks of pink and gold, fraying against a bruised blue canvas as our car snaked along the coastal road toward Finn's house, the horizon swallowing the last light. Shadows slithered across the dunes beyond, coiling like whispers of the Rogue River's hunger. Up front, Keith and Tami leaned close, their hushed murmurs a sharp, secretive hum that prickled the air—words too faint to grasp but thick with emotion. The rest of us, crammed in the back, sat in brittle silence, our lips locked by growing irritation. Keith's endless probing, his therapist's mask, had cut too deep into wounds we shielded. Tami was no better—her eyes would well at the faintest echo of that cursed November, her stifled sobs, a jagged reminder of the losses buried in the cave's shadows.

Tami turned, and her manicured hand touched my knee. The contrast between her new polish and her aged hand reminded me of my mother's twisted hands. "How's school going?"

I shifted slightly, which made her jerk her hand away. The lump in my throat felt like a frog squirming to get out.

Asher noticed my discomfort and then draped his arm over my shoulders, squeezing me against him. "It's good, Mom."

She must have realized he wasn't giving her more as she offered us a tight smile and turned around, whispering something to Keith. It made me uneasy, and I couldn't tell if I had changed more or if she had since Sadie's murder.

As we drove down the driveway to the Finns' house, a wave of emotions overwhelmed me, and the frog in my throat decided to go down. I coughed as Asher opened the door. As I pulled my gloves back, I took a deep breath and stepped out onto the frosted-covered concrete.

There were too many memories here. Sadie's presence still lingered like a ghost with an unresolved life, clinging to Earth. Maybe that's why Tami and Keith seemed to have aged so quickly.

They were haunted.

And a sense of being hunted refused to let me go.

2
Asher

I gazed at the frosted edges surrounding the painted glass of the windows while standing in the driveway. The house appeared as aged as my parents. What was once a refuge of warm childhood memories now felt haunted by ghosts.

"Asher?" Alexis took my hand, her gloves feeling cool against my skin. When I glanced at her, her face had a greenish tint. "I need a moment alone before I go inside." She nodded toward the house.

The cycle felt inevitable every time the road led back to Gold Beach. She nestled against my chest, her frame tense with a familiar anxiety, her head tucked under my chin. She was the strongest person I knew, having spent three years conquering the ghosts of her past, yet this town weighed on her shoulders like a physical burden. The nightmares always resurfaced here, and though she eventually found the strength to overcome them, the immediate toll was more devastating. She tried to hide the signs to spare me worry, but the trauma's stress always threatened to reignite her bulimia—a relapse I dreaded more than anything, knowing how hard she had fought to leave that battle behind.

"I'll bring our things in. You do what you gotta do." I kissed the top of her head. She pulled away and gave me a tight smile as I watched a tear slip from her eye. She wiped it away quickly, then walked toward the tree line, purposely avoiding the carved ladybug tree I so desperately wanted to cut down years ago.

"Ash, she'll be okay," Coop said, slapping me on the back. "It's freezing out here." He grabbed his bag from the back and jogged inside.

Tan stood there, staring at the setting sun, mentally cataloging the bleeding hues and shifting light to translate them into poetry later. "I don't understand why we torture ourselves by coming back here. It affects all of us, especially Lex."

"Yeah." There was no denying it, we all had a better life in Austin. No ghosts haunted us.

As we stepped into the house, it remained dark even though the lights were on. The only signs of youth were the old pictures still hanging on the walls. Nothing had changed since three years ago.

I heard raised voices coming from the living room. When I walked in, Aunt Kate was sitting on the couch, wrapped in a blanket. She'd come every year to pay respect to Sadie's grave; however, she usually didn't stay.

"I don't want to see her. Why are you okay with her being in your lives?" Kate's face turned red, and she stopped talking when she saw me. "Hey, Asher. It's so good seeing you. You look like a man now." Her tone turned sticky-sweet. It was fake.

She walked over and tried to hug me. I stepped back. "Are you talking about Alexis?" The blanket slipped off her shoulders, and she looked at Mom. "She's my girlfriend."

Tan walked in from the hallway. "And she's family. Our sister." He ran his hand through his hair and matched my stance.

Coop paused while looking in the fridge, staring at us. The guy was always hungry and couldn't wait for dinner.

Kate's face contorted into something fierce. "She's the reason my Sadie is dead." She balled up her fist. "If it weren't for that girl, she'd still be here."

That. Girl?

I dropped our bags on the floor, then took a small step closer as I weighed my words. Dad opened his mouth, then shut it. He knew Kate was off her rocker, but I couldn't let her keep thinking this was Alexis's fault.

"Sadie's dead," Kate's face twitched at my tone. "Because of the Rhyme Reaper, who was Nathan, who is dead." I looked around. Coop was by Mom, his arm over her shoulder. "Our family is in pieces because someone's choices took Sadie away from us. We can't let them keep taking our happiness, or Nathan wins. I refuse to let any of that happen."

I turned around, shoved my beanie on my head, and slammed the door behind me as I left. Pinks and purples streaked the sky as I headed toward Alexis. I paused at the ladybug-carved tree. Where Alexis found the image disgusting, I found it beautiful because it represented her strength. She kept doubting herself, doubting how amazing she was.

When I exited the tree line, Alexis was kneeling by the edge of the cliff. Her face was tilted toward the sky, and her long, wavy hair fell down her back, nearly touching the ground. Beautiful.

She was talking, but I could barely hear her over the crashing waves against the rocks. "I don't want to be here." She was sobbing now.

Was she going to jump?

She put her hands on the ground and looked over the edge. I rushed over and grabbed her shoulders, sliding behind her on the ground. I pulled her into my lap.

"Ash, what are you doing? You scared me!" she said as she tried to pull away from me.

"I got you, Lex!"

Her body tensed briefly, then relaxed as she turned to face me. Her eyes, rimmed with red, showed exhaustion rather than desperation—an accumulated weariness since we boarded the plane. "I wasn't... I wouldn't..." she began, but then she shook her head and pressed her face into my chest. The wind howled around us, carrying salty spray from the waves below, and I held her more firmly, my heart racing from that fleeting moment of fear.

"I know," I murmured into her hair, though part of me wasn't sure. Gold Beach had a way of reopening old wounds, making them bleed again. "I just... saw you there, and my mind went to the worst place. Sorry."

She pulled back slightly, wiping her cheeks with the back of her glove. "It's this place. It feels like Sadie's everywhere, and Nathan... even though he's gone, it's like he's still breathing down my neck." Her voice cracked on "breathing," and I felt a chill that had nothing to do with the December air. Wolves breathe quietly before they pounce—that stray thought flickered through my mind, unbidden, like a warning from some buried case file.

We sat there for a few minutes as the sky turned deep indigo and the cold seeped through our coats. "Come on," I finally said, helping her to her feet. "Let's get inside before Coop eats everything in sight."

She managed a weak laugh, clasping my fingers as we trudged back through the tree line. The ladybug carving stared from the shadows, and I squeezed her hand, guiding her away from it. As we walked, I told her briefly that Kate was there and, in a mood, but I kept her from the details. By the time we reached the house, the lights in the windows shone warmer, but the earlier tension still gnawed at me like undigested dread.

Inside, the air was thick with the smell of Mom's lasagna baking—her favorite comfort food for these visits. Aunt Kate was nowhere to be seen; maybe she'd stormed off after my outburst. Coop and Tan sat at the kitchen table, Coop halfway through a sandwich, while Dad paced the living room with his phone pressed to his ear. Mom hovered by the counter, her eyes flicking between us as we entered.

"Alexis, honey," Mom said, her voice gentler than before, tinged with that therapist caution Dad always used. She looked at Dad, who nodded subtly and ended his call. "We need to talk to you. Both of you, actually."

Alexis tensed beside me, her grip on my hand tightening. "What's wrong? Is this about Kate?"

"No, no," Dad said, waving it off, though his face looked drawn, older than when we'd arrived. "She left a bit ago—needed some space. This is... something else. Something we've been holding onto for a while."

Mom took out a bulky pile of envelopes from a sideboard drawer, the kind bound with rubber bands and stored away. Their edges were yellowed, postmarks indicating they were years old. She placed them on the table carefully, as if they might bite. "These are for you, Alexis. Over the past three years. We... we weren't sure if you were ready. But now that you both are here and things are settling, we decided it's time."

I huffed. "You decided? Seriously."

Dad was about to say something, but Mom placed her hand on his shoulder, effectively stopping him.

Alexis stared at the stack, her face paling. The top envelope bore a return address I recognized immediately—Two Rivers Correctional Institution. Where Ronny Moore, Nathan's dad, was incarcerated for aiding in his wife's death with Alexis's mom. "Letters? From Ronny?"

Mom nodded, her eyes welling. "He's been writing. Apologies, mostly. Stories about Nathan as a kid. We read the first few—to make sure they were safe—but we kept them from you. For your protection."

"I'm not that fragile. You shouldn't have kept these from me. And you shouldn't have opened them." Alexis reached out, her fingers trembling as she picked up the top one. The flap was already slit open. She pulled out the folded paper, her breath hitching as her eyes scanned the first lines. "Oh God... Asher, look at this."

I leaned in, my blood turning to ice. Scrawled at the bottom, in shaky handwriting that didn't match the rest: *We need to talk. I know who your father is.*

Another wound to be ripped open, and I couldn't shake the dread that was lurking.

3
Alexis

The stack of letters felt heavier in my hands than it should have, as if each envelope carried the weight of secrets I'd spent years trying to bury. Ronny Moore—Nathan's dad, the man who'd raised a monster and then disappeared into the fallout. And now, these words from him, hidden by Keith and Tami like some fragile artifact they thought I couldn't handle. They called it protection. But sitting at the Finns' kitchen table, with the lasagna forgotten in the oven and everyone's eyes on me, it felt more like a cage.

Asher stood behind me, his hand resting on my shoulder, warm and steady as usual. Yet even his comforting touch couldn't keep the cold creeping up my back as I opened the first letter. The paper was cheap, prison-issued, dated two years earlier. Ronny's handwriting was neat and almost formal at first, expressing regret for Nathan's actions and apologizing for the pain he had inflicted on Sadie, Luke, me—everyone. "I raised him wrong," he confessed. "Should have noticed the signs. As a boy, he harmed animals—stray cats in the yard, birds with broken wings. I would find them buried behind the shed, twisted as if they had suffered. I blamed neighborhood kids, but deep down... I knew."

The next letter was a blur of childhood stories. Stories about Nathan as a kid: quiet, too quiet, always reciting rhymes under his breath like prayers. "He had this old nursery rhyme book your mother gave me once," one letter said. "I wore it out, pages dog-eared. I thought it was innocent."

Unbelievable. How could a father miss that? Or maybe he didn't miss it—he just looked away, like everyone else in Gold Beach, whispering and watching the cave.

By the third letter, the words blurred. More apologies, pleas for forgiveness, hints at regrets he couldn't voice. And then, buried in the middle of one: "Go look in the old shed behind the house. Dug up things Nathan hid there—tokens, a book that matches yours. Proof of what he was. You need to see it."

Tokens? My mind flashed to the ladybug carvings, the rhymes etched in blood, and all the people he'd murdered. Had he taken things from them? I shoved the letter back into the envelope, my hands shaking. Ronny knew who my father was—he'd scrawled it like a taunt. If he thought this would wait, he was wrong.

"I have to see him," I said, my voice cutting through the silence. Asher's grip tightened, and I looked up to find Tami's eyes wide and Keith frozen mid-pace.

"Lex, we've only been here a few hours," Asher said softly, kneeling beside me. "It's late. We can plan this..."

"No." I stood, the chair scraping across the floor like a scream. "I'm not wasting time in this town. Gold Beach already took enough from me. Tomorrow, first thing, I'm going to Two Rivers Correctional Institution. He knows who my father is—he owes me that much."

Coop glanced up from his half-eaten sandwich, exchanging a look with Tan. "You sure, Lex? Ronny's... not stable. And jail visits aren't exactly a walk in the park."

"I don't care." My voice cracked, but I held firm. Three years in Austin had built me up—college, internships, nights with Asher when the nightmares faded. But here? It all unraveled. Sadie's ghost in the walls, Nathan's shadow in every rhyme. I couldn't linger, letting it pull me under again. "If Ronny's got answers, I want them now. Before we leave this godforsaken place for good."

Asher searched my face, his eyes dark with worry, yet he nodded. "Okay. We'll go together."

The room grew quiet afterward, the scattered letters on the table seeming like accusations. I headed to the guest room—our old shared space, still frozen in time with Sadie's posters on the wall—and pulled the blankets over me. Asher's arm settled around me soon after. Yet sleep slipped away. Ronny's words haunted me: harmed animals buried behind the shed, a book that matches yours.

Morning couldn't come fast enough.

The drive to Two Rivers the next day was a blur of coastal fog and silent tension, Asher's hand on my knee the only anchor. The prison loomed like a concrete beast, razor wire glinting under the weak winter sun. Security checks dragged on—IDs, pat-downs, the cold stare of guards—but finally, I sat at the visitation booth, the plexiglass divider smudged and impersonal.

Ronny shuffled in on the other side, older than I remembered, his dark face gaunt, eyes hollow. He picked up the phone, his voice raspy through the receiver. "Alexis. You came. It's good to see you."

"Cut the crap, Ronny. Just tell me," I said directly. "Who is my father?"

He leaned forward, a ghost of a smile twisting his lips. "Let's talk. How are you doing?"

"I'm not interested in small talk, Ronny. You obviously had more to say to me than I do." I pushed the pile of his letters toward the glass.

His proud smile fell as he noticed most of them hadn't been opened. "So you really don't care what I have to say."

"I'm only here for one answer." I spoke through clenched teeth, my determination sharpening with each word, and asked again, "Who is my father?"

His eyes bore into mine. "There were many men who wanted your mother. Have you ever wondered if you might never know?"

All the air left my lungs. "So, you want to play games. Are you mad at me for killing your son? Is that why you wanted me to come here?"

The right side of his mouth twitched. This was amusing to him.

I'll play.

"Fine. Yes, I wondered." I looked over at another table with a tattooed man talking to his wife and small child. Her hair was almost white as she sat by her mother, looking frightened.

Ronny cleared his throat, bringing me back to our conversation. "Well?"

"It's not news that my mother slept with many men. Over the years I did question if a few guys she brought home were my father and not Luke. In hindsight, I should have listened to that feeling."

His face softened. "I'm sorry about Luke."

I closed my eyes, remembering the good, the bad, and ugly when it came to Luke. "Don't be. He lied to me."

Silence stretched between us, but the chatter in the visiting room reminded me why I was there.

I stood. "It's obvious you want me here for something else, maybe loneliness. Who cares—but I only came here for one reason, and if you aren't going to tell me, then I don't want to do this—whatever it is." I gestured between us.

Retreating seemed like the only option, but then he spoke. "I am."

The words hit like a wave, drowning everything, and I braced myself on the table. But before I could respond, a whistle blew. Visiting hours were over.

Ronny's eyes flicked to the guard, then back to me, whispering urgently, "Nathan's not dead. He's out there—breathing, waiting. He's coming for you."

4

Nathan - The Wolf

The scar on my left side throbbed like a heartbeat under my shirt, a souvenir from my half-sister's desperate strike that morning in the water—the cold rush of the tide washing me out to sea like a discarded verse. But death? No, that was just another rhyme I bent to my will. Kessler's boat had been waiting in the shadows of the waves, engine humming low, with Becca at the helm, Kaitlyn and Zane scanning the horizon, and Trevor—Becca's sharp-eyed son—hauling me aboard like a drowned wolf. They'd patched me up, hidden me away, loyal to the end because they knew the truth: the Reaper doesn't die; he evolves.

The truth struck with the force of a physical blow when Dad spat it out, his eyes wild as I confronted his unraveling after Alexis was torn from California to Gold Beach. Half-sister? Blood or not, the fire for her—once a primitive urge to end her—had twisted into a hunger to claim her completely.

Three years later, the air in Gold Beach tasted of salt and unfinished business, her fear drifting from the Finns' house like an invitation. I crouched in the tree line, knife carving a wolf's paw into the ladybug tree—fierce, breathing, alive. Alexis would feel it soon. The pack was back, and the hunt had just begun to howl.

5

The Captive

The concrete cell had erased every trace of a life I could no longer name, leaving only a hollow madness in its wake I had run out of wall space for my wolf drawings, and the crude sketches crowded every surface. I spotted the rickety chair in the corner and dragged it over with a metallic scrape. If I climbed on it, I could reach the ceiling—my final canvas.

The chair's instability mirrored my breaking mind as I climbed up, wobbling dangerously, my hand trembling while I etched shaky wolf silhouettes overhead with a jagged nail. Each stroke felt like a defiance, a scream against the darkness that held me.

At night, when the faint light from the tiny window faded to darkness, the eyes of the sketched wolves glowed like fireflies in the dark, piercing and unblinking. Their stares prickled my skin, and I sank into the chair, staring back at them, locked in a silent standoff that led nowhere.

"Black sheep, wolf in sheep's clothing," I muttered, my voice a hoarse rasp. "Humpty Dumpty, so broken... can't be put back together." My fist thudded against my temple in time with the words as I rocked back and forth, the chains at my ankles clinking like a grim melody. It was a habit now, this muttering, this rhythm, as routine as the hunger gnawing at my gut.

Echoes of whistling reverberated through the tunnel, a dissonant melody that made my teeth grind. I rushed back to the narrow, grimy mattress, curling into a fetal position and squeezing my eyes shut so tightly they throbbed. Slowly, I managed to relax my body as the door creaked open.

"Don't pretend with me—I know you're not asleep. I can hear your mumbling down the tunnel," he said. I didn't care if he knew; I kept my eyes closed, willing him away like a bad dream. A bucket clattered to the concrete, water sloshing out and splashing my bare feet, jolting my eyes open. "You reek. Clean yourself up."

He limped across the cellar, clutching his side with a wince, and grabbed another bucket—one that smelled just as foul as me. Without another word, he turned and hobbled out, the door clicking softly shut behind him—only to pop ajar moments later, a sliver of dim light bleeding through the crack.

I froze, my breath catching in my throat, expecting the final slam that would seal me in my prison. But it never came. A faint flicker of hope sparked in my empty eyes as I leaned against the damp wall, loose chains softly rattling with each cautious step. I moved forward slowly, hesitating to touch the door, and gazed through the narrow crack into the moss-covered tunnel beyond. A rat scurried past, clutching a wriggling cockroach in its jaws, disappearing into the engulfing darkness.

My skeletal frame, worn down by starvation and despair, was just slim enough to slip through the opening. My heart pounded as I moved forward carefully, the chains dragging behind me like accusing whispers across the gritty floor. I tried not to make a sound, but the terror that the metal would betray me clawed at my chest. The tunnel stretched ahead, cold and echoing, until—at the very end—a faint glow cut through the gloom. Light. Real light. For the first time in what felt like forever, a ghost of a smile tugged at my cracked lips.

Then, from the shadows behind me, a soft, eerie melody drifted through the air, unseen and disembodied: "Ring around the Rosie, a pocket full of posies..." The words curled like smoke, twisting into my ears and freezing me in place.

Before I could turn, a brutal force slammed into my back—his fist, unrelenting and savage. Pain exploded through my ribs as I crumpled to the ground, the rhyme dissolving into my gasps. "Ashes, ashes," he growled, his boot connecting with my side in a vicious kick. "We all fall down."

6
Alexis

The drive back from Two Rivers felt endless, the coastal fog wrapping around us like a veil, mirroring the confusion clouding my mind. Ronny's words played on repeat: *"I am."*

The revelation of my paternity felt like a physical assault—the man who had brought into this world the monster responsible for shattering my life. And Nathan? To think he was still breathing seemed impossible, yet it finally provided the missing piece explaining why Luke had despised Ronny with such ferocity.

I could still feel the warmth of Nathan's blood on my hands, the tactile memory of his weight slipping off my steel before the ocean swallowed him whole. Yet, a gnawing doubt took root in the pit of my stomach, a persistent, jagged edge that whispered he had survived.

Asher's knuckles whitened on the steering wheel, his eyes flicked to me every few miles. "Lex, say something. What's going through your head?"

"I don't know," I confessed, my voice a hushed murmur. "Part of me wants to torch those letters and pretend none of this happened. But... the shed. He mentioned tokens and a book like mine. If there's evidence that Nathan was this deranged from the start, or if Ronny's just spinning lies..."

"We'll investigate," Asher replied resolutely. "But not alone. And not without consulting someone. Genevieve?"

I nodded and fished out my phone. Genevieve Steinfeld had been my lifeline since the chaos after Sadie's murder—referred by Keith, of all people. At sixty-four, she ran her practice from her home office in Austin, and her wisdom was a steady anchor through video calls that spanned the miles.

I messaged her: *Urgent video session? In Gold Beach, major problems.*

Her response pinged back almost immediately: *Logging on now. Link incoming.*

We pulled over at a scenic overlook, the Rogue River churning below. I set up the call. Genevieve's face appeared on screen, her silver hair neatly pinned, her kind eyes sharp despite the lines etched by years of listening to trauma. "Alexis, Asher. You both look exhausted. What's happened?"

I dove in, recounting Ronny's claims—his paternity claim, Nathan's supposed survival, and the letters urging a search of the shed. "It feels like the ground's crumbling again," I finished, my voice cracking. "If Ronny's my dad, that makes Nathan my half-brother. And if he's alive... everything we've rebuilt—college, the internship, our life—it's all fragile."

Genevieve moved closer to her camera, her face steady yet compassionate. "That's a heavy load to bear. Betrayal, disgust—those feelings are understandable. Your mother kept secrets, maybe for protection, but uncovering them now changes your sense of self. As for Nathan, the official record says he's gone, but survivors like you know fear isn't bound by facts. What feels right to you?"

"The shed," I said without hesitation. "I need to see what's hidden there. Proof could end this... or confirm the nightmare."

She nodded thoughtfully. "Action can reclaim control. Be cautious, though. Involve trusted people and loop back with me afterward—we'll dissect what you uncover."

The call ended, leaving a sliver of clarity amid the storm, but the question lingered: Would I ever recover?

Asher started the car again. "Shed next?"

"Yeah. But let's loop in Coop and Tan first."

After we picked them up, we explained the basics on the way to Ronny's abandoned house on the outskirts—a run-down shack by the Coquille, seized and boarded up after his arrest and Nathan's 'death'—disappearance. No one was around, so we parked quietly and slipped through the overgrown yard.

The shed loomed in the back, its door sagging on corroded hinges. Asher pried it open with a crowbar from the trunk—echoes of our old sleuthing days when Nathan hunted me. Inside, the air reeked of mold and rot, with tools strewn like abandoned memories. "Check for hidden spots—floorboards, walls," Asher directed.

My pulse thundered as I probed a loose plank in the corner, lifting it to reveal a rusted metal box. I set it down on an old makeshift bench, then Asher cracked the simple lock. We all huddled around as the lid creaked open.

Tokens. A ghastly collection that punched the air from my lungs. Megan's car keys, dangling from a keychain etched "Little Miss Muffet sat on a tuffet." Items pilfered from the boys: Asher's old pocket knife, Cooper's small sketchbook, Tanner's poem he had written for Sadie—bundled as *"Three blind mice, see how they run."* A faded photo of Mark and Laura Hensley, crumpled with *"Jack and Jill went up the hill"* inked across their faces. A simple wooden cross, stained dark, invoking *"Mary, Mary, quite contrary."* My track trophy from high school, the base carved with *"Ladybug, ladybug, fly away home."*

The last one was a velvet bag with a tag marked 'Nicole.' It felt like sticks inside. I opened the drawstring and spilled the contents into my hand—which I instantly realized was a huge mistake.

"Are those bones?" Cooper said, shocked. I dropped them on the wooden floor, and they clanked like marbles.

A flash of that fateful day hit me: the pumpkin, the blood-smeared walls and bed, my mom's finger... and here was yet another one.

Had he taken one for a trophy?

"Guys, there's something etched on it," Tanner whispered. None of us wanted to touch them, so we leaned in closer.

A tear slipped down my cheek. "Pumpkin Eater." My knees buckled, but Asher caught me and eased me to the ground, ignoring the grime that would cling to us.

"You okay? We can stop," Asher said, though his voice hummed with curiosity. I shook my head.

"Look at this..." Coop pointed to a book.

And at the bottom: the nursery rhyme book. Identical to mine, but defiled—pages crammed with Nathan's alterations, innocent verses warped into sinister prophecies. Drawings accompanied each: crude sketches of crimes, victims' faces contorted in agony, rhymes rewritten to mock their fates. *"Humpty Dumpty"* showed a figure shattered at a cliff's base; *"Ring around the Rosie"* depicted bodies in a collapsing circle, ashes raining down.

"Oh God," I whispered, flipping through the horrors. " This... it's his game plan. But some of these drawings, the symbols—I can't make sense of them. The words are coded, layered."

Cooper leaned in, his gaze following the jagged strokes of the illustrations. "Let me take some photos of these. I spent enough time in studio sessions to know when lines aren't just lines—there might be a sequence or a repeating pattern hidden in how he layered the charcoal." He looked over at me and gave me a small, tight smile. "And this reminds me of when we found the Hensley's on the hill."

I closed my eyes, unfortunately, being taken back to that scene.

Tanner nodded, taking the book with care that bordered on reverence. "I can handle the rhymes. I've spent enough time breaking down meter and subtext to see where he's butchering the structure—if he's twisting the original verses, there's usually a reason. He might be hiding a timeline or a specific target in the cadence. He might also rewrite them to fit his agenda."

As they worked, I stepped outside for air and dialed a number from memory. Detective Jacobs—the one honest cop from the original case. It rang twice before a gruff voice answered. "Jacobs here."

"It's Alexis. From Gold Beach. I... need your help."

A pause, then a sigh. "Kid, I'm retired. Fishing in Bandon these days. But... what's going on?"

I spilled the essentials—Ronny's claims, the tokens, Nathan possibly alive. "The book's got drawings of old crimes, maybe new ones. I need someone who knows the case files."

He chuckled dryly. "Retired, not dead. Send me photos. I'll poke around quietly—old contacts owe me. But stay safe."

Hanging up, I watched fog swirl thicker, a distant howl cutting the air—imagination? Or a warning? I went back into the shed and grabbed the all-too-familiar nursery rhyme book. There was no ladybug sticker, and it was more worn. I wiped off the dirt and opened it.

"Oh God," I whispered, flipping through it. "This matches mine exactly. How did he...?"

A crunch of gravel outside snapped us to attention. Asher peered through a crack in the door. "Someone's here."

The house door creaked open as Kaitlyn emerged, her eyes widening in an expression that hovered between shock and calculation. I almost didn't recognize her. The long blonde hair she'd carried through high school was gone, replaced by a jagged, short-cropped cut dyed a deep black. She looked thinner and edgier now, her rumpled clothes giving her the frantic appearance of someone who had been sleeping rough or living on the run.

"Kaitlyn?" I called. The others joined me outside the shed as she turned, her body tensing like a startled deer. Before I could say more, she sprinted toward the tree line.

"Hey, wait!" Asher shouted, and we took off after her, feet pounding the dirt. She was fast, weaving through the fog, but Cooper lunged and grabbed her sleeve just before she vanished into the mist. She stumbled, panting, as we caught up.

"What are you doing here? Where have you been?" I demanded, my voice sharp with suspicion.

Kaitlyn froze, glancing nervously at the shed. "I... I've been crashing here sometimes. Sneaking in to see my parents without the town knowing. The place is empty, right? What about you guys?"

Asher crossed his arms, his gaze hardening as he leveled it at each of us in turn. "I'm struggling to see why you think this is your business."

I interjected, wanting to test her. "Just looking through some old things of Nathan's."

Kaitlyn's face paled, but she averted her eyes, shifting uncomfortably. "Nathan? That's... ancient history. He's dead. Why dig it up?"

"Because Ronny says he's not," I pressed, stepping closer, getting angrier. "You were part of his team—what do you know?"

She backed up, shaking her head. "Nothing. I don't want to talk about this. It's over."

Cooper frowned. "Come on, Kait. You know something. Where's Nathan? You helped tie us up in that cave! You helped get Sadie killed!"

"No, I'm so sorry about Sadie. I didn't want any of you hurt," she snapped, voice rising. "I said I don't know anything. Leave it alone."

Tanner pulled out his phone. "Fine. We'll call the cops—tell them someone's squatting in a seized property. Maybe they can ask the questions."

Kaitlyn's eyes darted to the road, panic flashing. "Don't. Just... not here. It's not safe. I missed my family. I wanted to see them. I'll be in touch if I think of anything." She yanked her arm free, bolting toward the tree line again, vanishing into the fog before we could react.

We stood there, stunned, the box heavy in my hands. "That was weird," Asher muttered. "She's hiding something. Where has she been?"

7
Asher

The encounter with Kaitlyn left a sour taste as we piled back into the car, the metal box wedged between my feet like a ticking bomb. Her evasion, the panic in her eyes—it screamed secrets, and in Gold Beach, secrets had a way of turning deadly. Alexis stared out the window, her face pale, fingers absently tracing the edge of the nursery rhyme book. I tried to have faith she wouldn't start purging again but doubt crept in the more we brought the pain of loss to the surface.

Coop and Tan murmured in the back, debating the etched bones, but my mind was already dissecting: Kaitlyn hiding in Nathan's old house? Coincidence, or something more sinister?

"She's lying," I said finally, breaking the silence as we pulled onto the coastal road. "About why she's there, about not knowing anything. We should've followed her."

Alexis shook her head. "She looked scared, Ash. And rough—like she's been on the run. But yeah... she dodged every question about Nathan."

Coop leaned forward. "She helped him before. Tied us up in that cave. If Nathan's alive, she's probably in on it."

Tan's voice was quieter. "Or trapped. Either way, we need to dig deeper. Those drawings in the book—some look recent, fresher ink."

I nodded, gripping the wheel. At the house, we spread the tokens on the kitchen table, away from Mom and Dad's prying eyes—they were out 'running errands,' but I suspected they were giving us space after last night's tension. The room felt heavier with the artifacts laid out: Megan's keys mocking *"Little Miss Muffet,"* Coop, Tan, and my stolen items bundled together; the Hensleys' photo crumpled under *"Jack and Jill,"* the stained cross whispering *"Mary, Mary,"* Alexis's trophy scarred with ladybugs. And those bones... *"Pumpkin Eater."* Nicole's—Alexis's mom's—finger bones, a gruesome echo of the past.

Alexis shivered as she stood beside me. "He kept these like trophies," she whispered, her voice brittle. "Proof he was always this monster. He was too proud to hide it."

"It's more than just pride," I muttered, picking up the book with a caution usually reserved for unexploded ordnance. The pages resembled a nightmare gallery: twisted rhymes intertwined with crude, hyper-detailed drawings—victims caught in the throat of a scream, bodies mid-fall, scenes of total collapse. "These aren't just memories; some of them seem as if they are blueprints. This Humpty Dumpty sketch—look at the line of the cliffs. That's Bandon. And these symbols...they aren't random. They're code."

Coop's phone flashed rhythmically as he documented the carnage. "Tan, I don't think any logic we apply to this is going to get us close to the rot inside that bastard's head."

Tan flipped through the rhymes, his fingers visibly trembling. "Yeah, and honestly? I'm not sure if I want to go there. I can try to deconstruct the structure, but my brain isn't wired to think like a predator. Let's just send whatever we find to the authorities."

A heavy silence followed, which I tried to puncture by clapping them both on the shoulders. "You mean to tell me you're not psychopaths?" The chuckle that left my throat felt dry. "Well, that's a relief."

The laughter that followed was short-lived and forced, but Alexis's was the worst—a hollow, rattling sound that stayed in the air long after she had turned and walked toward the bathroom.

The heavy silence of the yard pressed against me as the afternoon bled into a gray, suffocating twilight. I paced the perimeter, my mind a jagged loop of Kaitlyn's frantic escape into the fog—her terror felt too real, a reflection of the cold knot tightening in my own chest. Drawn by a pull I couldn't explain, I wandered toward the tree line, my boots crunching softly until I reached the ladybug tree.

The air left my lungs in a sharp, painful hiss. I froze.

Where the familiar, innocent ladybug once sat, a fresh carving now snarled from the trunk. It was a wolf's paw, the claws dug deep and predatory into the wood. The bark was still raw, weeping sap resembling an open wound, the scent of fresh timber stinging my nose. It was a brand. A promise. He had been standing right here, watching us, while the wood was still wet.

"Guys!" I screamed, my voice cracking under the weight of a sudden, paralyzing dread.

8
Nathan - The Wolf

The stale air in the old Bandon warehouse clung to my skin as if it was a second layer, thick with the metallic tang of rust and the faint, sour smell of the Coquille River seeping through the cracks. Shadows slithered across the crumbling walls, whispering secrets in the dim flicker of the single bulb swinging overhead, its angry hum a constant buzz in my skull. I slammed cans of beans onto the rickety shelf, each thud echoing similar to a heartbeat—mine, racing with fury, or hers, soon to stop if she pushed me further.

"How much longer do you think I'm going to take your shit, Kaitlyn?" I snarled, my voice bouncing off the concrete as if a rhyme had gone wrong—jagged and unhinged. I didn't wait for her pathetic whining. "You think I'm some idiot? I send you back to Gold Beach to keep an eye on Alexis, and you slink off to visit your family. We made a pact—lay low, vanish like ghosts in the fog! But you... you trot out resembling a lamb to the slaughter, risking everything for what? Mommy's hugs?"

Her sobs began then—wet and choking—filling the cramped kitchen with a sound that grated against my eardrums, sharp as nails on bone. "I'm sorry... I can't stand not seeing them. I miss them, and my little brother—Benji—he's so sick. They've been running tests. His cancer is getting worse..." The words dissolved into hiccupping gasps, her body shaking as if she were the one rotting away, not that sniveling brat who'd make a perfect posy—him and a circle of other wide-eyed children, falling down in ashes, their tiny hands clutching at nothing. A surge of excitement ran through me, igniting more kills. It's been too long, and my self-control was withering away.

Pathetic. I downed a beer then slammed the cooler shut, the cold metal biting into my palms, and followed her as she fumbled with boxes of macaroni and cheese in the cupboard. The sharp stench of her fresh hair dye assaulted my nostrils—a cheap black that turned her once-blonde hair into oily midnight strands, a weak disguise for our escape. It mixed with the warehouse's moldy smell, making my stomach churn and fueling the rage burning like acid in my throat.

"You asked for this!" I growled low in her ear, my breath hot against her neck, tasting the salt of her fear-sweat on my tongue. She let out a high-pitched squeal, spinning around. Her skin, once smooth porcelain, was now sallow and stretched tight over bones, aged by three years of shadows and secrets. Those blue eyes—sunken into black pits—darted wildly, pleading.

Her chocolate-scented breath washed over me, sweet yet overwhelming, as she stammered, "I'm only here because you promised me money to help my parents keep our house." I raised an eyebrow, my fingers twitching, tempted to wrap around her throat and squeeze until the rhymes in my head went silent. "Which you did, and I'm so grateful, but they're struggling again with Benji's medical bills now, so I was hoping... more? Please, Nathan. That's why I'm still here."

More? The word ignited a fierce, primal rage inside me, making a wild laugh burst from my chest—ragged and echoing similar to a wolf's howl trapped in a cage. "Money? That's all you care about, you greedy little sheep. Not the pack, not the hunt, not me—the Rhyme Reaper, bringing the verses that hold us together! You just want to eat away my mother's life insurance. I'm already paying for every goddamn thing this pack has!" My voice cracked and shot up into a scream, as the warehouse seemed to pulse with my madness. The air grew thicker and heavier, pressing down resembling the weight of all the bodies I've buried.

I lunged forward, grabbing her by the arms, my nails digging into her flesh—soft, yielding, warm with the pulse of life I could so easily snuff out. She yelped, the sound piercing my ears, her body trembling under my grip, the fabric of her shirt rough against my palms. "You think you can bleed me dry like some pathetic rhyme? You're crying for coins while the wolves circle!"

The door burst open, a gust of damp river wind carrying the salty brine of the outside world, slamming against the wall with a crack. Zane stormed in, his broad frame filling the space, eyes blazing with that loyal-dog fire. "Get your hands off her, Nathan!" he roared, his voice a deep rumble that vibrated through the floorboards. He'd follow Kaitlyn to the ends of the earth—no family of his own, parents lost to needles and haze, just her as his anchor in the storm.

I shoved her away, making her stumble into the counter, the clattering of falling boxes resembling scattered bones. Laughter erupted from my throat again, wild and bitter on my tongue. "Oh, the knight in rusted armor! Zane, you pathetic stray—drug-addict spawn, trailing after her like a lost pup. Defend your bitch if you want, but remember: wolves eat dogs. And the pack's hungry."

Zane stood ready, fists clenched, the air thick with the salt of his sweat and the heat of his rage.

"Nathan, back off! This isn't the plan," William barked, stepping forward from the shadows of the hallway, his voice tight with the authority he thought he still held. Behind him, Becca moved with predatory grace, her hand resting on the hilt of the knife at her belt.

"He's right, Nathan. Cool it," Becca urged, her voice a low, dangerous honey. "We're a team. We don't tear each other apart in the kitchen like common strays."

Trevor, Becca's sharp-eyed son, hovered by the door, his gaze darting between us. "The heat's rising outside, man. We can't afford this noise. Let her go."

Look at them, I thought, my pulse a frantic drum against my ribs. *The architect, the mother, the scout... and the dog.* They thought they were the pack, but they were just weights dragging me down. The doubt I'd felt earlier had hardened into a cold, crystalline certainty. I didn't need them; I needed them gone. The rhyme was evolving. I'd built this circle, and now, I was the only one who wouldn't fall. I'd start with the weakest links and work my way to the heart.

I stepped back, my chest heaving as the rhymes spun in my mind—posies, ashes, falls. My hands twitched, an itch deep under the skin. I needed my book. I needed the ink. Going back and forth to Gold Beach was growing old, and the final verse required a sacrifice the "pack" wasn't prepared to give.

"Fine," I spat, raising my hands in a mock gesture of peace. "The wolf is fed for now."

As I prowled the rotting husk of the house I once called home, a frigid gust twisted around me, conjuring Mom's ghost—her noose-tightened neck, purple lips, dead eyes staring, red hair knotted in the rope, fingernails caked with blood from clawing her throat. I watched it all, a boy silenced by weakness, and it set my veins on fire—rage choking me, not anymore. I'm no coward now, but the memory gnaws, a blade in my skull.

I stopped in my tracks, not because of the image that assaulted me, but because the shed door was wide open and hanging by one rusted hinge, grinding in the wind.

Not the way I left it.

Was this recent? I looked around but didn't see or feel eyes on me. The sound of the ocean filled the air. I walked backwards, still scanning the area, and stopped at the entrance of the shed. I peered inside. My hiding place with my collection had been obstructed. Shit. Did the police find it? I was stupid to think they wouldn't.

I examined the footprints in the dirt. One set was small enough to belong to a child, and there were three other sets that looked different.

My blood began to boil, and I snatched up a handful of dirt—only to find it gone, every single one of my tokens had vanished.

9

Alexis

The heavy silence of the kitchen was broken only by the rhythmic steam of my chai latte. The warmth curling against my tired face was a fleeting comfort against the chill seeping through my skin. Sleep had dodged me all night, replaced by nightmares of the ladybug tree—its carved wings clawed away by a wolf's jagged paw. I had jolted awake with sheets tangled around my legs and my heart racing, only to find Asher watching me with a quiet, devastating intensity. He didn't have to say it; the faint scent of bile and the raw puffiness of my eyes gave me away. He knew I was purging again. The distance of Austin had softened the urge, but Gold Beach had dragged the darkness back to the surface.

As I approached the table, the clink of silverware and the low, uneasy voices of Cooper and Tanner spiked my anxiety. They were hunched over Nathan's twisted nursery rhyme book, their excitement over his "blueprints" feeling misplaced. I closed my eyes, seeking calm, but the image of that raw, carved tree flashed behind my lids, making me flinch.

Asher's arm slid around me, and I leaned into his warmth instinctively, even as the guilt of my relapse sat heavy in my stomach. I never wanted a life without him, yet I couldn't stop destroying the one I had. "Hey, you holding up?" he murmured. His voice was soft, but his eyes were searching—looking for the girl who had vanished into the bathroom earlier that morning.

"Maybe a fraction," I said, holding up my thumb and forefinger, the gap between them barely visible.

He kissed the top of my head, a lingering touch that felt as if it was an unspoken plea for me to be okay. "I'm sorry this is happening. I wish things were different."

"Me too." I pulled back to meet his gaze, hating the concern that always seemed to mirror my own unraveling. "Let's hand this over to the authorities. Give them everything we've found and head back to Austin."

"Alexis, Christmas is in three days. You can't leave now," Tami said, her voice laced with full-on panic as she twisted a dish towel between her hands. She sighed, her expression sagging into a deep, weary sadness. "It's just so heavy around here lately. It breaks my heart that Kaitlyn doesn't come back to visit anymore. She has no idea how much her family needs her." Tami looked down at the towel, her voice dropping to a ghost of a whisper. "Her younger brother, Benji... the leukemia is taking a toll. He's so sick, and she's just... gone."

A wave of nausea that had nothing to do with my eating disorder rolled through me. Benji. I remembered him as a bright-eyed kid, all laughter and scraped knees, and the thought of him wasting away in a hospital bed while his sister lived like a ghost in the woods was a special kind of cruelty. My heart ached for that little boy; he was an innocent caught in the wake of the wreckage Nathan had left behind. It was devastating to think that while we were hunting a monster, Benji was fighting a war inside his own blood.

A heavy, suffocating silence fell over the room. Tami had no idea we had just seen Kaitlyn at the shed—haggard and cagey—while she sat here mourning an absence that was killing a little boy's spirit.

Asher, brushing off his mom's plea but clearly darkened by the mention of Benji, turned back to me. "I want to go back to Austin too. What if we leave on the twenty-sixth? We could spend New Year's together—just us."

I smiled, a wave of gratitude washing over me. We were on the same page, as always, though I knew the "just us" would still include the ghost of my relapse and the shadow of the Reaper.

Cooper leaped up from the table, shouting, "Yes! My buddies wanted me to spend New Year's Eve with them so we can go party with some chicks." He paused, raking a hand through his messy hair. "If you guys don't mind me tagging along too."

The thought of the cozy house Keith and Tami had bought us near the university offered a flicker of hope. With enough rooms for all of us, Austin truly felt like the only sanctuary left.

"I'd like all of us to go back," I admitted, a pang of selfishness twisting inside me. With Nathan's shadow possibly lurking, Gold Beach felt comparable to a tomb.

Tan let out a relieved breath. "Whew... I thought you guys were ditching me here."

We all laughed—except for Keith and Tami, whose faces remained etched with a worry that the sound of our laughter couldn't reach.

While Asher worked on our flights, I called ex-detective Jacobs to tell him we were stepping back. He gave me the new contact information for Detective Fields from the Ventura office, who was now a Special Agent for the FBI.

"He'll be expecting your call," Jacobs cleared his throat. "Alexis, I think this is a smart move. For what it's worth, I think Nathan is dead. You should move on and try to be happy."

I shifted onto the oversized sofa, finding no comfort as the uneasy feeling in my gut grew. "Thanks." I ended the call quickly. I appreciated his hope, but Nathan's words on that beach were etched into my soul: *"I need her; she needs me. We are more alike than you know."*

The Trips and I decided to head out for a walk to call Agent Fields. They insisted on being there, teasing me about my "noble rogue" phase from years ago to keep the mood light.

"Come on Lex, whatever problems you have are our problems too," Tan said, refusing to let me shut them out.

I dialed Agent Fields and put him on speaker. A familiar, gruff voice answered. "Special Agent Fields, who's this?"

"Agent Fields, it's Alexis Harper. I'm with Asher, Cooper, and Tanner. We're calling about the Rhyme Reaper case in Gold Beach."

"Harper, yeah, I remember you," Fields said, his tone warming slightly. "I'm in Seattle, but I can be in Gold Beach tomorrow. What've you got?"

I took a deep breath. "We found a shed with letters from Ronny, tokens, and a nursery rhyme book with Nathan's writing. We believe Nathan Moore might still be alive."

There was a brief, calculating pause. "Alive, huh? That's a bold claim. Tell me about it."

Asher leaned in. "We ran into Kaitlyn at the shed last night. She was squatting there. When we confronted her about Nathan, she got spooked and bolted into the woods."

"Kaitlyn, yeah. Not surprised she's still lurking," Fields said, his voice carrying a steady, unshakable calm. "Alright, get everything to the Gold Beach station by tomorrow morning. I'll meet you there."

"Absolutely," I said. "We'll hand it all over."

"Good. Don't go digging further. This is FBI business now. Stay safe, Alexis."

The line clicked off, leaving us in the swirling fog of the ocean breeze. "He didn't seem shocked about Kaitlyn," Tan noted, frowning. "Or Nathan."

"Yeah," Coop agreed. "Like he's already got pieces of this puzzle we don't."

I clutched the box tighter, the Reaper's twisted verses echoing in my head. Fields' lack of surprise felt less professional and more as a warning I was terrified to decode.

10
Asher

How did I manage to be so lucky and yet feel so awful at the same time? Alexis has been my entire world, and I loved her more than I loved myself, but were we ever truly going to escape the constant nightmare we've been trapped in? I seized the moment she decided to give up everything to the authorities, hoping we could finally regain some of the normalcy we once had in Austin.

Everything was ready; we'd fly back to our normal life the day after Christmas. My parents weren't too happy, but I couldn't bring myself to care. They had been acting overprotective and odd since coming back. Maybe it bothered them that they didn't have much say in our decisions anymore.

My head shook as I kept searching for Alexis, whom I hadn't seen since our conversation with Agent Fields. As I climbed the stairs, I could hear my parents speaking in frustrated tones in the office. I stopped at the top of the stairs and spotted Alexis outside the office—listening in. I smiled and tuned out my parents, just gazing at her. She was stunning, leaning against the wall with her long, wavy dark hair trailing down to her waist. The skylight cast just enough sunlight to highlight the red undertones of her hair. She was wearing my favorite color on her—green.

The stairs creaked softly, and she spun around in shock, as if she'd seen a ghost. But then her emerald eyes brightened, and she smiled when she recognized me. She put her finger to her lips, signaling me to be quiet, and then motioned for me to come closer. I walked over, resting my hand on her waist, and gave her a kiss on the top of her head. The coconut scent that surrounded her was calming, as we both listened to my parents.

"We are still dealing with the choices you've made years ago," Mom said as she choked out a sob. Alexis bent her head back and looked at me. My fist tightened and I wanted to barge in there but Alexis mouthed 'just wait'.

"I don't know how many times I've had to apologize. I've tried making up for it but nothing seems to be working. We were doing so well...."

Mom cut him off, "Yeah we were doing well up until Alexis came back to Gold Beach and you thought you had to help her then we almost lost our sons because of her, because of you."

"Tami," Dad warned. "You know why I had to help her."

Mom was not doing well. What the hell was happening? What was Dad trying to make up for?

"If you hadn't read that letter from Ronny you would still believe that there was a chance Alexis was..." she coughed then cleared her throat, "was your daughter."

WHAT!?!?!

Alexis immediately wrapped her arms around her waist and fell to the floor, making a loud thud. I fell to the ground pulling her into an embrace as her sobs shook through me. My stomach churned as my mind reeled then settled on realization.

Dad cheated on Mom.

Dad cheated on Mom with Nicole.

Dad's a cheater.

As I looked up, Mom and Dad were standing in the office doorway. Dad's eyes were filled with shock and pleading, but I didn't care. My focus turned to Mom, who had black mascara streaks on her cheeks, and eyes, and her nose was red. She held a balled-up tissue to her lips, broken and emotional. I was furious.

Footsteps pounded up the stairs behind us. Cooper and Tanner appeared, their faces a mix of confusion and alarm.

"What the hell's going on?" Cooper demanded, his eyes darting between Alexis, crumpled in my arms, and our parents in the doorway.

Tanner's brow furrowed. "Lex, you okay? What happened?"

Alexis was trembling, her face buried in my chest, unable to speak. I glared at Dad, my voice low and sharp. "You want to tell them, or should I?"

Dad ran a hand over his face, his shoulders sagging. "This was before you boys were adopted," he said, his voice heavy. "Mom and I... we were struggling. We wanted a family so badly, but we couldn't have kids. The doctors said it was unlikely, and it tore us apart. I was weak. I had an affair with Nicole, Alexis's mom. It was brief, and I ended it, but for a while, I thought... I thought Alexis might be mine."

Mom's sob broke the silence, her voice raw. "I wanted a family so much, and when I found out about Nicole, I hated her. And when Alexis came into our lives, I... I resented her. I know it wasn't fair, but every time I looked at her, I saw Dad's betrayal. I've tried to move past it, but it's hard."

Cooper's jaw dropped, and Tanner took a step back, as if he'd been slapped. "You're saying Lex could've been... our sister?" Cooper's voice was tight, his eyes wide with disbelief.

"No, yes. Well, not now, but when she came to Gold Beach after Nicole died, I thought she was," Dad said quickly, glancing at Alexis then back to the ground. "It took me seeing Ronny's letter and... and talking to Ronny. Alexis isn't mine but..."

Alexis lifted her head, her eyes red and glistening. "Back up. Not only did you open my letters from Ronny, you...you went and saw him?" She was standing now, shifting into the warrior I knew she was—about to fight.

Dad's face crumpled. "I'm so sorry, Alexis. I've wanted to protect you all this time." He cleared his throat, "even before you came back, before your mom took you away from Gold Beach."

I held her tighter, my anger boiling over. "You should've told us," I snapped. "All of us. Instead, you let this fester, and now look at us, especially Mom."

Tan put a hand on my shoulder, his voice steady but shaken. "Hey, we'll figure this out."

Coop nodded, still processing, his eyes flicking to Mom. "You should've said something. We could've handled it."

Mom wiped her eyes, her voice barely above a whisper. "I was ashamed. Of the resentment, of how I let it affect me. I love you boys, and I've tried to love Alexis, but it's been hard."

The air felt thick and heavy with too many truths. Alexis clung to me, her sobs gone. I pressed my lips to her forehead, whispering, "This changes everything. I'm not sure if I could ever forgive you, Dad?"

I couldn't recognize my parents, my life.

Was it all lies?

The truth about Nathan and Ronny was heavy, but this—this betrayal—cut deeper.

11
Nathan - The Wolf

The wind howled like a choir of the damned, tearing across the cliffs of Cape Sebastian, whipping salt and spray into the air. Below us, the Pacific convulsed in a frenzy of white-capped waves, thrashing against the rocks as though the sea itself wanted blood. The iron grate I'd dragged here glowed against the backdrop of the crashing surf, fire licking high, its smoke snatched by the wind and carried out into the endless black horizon.

Becca's screams ripped through the gale, shredded and raw, her wrists bleeding as the chains bit deeper with every frantic lunge. William strained beside her, his curses drowned by the storm. William, the fool who thought he could play hero. He'd come to me months ago, trying to negotiate, trying to "rescue" Becca and Trevor from my grasp as if they were property he could reclaim. I'd given him a simple choice: stay with the pack and serve the wolf, or die with the sheep. He'd chosen to stay, thinking he could undermine me from within. He didn't realize that in my pack, there is no exit strategy.

None of it touched me. Not really.

Because it had been years. Years since I killed. Years since I felt the fever in my veins, the world sharpening to a single, perfect point—the moment I chose who lived and who burned. Alexis had stolen it from me when she slipped away. The little spider thought she spun herself free, thought she proved I was fading. That I was weak.

But Alexis was wrong. She had no idea what she woke in me when she ran. She sparked the hunger again.

All my tokens were gone. I needed more. And a new plan to get Alexis—forever my ladybug. No one would ever understand me. I called myself the Black Sheep once, because I never fit in with their flock. Different. Broken. Unwanted. I wore the name like a curse. Then the world crowned me with something else—the Rhyme Reaper. The press. The FBI. The bleating sheep with microphones clutched in trembling hands. A monster who carved blood into nursery songs. That name I embraced. It wasn't a curse. It was power. It was a legacy.

But it was still a mask. Because the truth had always been something worse. I was the wolf in sheep's clothing. Moving among them. Wearing their wool. Waiting for the night, I could tear it off and let them see my teeth.

I had planned this from the very beginning. A pack is only useful until it becomes a liability, and their doubt was beginning to smell. It was time to clear the board.

Trevor saw the teeth first.

I stepped closer, the fire painting my shadow long and black across the stone, stretched like a demon over the cliff. The heat curled against my skin, carrying with it the sharp tang of burning denim and the copper-sweet perfume of blood. Salt from the sea stung my tongue, the air thick with smoke and char. Fear had a smell—the sour, animal reek of sweat and terror spilling off Trevor in waves.

"Please, Nathan! Please!" Trevor sobbed, his voice thin and cracking as he hovered at the edge of the grate. "I'll do anything! I'm loyal, I swear! I'll kill for you, I'll hunt for you—just don't do this!"

I looked at him, his begging eyes reflecting the orange glow of the flames, and felt nothing but a cold, clinical boredom. He was a resource spent.

"Jump, Trevor," I crooned, my voice a silk thread woven through the roar of the sea. "Jack be nimble, Jack be quick... Jack jump over the candlestick. You know the rule."

He leapt, shrieking as the flames caught his jeans, his body jerking. His fear was delicious, but it wasn't enough. I didn't want his loyalty. I wanted his ending.

The wind howled, a jagged blade of sound that seemed to cheer as Trevor scrambled back across the iron grate. He was a broken thing now, his movements jerky and uncoordinated, his face a mask of soot and tears.

"Again," I whispered, the word barely a breath, yet he heard it over the thunder of the surf.

Trevor lunged into his third jump, his legs giving out mid-air. He landed hard on the glowing metal. The hiss of skin meeting iron was a sound more beautiful than any rhyme I'd ever written. He shrieked—a high, thin sound that peaked and then broke into a wet gurgle. He tried to crawl off, his fingernails scraping uselessly against the hot bars, leaving charred streaks behind.

"Nathan, please! Look at me!" William's voice was hoarse from screaming, his body straining against the chains until the links groaned. "He's a kid! He did everything you asked!"

I didn't turn. My gaze was locked on Trevor, who was now huddled in a fetal position at the edge of the grate, his breath coming in ragged, whistling heaves.

"You said you'd do anything for me, Trevor," I said, stepping closer until the heat of the fire kissed my cheeks. "This is the only thing left. Be the spark. Be the warning."

"I... I... can't," Trevor wheezed, his eyes rolling back in his head. The smell of him—the salt, the sweat, the scorched denim—was reaching its crescendo.

"Jack was nimble," I recited, my voice dropping to a low, melodic thrum. "But Jack grew slow. Now the fire begins to grow."

With a slow, deliberate movement, I planted the toe of my boot against Trevor's shoulder. He looked up at me one last time, a flicker of recognition in his eyes—the realization that the man he had worshipped was nothing more than a hollowed-out cavern of hunger.

I pushed.

He didn't scream this time. He just fell. The flames roared upward as they accepted his weight, a bright, orange bloom that illuminated the jagged cliffs and the black, churning mouth of the sea below. He disappeared into the heart of the pyre, his body becoming part of the light, part of the heat, part of the legacy.

Becca collapsed, her sobs turning into a low, rhythmic keening that matched the wind. William went silent, his head hanging low, the fight finally drained from him. He knew now. The pack was never a family. It was merely a group of pawns.

I stood at the edge, and the dark cloak of smoke billowed around me. I wasn't the Reaper tonight. I wasn't the Black Sheep. I was the apex, the end of the line, the wolf standing over the remains of a feast that had barely begun.

I didn't care. I was still here. Still pulling the strings. Still in control.

When Trevor finally fell into the fire, and the flames devoured his screams, I inhaled deeply, drawing the moment into me. The reek of burning hair, the sweet-metal edge of blood, the panic-sweat stinging my nose—it was a symphony. Every scent, every scream, every crackle of flesh in the fire played its note.

He wasn't dying at the hands of the Reaper. Not some rhyming phantom the news could twist into headlines. He was watching the wolf—and the wolf doesn't kill cleanly. The wolf savors.

The Black Sheep is dead. The Rhyme Reaper is only a mask. The wolf is alive. And when wolves breathe, they must hunt.

12

The Captive

It was moving day, and my stomach twisted with a grotesque mix of emotions—excitement that I might be leaving this hell, relief that change was coming, and grief that felt comparable to a funeral already held inside my chest. But when the door scraped open, and he stepped in, dragging a large gray dog crate, the air soured. I shrank into the corner, clutching at the paw-carved concrete as if the claws might dig in and pull me free.

The rules echoed in my mind—never speak his name, never resist, never forget. The one time I broke them, I paid in blood and darkness. I still remember the blackness that swallowed me, the sting of chains cutting into my skin, his shadow erasing even my screams.

I couldn't go through that again. Not today. My mind was exhausted, my body fragile.

To only me, he was known as The Wolf. If I ever said it out loud, I knew I'd end up pressed against the wall, his tuneless humming seeping into my ears until I begged for quiet.

The Wolf—always a predator.

His smell filled the room—waxen smoke, mixed with the sour musk of sweat soaked into his clothes. It crawled down my throat, coated my tongue, and made me want to gag. It wasn't just a smell that lingered—it dominated the air.

He squatted down and popped open the crate's door. Its hollow interior yawned—a coffin waiting to be filled. He jabbed a finger at it. "Get in. Now."

I froze for a brief moment, and he noticed it, his predatory eyes narrowed—sensing weakness. My chains screeched across the floor as I dragged myself forward. Each movement tore at my pride, stripping away the layers until I was just the little girl I used to be—the one who still believed monsters couldn't be real.

I stopped in front of the crate, heart pounding so hard I could taste iron. When I raised my hands as if I was a beggar, they shook like paper in a draft.

He chuckled. Low, cruel. Then the humming started. That cursed tune, the one that only came when he was happy. And he was only happy when he'd taken a life—or was planning to.

The tears came before I could stop them. Because I knew the truth: stepping inside wasn't just obedience. It was a rehearsal. Practice for the grave.

The crate smelled of rust and dog, its plastic walls pressing close before I even entered. My breath hitched as I crawled inside, my shoulders scraped the narrow doorway, and chains dragged. The moment I folded myself small enough to fit, something in me broke. The crate wasn't a cage anymore—it was my coffin, and he was sealing me inside.

And the worst part? I knew he could lift me, carry me away as if I were merely luggage or trash, because there wasn't much left of me to carry. Flesh and bone, hollowed by fear. He didn't need strength to own me. Just will.

The humming swelled, vibrating through the air, vibrating through me as I laid myself down in my own grave.

13
Alexis

The vibration of my phone cut through the silence, sharp enough to make me jump. Agent Fields's name lit the screen.

"Alexis," he said without preamble, his voice clipped and tight. "There's been a development. Close by. I need you to come down here immediately—and bring everything you and the Trips found. All of it."

My stomach dropped. "What happened?"

A pause. I could hear wind whipping through the end of his line, maybe even the distant wail of sirens. "It's better if you see it yourself. I'll text you my location. Sorry, I need to go. See you soon." Then the line went dead.

I stared at the phone until Asher's voice broke through. "Well? What did he say?"

I swallowed hard. "He wants us. And the evidence." I look at my phone. "At Cape Sebastian. That's just down the coast."

So close. My body buzzed, and I knew. This was about the Rhyme Reaper.

Minutes later, we were crammed into Tami's old Jeep Cherokee, headlights cutting through the Oregon fog as the coast highway twisted ahead. The air inside the car felt heavy—the silence before a storm.

When we finally pulled up behind the line of flashing cruisers and crime scene tape, my chest seized. The cliffs. The black surf hammering below. The smell of smoke was still clinging to the air.

I didn't need to step closer to know. I'd seen this place before—on the page.

Cooper jumped out of the Cherokee. "Oh my God," he whispered. "It's the rhyme… it's undoubtedly how it was written."

The three of them exchanged a look that said everything without words.....

Nathan was alive.

The Rhyme Reaper had returned.

I didn't want to be here. And I especially didn't want to be part of it anymore. I sat frozen, gripping my fingernails into the leather seat. They can't really expect me to go out there and look at a damn crime scene. Memories of my mother's blood-splattered room in Ventura flashed in my mind: the pumpkin and the rhymes, news clips, and other victims.

"Nope," I said, squeezing my eyes shut and shaking my head. "I am not going over there. I can't."

Asher exited the car, and before I knew it, he was by my side, pulling me into his chest. "You don't have to. We can tell Fields to back off."

"Why does he want me here? Can't they take care of this without me?" I started to cry. I hated this version of myself. I sounded so weak.

Asher tilted my chin up, and our eyes locked. "I don't know why he wants you here. I know this hits closer to us; however, our internship will be helping those who have been victims of crimes like these. If we can't face this, then we won't be able to help others face their trauma." He kissed me softly. "If you can't do this, we understand. Would you like a moment?"

I nodded and got out of the car. I turned my back to the impending scene but couldn't block it out as the smell of smoky death assaulted me.

I knew he had a point. And I knew I needed to buck up and put on my big girl panties; however, I just wasn't ready.

Nathan. I failed to kill him. One stab. I should have stabbed him more. I've watched countless movies and should have known better.

We slipped past the yellow tape under Fields's glare. His suit was damp from the mist, his tie crooked, and his expression—harder than I'd remembered.

"Alexis, it's been a while," he said, eyes flicking from me to the boys. "You brought backup."

"They're part of this," I shot back, hugging the notebook and the nursery rhyme book against my chest. My palms were damp around its spine. Another agent approached, collecting the evidence we found from the shed

Fields didn't argue. He just gestured for us to follow him down the slick dirt path. The ocean thundered below, waves crashing themselves apart against the cliff face.

The air hit me first—smoke and saltwater, thick enough to claw at my throat. Fields led us down the muddy cliffside path, the ocean below roaring as if it wanted to swallow the whole scene.

Then I saw it.

The clearing glowed with the aftermath of fire—charcoal-black earth, wax congealed in glistening rivulets, and in the center, the body.

His face was still there, blistered, but unmistakable. The curve of his jaw. The bridge of his nose. Even the melted outline of his glasses, which I remember him sometimes wearing. He was gone, and yet staring at us, accusing, like the fire hadn't finished its work.

Cooper's voice cracked. "That's—no. That's Trevor. But... he was one of Nathan's. Why the hell—"

Tanner shook his head, pale. "He burned his own guy?"

Asher clenched his fists, fury simmering beneath the horror. "To him, nobody's safe. Not his crew. Not us. Not anyone."

But it wasn't just Trevor.

My eyes dragged away from him to the circle around the pyre—and my blood froze.

Mannequins. Dozens of them, propped on wooden chairs, their plastic faces twisted into false, painted smiles. They sat in grotesque stillness, as if an audience frozen mid-applause. And in the front row—two empty chairs. Waiting.

Pinned to the chairs were Polaroids, edges curling from the heat. I staggered closer, heart pounding, and saw them.

Becca and William. Trevor's parents. Bound. Mouths gagged. Eyes wide with terror in the frozen flash of the camera.

"Oh my God," I whispered.

The Trips followed my gaze. Cooper swore under his breath, Tanner took a sharp step back, and Asher's jaw tightened. I was afraid he'd break his teeth.

Fields crouched, tearing the Polaroids free. His voice was flat, cold. "They're alive. Somewhere. He wants us to know it."

Then—etched into a jagged rock just behind Trevor's corpse—were the words:

> *Jack be nimble, Jack be quick,*
> *Jack jump over the candlestick.*
> *But flames don't fade, they cling, they crawl,*
> *And Jack can't run when the fire takes all.*

Beneath it, carved deep enough to bleed stone:

> *—Rhyme Reaper*
> *PS I'm breathing.*

I felt my stomach sink, not just from the horror, but from the difference. The book we found, the sketches, the evidence—all of it pointed to murders staged like illustrations, each rhyme accompanied by drawings as though it were a collection in a child's storybook.

But this?

This was theater. This was an audience, a performance, a message.

Asher exhaled sharply. "He's changing it. Switching his whole M.O."

Tanner swallowed hard. "He knows we're following the drawings... so he's throwing us off. Making new rules."

"New rules," Fields muttered, eyes narrowing at Trevor's charred remains. "And he just told us—he's always one step ahead."

The mannequins sat as silent witnesses to it all.

Watching. Waiting.

And in the smoke, I swore I could still hear his laughter.

14
Asher

Alexis stood rigid before Fields, her arms locked tight across her chest, as if sheer defiance could hold her fracturing world together. Her eyes blazed—not with anger, but with a raw, desperate fire, the kind that flares when you're one step from breaking. Beneath that glare, though, was something softer: fear, flickering like a shadow she couldn't shake. She'd always been tough, the kind of person who'd stare down a storm and dare it to blink first. But now? Now, her edges were fraying, and I could see the ghosts of her past in the way her hands trembled, betraying the weight of memories she'd buried deep.

"I don't understand why I'm even here," she snapped, her voice sharp but brittle. "You've got a whole damn team—agents, investigators, specialists. Why me?" The question wasn't just defiance; it was a plea, a demand to know why her life kept circling back to this nightmare named Nathan.

Fields didn't flinch. His hands stayed clasped behind his back, his posture as unyielding as the truth he carried. "Because, Alexis, whether you like it or not, you know Nathan. Better than anyone. His patterns. His obsessions. The way his voice lingers in a room, even when he's gone. He's circling you, and that makes you the center of this investigation. He's your half-brother." His tone was steady, but there was a weight to it, an acknowledgment of the burden he was placing on her already bruised shoulders.

Her jaw clenched, teeth grinding so hard I could almost hear the strain. "So, what—you're basically asking me to be bait?" The word landed, cutting through the room's tension.

Silence. A muscle twitched in Fields' cheek, the only crack in his stoic facade. He didn't confirm it, but he didn't deny it either. That silence was louder than any admission.

My gut twisted as I watched her. Alexis, who'd once laughed so freely it could light up a room, now stood as if a statue under the weight of it all. Her shoulders sagged, not from defeat but from exhaustion, and her eyes drifted, unfocused, as if she were already back in Austin—back to the porch swing where she'd sip coffee at dawn, pretending the world was still whole. She was unraveling, thread by thread, and I knew if she stayed in this game much longer, we'd lose her. Not to Nathan's schemes, but to the quiet despair eating her from the inside.

"I want to go back," she said suddenly, her voice cracking, raw with a vulnerability she'd never let show before. "I want to go home. To Austin. I can't..." Her fists trembled, and she stopped, swallowing the rest of the words as if they burned. Austin wasn't just a place for her—it was her haven after the storm, after she thought she killed Nathan, and after the fear, the riddles, and the endless running. It was where she'd taught herself to hope again, after years of building walls around her heart.

My chest tightened. If Fields pushed her now, she'd break. And if she broke, there'd be no piecing her back together—not the Alexis who'd once believed in second chances, who'd stayed up late telling stories about when she was three in her grandmother's kitchen, where the smell of fresh bread could fix anything.

Before I could step in, Cooper's voice cut through, calm and steady—a lighthouse in a storm. "What if we helped?"

All eyes turned to him. Cooper, with his quiet intensity, the kind of guy who noticed the smallest details—how a shadow fell wrong, how a word didn't fit. He wasn't loud or showy, but his mind was a steel trap, and right now, it was locked on saving Alexis. He lifted his chin, unshaken by the room's tension. "The pictures Nathan left behind? I can work through them. I see the patterns, the details—what doesn't belong. I can find the threads."

Tanner stepped up beside him, his usual easy grin replaced by a grim nod. "And the rhymes—those creepy riddles he loves? They're codes. They point to who he's targeting next. I can break them apart. Together, we can actually stay ahead of him for once." Tanner was the optimist, even after losing Sadie, but even he carried a shadow now—a flicker of guilt for not protecting Sadie and now the look in his eyes showed he'd do anything to protect Alexis.

Fields' eyes narrowed, his gaze flicking between them, calculating. He was a man who lived by control, by plans and protocols, and I could see the gears turning as he weighed their offer against the risks.

"They're not wrong," I said, my voice rougher than I meant, scraping against the tension. "We've been part of this from the start—deeper than your agents, deeper than anyone." I wasn't just defending them; I was pleading for Alexis, for a chance to pull her back from the edge.

Fields' gaze moved from Alexis, whose eyes were still locked on some distant point, to Cooper, then Tanner, and back again. His jaw tightened, the decision warring with his instinct to keep things tight and professional. "This isn't a game," he muttered, low and clipped. "And we have his book. Things will be different."

"So is Nathan," Cooper shot back, his voice quiet but sharp, cutting through the fog.

The words hung there, undeniable, a truth none of us could escape.

After a long, heavy silence, Fields exhaled, dragging a hand over his face, his composure fraying just enough to show the man beneath the badge. "Fine. You work alongside the team. No solo missions, no wandering into danger without backup. You coordinate, or you're out. Understood?"

Cooper and Tanner nodded with steed resolve. Alexis stayed silent, but a flicker of relief softened her eyes, a sign she wouldn't be forced to stand alone against Nathan's shadow. Not yet.

But I still saw it—the exhaustion carved into her face, the cracks in the armor she'd built over years of surviving. She was holding on by threads, and every day in this fight pulled another one loose. Alexis wasn't just fighting Nathan; she was fighting herself, the part that wondered if she deserved this, if she'd ever escape the orbit of his chaos.

Right then, I knew my job. Forget the case, forget Fields' strategies or Nathan's games. If I didn't find a way to anchor her—to remind her of the girl who'd once danced barefoot in the rain, who'd believed in tomorrows—she'd drown in her own doubts. Nathan wouldn't need to touch her to win.

Christmas was coming, maybe the last good one we'd have together in a long time. I thought of the way her face used to light up at the sight of twinkling lights, how she'd hum carols under her breath, thinking no one could hear. I'd be damned if I didn't make this one count, if I didn't give her something to hold onto when the darkness closed in.

15
Nathan - The Wolf

The captive's body was folded nicely into the crate, knees bent at wrong angles, wrists bound so tight the rope bit into flesh. Her head down as I had told her to—she obeyed without hesitation. The lock clanked against the crate. Perfect fit, isn't it? As if she were made for this box, this moment. Just like the others. No fuss, no fight. They learn quickly when the cage shuts.

Dog crates. Stackable. Containable. The perfect way to teach them that they were no better than mutts. Humans broke quicker when you stripped away the illusion of dignity. A cage shrank them, bent them, made them into things. Animals waiting for commands. Look at her, curled up like a kicked pup. Makes you wonder why they ever thought they were more. Dignity's just a lie they tell themselves.

This crate was lighter than the rest. She hardly weighed more than a bundle of bones wrapped in skin, and carrying her to the van took almost no effort. The silence inside it was a melody sweeter than any hymn, a hollow lull that thrummed against my ears, far better than the ragged, muffled breathing of the others. They knew what would happen to them if they disobeyed. Quiet now, aren't you? This one's smarter. Knows the rules. Silence is obedience, and obedience is life. For now.

Fear had its own perfume—sharp, metallic—copper coins ground against sweat-slick flesh. It clung to them, seeped out of their pores, and filled every breath they took. The van was drenched in it. The stink of terror had sunk deep into the padding on the walls, into the old carpet scraps I'd tacked across the floor. It never faded. Breathe it in. That's it. That's the good stuff. A vintage wine, only better. This is what they give you when they break. This is truth.

I inhaled deep, letting it crawl into my lungs, into my blood. It was better than smoke, better than whiskey, better than anything this world offered. Nothing else comes close. Not a single damn thing. This is what it means to be alive.

I checked the latch twice. Always twice. Never trust the drug completely. Eyes could still open, fingers could still claw. But mine didn't. Not anymore. My formula held—syringe precise. It took years of trial and error on any animal I could get my hands on to find the sweet spot between sleep and death. Too little, and they'd scream. Too much, and they'd spoil too early. I had perfected it. Years of work, and now it's art. One slip, and they're gone too soon. One drop too little, and they're howling. But I've got it down to a science. My science.

Pain ripped across my side when I straightened. My hand gripped my hip where the scar still burned—a souvenir from the blade that had come too close, carving heat against bone. It never healed right. Scar tissue knotted deep beneath the skin, flaring whenever I bent too fast or lifted too much. Sometimes I swore I could feel the knife again, sawing against me, a phantom cut that never stopped. Still there, huh? Still biting. Good. Keeps me sharp. Keeps me honest. You don't get to forget the ones who fight back.

But I didn't curse it. Pain wasn't punishment. It was scripture. Every throb reminded me of the lesson: that weakness could become ritual, that scars could sanctify. Pain's a teacher. Pain's a preacher. It's the only thing that never lies.

I dragged another crate toward the van. Becca and William slumped inside theirs, Polaroids already left at the last scene. Their heads lolled, mouths taped shut, alive but half-gone. I liked them better that way. Puppets with strings pulled too tight. They would last, I decided.

Look at you two. Perfect little dolls. Ready for the show. You'll see it all, won't you? Every verse, every scream.

Three more crates waited in the corner, small, medium, and large, like the Three Bears—faces nameless for now. Their roles would come soon enough. Every nursery rhyme had its cast. Trevor had already played his part in the fire, Jack be nimble, Jack be quick. I could still smell the char on my hands, and could still see his face even though the skin bubbled and cracked. He had lasted longer than I thought he would. Trevor, Trevor. You burned so bright. Didn't think you had it in you. Almost made me proud.

That one had been special. The flames didn't just burn—they performed, curling and bowing as if they knew they were being watched. I remember the heat blooming against my skin and the thrill rising with it, bright and effervescent, the way it used to when I was a child holding sparklers in the dark, convinced I was controlling the stars.

And Alexis—God, Alexis.

The way she looked when she saw him. The way the truth finally reached her eyes. They went wide, luminous with terror and recognition, her lips trembling as if they were trying to form a word her mind wasn't ready to accept. That moment was perfect.

Oh, Alexis. You should have seen yourself through my binoculars. Framed. Still. Exactly where you were meant to be.

As if you finally understood.

As if you'd been handed the story at last—and realized you were never the reader.

You were the art.

A soft mewl cut through the silence. My cat padded out from the shadows, brushing against my leg, tail curling like smoke. I bent to stroke her back, the only living thing in my world free to come and go. There you are, my little shadow. Always watching, aren't you? You get it. You know why I do this.

Funny. Years ago, I killed cats. Snapped their necks, drowned them, burned them, gutted them, tore them apart—testing myself, testing God, seeing if I'd flinch. I didn't. Not once. I kept going until there was no thrill left in their deaths. That's when I knew. Cats were wasted on killing. Humans gave me the real rush. The real hymns. Cats were practice. Stepping stones. They taught me how to hold a life in my hands and squeeze. But humans? They're the real song. They scream so much prettier.

Now, she was the exception. My companion. My confessor. Her purrs filled the spaces between my thoughts, low and steady, grounding me in the moment. She was the one voice that never judged, never screamed. She approved of me. I could see it in her eyes. You're the only one who stays, aren't you? The only one who doesn't run. You see me, and you stay.

I packed the last of my tools into the van—my blades, my rhyme cards, the accelerants, the new notebooks filled with jagged sketches. No chaos here. Every jar, every rope coil, every syringe belonged. This was my cathedral. Each object had its place, each weapon a hymn, each rope a verse. Everything in its place. Every tool—a prayer. This is my church, and I'm the high priest.

The van's walls were padded with old blankets to muffle sound. I had glued scraps of nursery rhymes across the roof in my own handwriting. Some scrawled in black ink, others in rust-colored streaks. Sometimes, when the engine rumbled and the crates rattled, I'd recite them out loud until the captives wept. Sing with me, now. You know the words. You've heard them before. Cry if you want. It only makes the song sweeter.

As I slammed the doors, a faint whimper leaked from the crates. A muffled cry. The sound made my skin prickle with warmth. There it is. That's the sound. That's the music. Keep singing, little ones. Keep singing for me.

"Jack be nimble," I whispered, testing the words on my tongue. "Jack be quick. Jack jump over—" I grinned at the silence that followed, finishing it in my head. Oh, you know how it ends. Don't you? You all do.

Sliding into the driver's seat, I felt the cat leap gracefully into the passenger side, curling small and perfect, her yellow eyes watching me. She was calm. She understood. She always understood. Good girl. You're my witness. My muse. You see the beauty in this, don't you?

The van's engine growled, cages rattling in the back. I steered southeast. Always southeast. Alexis wouldn't linger in Oregon. Not after Trevor. Not after seeing what I'd carved into her story. Our story. She's running now, isn't she? Thinks she can escape. Thinks she can rewrite the ending. But this is my story, Alexis. And I know where you're going.

She'd run back to Austin, to safety, to her ghosts. And I'd be there waiting. You can't outrun me, Alexis. You can't outrun the rhyme.

The scar at my hip burned hot, pulsing with each turn of the wheels. My cat purred, vibrating against the rumble of the van. My captives breathed— shallow and terrified. Listen to that. The rhythm of it. The pulse. It's all coming together now.

And I whispered the rhymes to myself. Sing it, sing it. Let it fill you up. This is your hymn, your gospel. This is forever.

16

The Captive

I sucked in a breath as my body hit hard against the crate—another pothole, another bruise—which I was sure my body was covered in by now. Hours, maybe days, had gone by since seeing any light. There was a divider between the back of the van and the front seats; however, I could hear The Wolf whistling his rhymes and talking to his mangy cat.

I shifted, the crate's plastic pressing into my ribs. My mouth was dry, my tongue thick and sandpapered. The drugs he gave me were wearing thin, leaving my head foggy, my stomach sour. For so long, I thought I was the only one back here. Alone in the dark with my own heartbeat. But then—

"You awake?" a voice rasped, low and male, from somewhere to my left.

I froze, unsure if I had imagined it. My pulse hammered in my throat. "H-hello?" My voice cracked.

A pause, then: "You're not alone. I thought I was." His voice was weak and raw but steady enough to send a chill down my arms.

I pressed my forehead to the side of the crate, straining to hear. "Who are you?"

Silence. A cough. Then, softer: "Doesn't matter. Not here. Not yet."

I knew that voice. Somewhere in the fog of memory, I recognized it. Familiar, but slippery. My brain, heavy with chemicals, wouldn't cooperate. As if I were trying to grab smoke with my bare hands. The more I tried to cling to it, the further it slipped away.

Before I could ask again, the van lurched and then slowed. Gravel crunched under the tires. The Wolf's whistle stopped. I heard him take a long drag of something and hold it for a moment before muttering to the cat.

Through the cracks of the crate, I caught sight of a looming shape in the distance, illuminated by the headlights. A sign, rotted and leaning, its paint flaking in strips. The letters were ghostly in the wash of light: Lockhart Veterinary Hospital.

The bulbs inside the sign were long dead, the glass casing shattered, but I could imagine it glowing once, welcoming pets and their owners. Now the building was a husk, its brickwork cracked, its windows yawning empty—sockets in a skull.

The van rattled to a stop. The back doors squealed open, flooding the compartment with cold night air. The Wolf's shadow stretched long and bent, just like his gait. He dragged the first crate out, humming as he went. One by one, we were carried inside.

When it came time for the man's crate—the one who had spoken to me—I heard a violent clatter. The Wolf cursed, a guttural sound, and the van shook with the struggle. The sound of plastic scraping, fists hitting metal. A thud. Another.

Then the voice again, no longer weak but raw and fierce: "You're not taking me!"

For a heartbeat, hope surged hot in my chest. Someone was fighting back. Someone strong.

But The Wolf laughed, wheezing between the blows. "Oh, I've got something special planned for you." His tone was a lullaby of cruelty, a promise wrapped in sing-song. A heavy grunt, the crack of bone on metal, and then the fight went silent. When he spoke again, his voice dripped with amusement. "Don't worry. Your time will come."

The next sound was the squeal of rusted hinges. A cage door clanged shut, rattling against its lock.

By the time it was my turn, I was shaking. He hefted my crate as though I weighed nothing, humming louder now, pleased with himself. Inside the building, the air was colder, staler. The scent of ammonia and mildew burned my nostrils.

The Lockhart Hospital was a corpse. Faded posters of dogs and cats peeled from the walls, their cartoon smiles warped. Metal tables with cracked ceramic tops were shoved against the walls, rust spiderwebbing their legs. Old leashes and muzzles dangled from hooks resembling nooses. Dried stains—maybe blood, maybe something else—darkened the tile floor.

He lined the crates against the wall of what had once been an operating room. His cat jumped onto one of the counters, its tail flicking, its eyes reflecting the dim light like twin coins. The Wolf stroked its back as though it were royalty, humming all the while.

The drugs still churned in my system, and reality wavered. At first, I thought I saw myself step out of the crate, smiling, helping him arrange the others, lining them up. My fingers brushed his. I handed him the leashes. I laughed when he whispered rhymes into my ear.

The sickness came quickly, hot in my gut, twisting. No, that wasn't me. That couldn't be me. I gagged, bile burning my throat. My body convulsed, pressing me harder against the plastic walls of the crate.

I couldn't tell anymore if I was imagining it or if The Wolf really glanced back at me with that crooked smile—as though he knew exactly what I'd seen, exactly how the drugs twisted me into believing I could ever help him.

And the worst part was, for a split second, some dark corner of me wanted to.

17

Alexis

The scent of cinnamon rolls, sweet and laced with cloves and nutmeg, should have been a warm embrace, a tether to childhood mornings when "home" was a word that held weight. Instead, it sat heavy in my chest, a bitter reminder of how long it had been since that word meant anything but an ache. Each breath dragged me further from comfort, tying me to memories of a life that no longer existed.

I blinked awake on the Finns' couch, the faint glow of Christmas lights—soft reds, greens, and golds—its flickering reflection against the frosted windowpane resembling a heartbeat struggling to keep time. Tami had strung them up with desperate care, as if their fragile twinkle could hold her crumbling world together. From the kitchen, her humming clashed with the sharp clatter of mugs and plates, each sound too forceful, betraying the strain beneath her forced cheer.

Keith drifted through the house, a ghost in his own home, his dad jokes dissolving into the silence his children left behind. His voice cracked with a quiet desperation, as if he could will normalcy back into existence if he just kept pretending. But Cooper stayed silent, his eyes fixed on nothing. Tanner's gaze never left the floor. And Asher's silence screamed louder than any words could.

I curled into myself on the edge of the couch, knees pressed to my chest, feeling like an interloper in a family unraveling at the seams. The Finns were fracturing, each splinter a slow bleed, and I was at the center of it, a jagged piece in their broken mosaic. Keith's betrayal wasn't mine, but my mother's absence was. Now he faced his children's quiet hatred over breakfast every morning. And maybe—maybe I did too.

It didn't feel like Christmas.

Asher found me first.

He sank onto the couch beside me, his presence soft but heavy—a shadow that carried too much weight. His hair stuck up in wild, uncombed tufts, his hoodie half-zipped, as if he'd given up on himself before the day even began. His knee bounced, a nervous rhythm that mirrored my own racing pulse.

"You okay?" His voice was low and cautious, as if he were afraid of breaking something fragile.

I nodded too fast, the lie automatic. "Yeah."

"You're not sleeping." It wasn't a question.

My throat tightened, choking on the truth I didn't want to voice. The dreams—rhymes that slithered through my sleep, faces that shifted between Nathan's cruel smirk, my mother's pleading eyes, and Trevor's burned, accusing stare—haunted me. I couldn't let them spill out.

"I hear you," Asher said, softer now, his eyes searching mine. "Pacing at night. Muttering to yourself."

I pressed my forehead to my knees, hiding from his gaze. "It's nothing."

"It's not *nothing*." His voice broke, raw and cutting through. "I can't lose you, too. Maybe we should get a dog... you know, an emotional support animal."

The words hit like a fist to my chest, stealing my breath. He looked away, his jaw tight, swallowing hard against what he couldn't say. Silence stretched between us, heavy with unspoken fears, and neither of us dared break it.

And in that quiet, Ranger came back to me.

Not whole. Never whole.

Just flashes—his body on the ground, the wrong stillness of it, the way his eyes hadn't closed no matter how much I begged them to. Blood dark against fur. The sound I made when I realized he wasn't alive ripped from my throat before I could stop it. The memory slammed into me without warning, sharp and merciless, as if my mind had decided this was the moment to remind me what loss really looked like.

I clenched my teeth, forcing the images back down and myself to stay in the room. Because if I let them surface—if I let Ranger's death take root between us—something in me would fracture beyond repair.

Cooper was fully absorbed in his work. In the dining room, he hunched over a sketchpad, with crime scene photos spread out like a dark tarot card. His pencil deliberately drew sharp lines, transforming shadows into faces and symbols into patterns. His jaw was clenched, and his focus was intense and unrelenting, as if the monsters he drew were just equations waiting to be solved, not nightmares brought to life.

"Fields needs these by tonight," he said quietly, without looking up, his tone sharp and cold.

I looked at the photos—blurry mannequins arranged in disturbing displays, their limbs contorted as if mocking life. My stomach tightened, and bile rose in my throat. "You're... good at this," I said, the words sour in my mouth because, deep down, I knew it was all pointless.

"I don't have time to be good," he snapped. "I just need to be useful."

Keith appeared in the doorway, clutching two steaming mugs of coffee, his smile fragile. "Coop, take a break. It's Christmas morning."

Cooper didn't flinch, didn't look up. His pencil kept moving, scratching louder than Keith's plea. Keith's face fell, the mugs trembling in his hands as he set them down and retreated, leaving silence in his wake.

Tanner was quieter, but his intensity burned just as fiercely.

He sat cross-legged by the fireplace, a notebook open on his lap, filled with nursery rhymes written in flowing ink. Each line was annotated with notes on rhythm, cadence, and meaning. His phone was beside him, with Fields' email visible on the screen like a warning.

"The rhymes aren't random," he murmured when he caught me watching, his voice low but certain. "They're steps. A sequence."

"Steps to what?" My voice wavered, barely audible.

His eyes darkened, shadows pooling in their depths. "Fields is trying to figure that out."

The room seemed to tilt, and I caught myself against the wall, each word pressing me down more. Every rhyme and clue felt like nails driven deeper into the coffin I was already in. Christmas dinner felt fake, just an empty show. Tami had gone all out—her glazed roasted ham was perfect, served with carrots, mashed potatoes, and green beans with almonds. Candles flickered on the table, their light mocking any real warmth. She smiled too wide, laughed too loudly, and her wine glass was refilled one too many times.

Keith carved the ham, his hands unsteady, his knife slipping. He tried a joke—something about his slices belonging in a commercial—but it fell flat. Cooper didn't speak. Tanner kept his eyes on his plate. Asher pushed his food around, each scrape of his fork a quiet act of defiance.

I forced myself to swallow, but every bite tasted bitter.

Keith raised his glass, his voice trembling yet resolute. "To family."

The silence that followed was a living thing, suffocating us all. It was louder than Cooper's pencil, louder than Tanner's pen, louder than the sing-song cadence of Nathan's rhymes echoing in my head. *To family*. I pictured the mannequins again, frozen around their eternal feast, their glass eyes staring, their smiles empty. A staged family, dead and perfect.

That was us. But our cracks were starting to show.

Later, I felt like the air was too thick to breathe. I stepped outside, the cold piercing my coat as snow crunched under my boots. The neighborhood shimmered with Christmas lights—reds, greens, blues, and golds—twinkling in patterns that seemed almost intentional, a mysterious code I couldn't decipher. The quiet night offered no comfort; instead, it only made the voices inside my mind louder. I heard my mother's soft, pleading whisper. Luke's sharp, police-detective tone. Trevor's raw and accusing scream. Ronny's rough I'm-your-dad voice. And Nathan, my half-brother, his sing-song voice weaving through the background dark: *Jack be nimble, Jack be quick...*

I pressed my hands to my ears, but the rhymes were inside me, clawing at my skull. I wanted to run, to escape, but there was nowhere left to go. Fields had called me bait, said Nathan wouldn't stop until he had me. I was living in a house of broken people, pretending we could be whole, when I was just the worm on the hook, writhing, waiting.

I crouched in the snow, hugging my knees as the cold seeped through my jeans. My breath fogged in the air, my tears freezing on my cheeks. "You won't win," I whispered, but the words were frail, hollow.

Deep down, I wasn't sure I believed them. The rhymes, the lights, the Finns' fragile hope—they were all closing in, and I was running out of places to hide.

I wanted to get rid of everything.

I needed to purge.

18
Alexis

Christmas felt like a lie, a cruel illusion of warmth that fell apart as my world unraveled. The Finns' house, with its shimmering lights and cinnamon aroma, as if it was a stage for a play I couldn't act in. I sat curled on their frost-covered lawn, knees pulled to my chest, breath visible in the cold air. My fingers clenched my jeans, nails digging into the fabric, as if pain could ground me when everything else—Sadie, Mom, my sense of safety—had been taken by Nathan. The Rhyme Reaper. My half-brother. The monster I believed I had killed is now shadowing me.

I was no longer the girl I once was. The old Alexis—who used to laugh with Sadie beneath the Gold Beach stars, believing Austin's bright lights could wash away the blood on my hands—had been transformed into something sharper and more resilient. Wings of steel, hardened by pain, now carried me. Agent Fields' bait jabbed like a blade in my mind, not merely a tactic but a challenge to confront Nathan and tear him apart. My stomach twisted, not out of fear but with a blazing fury—shame for missing his heart in that cave, my knife too shallow, fueling a resolve to end him. He thought he could trap me with wolf-like paws and clever rhymes, trying to provoke me into breaking. But he was mistaken. I was no prey; I was the hunter, and his mocking words would become his last send-off.

The cold sliced through my coat, but it couldn't touch the fire in my chest. I glared at the snow-dusted grass, visions of the cave from three years ago clawing at me—Sadie's lifeless eyes, Nathan's smirk, my mother's finger in that cursed pumpkin. I'd tried to outrun it, to build a fortress with Asher, Cooper, and Tanner in Austin's sunlit streets. But Gold Beach had dragged me back, and Nathan's ghost wasn't just haunting me—it was carving me open, daring me to fight. I'd meet that dare with steel.

Asher's voice cut through the frost, sharp with worry yet steady as always. "Alexis?" He crouched nearby, his hoodie a flimsy shield against the chill, his breath a fleeting cloud. I met his gaze, unflinching, letting him see the fire, not the cracks. He hovered, cautious, as if I were a blade he feared might cut. "It's freezing. You shouldn't be out here."

I didn't flinch, didn't soften. Words were weapons now, and I'd wield them. "I'm not running," I said, my voice low, forged in resolve. Inside, Keith and Tami's voices bled from the living room, their argument a bitter echo of betrayal—Keith's affair with my mom, a wound that had fractured their family as deeply as Nathan had shattered mine. Cooper and Tanner were ghosts, hiding from the poison in the air. We were all scarred, but I wasn't the jagged edge anymore—I was the sword.

My phone buzzed, a jolt in the silence. Fields' name burned on the screen, and my pulse surged, not with fear but with purpose. "Alexis," he said, his voice taut and urgent. "We've got a lead from Trevor's crime scene. It points to a warehouse in Bandon. I need you there—bring the evidence, everything you've found. Cooper and Tanner aren't answering."

My jaw tightened, teeth grinding. "What's in Bandon?" I demanded, my voice like iron.

A pause, wind howling, sirens faint in the background. "You need to see it. I'm sending you the address. Hurry." The line cut out. I clutched the phone, my heartbeat pounding.

Nathan. This was his territory, his song, his game meant to draw me in. But I wasn't his pawn—I would be his reckoning. Asher watched silently, waiting, but I stayed steady. "We're going," I said, standing, voice sharp and cold. "Fields found something. Bandon." Asher's hand brushed mine, his fingers cold but firm, a tether I didn't need but welcomed. "Let's get you inside first," he said, his tone tense but composed. He led me to Tami's Jeep Cherokee; my steps were sure despite the fire burning inside me. I wasn't fleeing Nathan's shadow—I was stepping into it.

The drive was a haze of frost and silence, Gold Beach's streets fading into Bandon's jagged skyline. My breath fogged the window, but I didn't see the road—I saw the cave, the blood, the ladybug carvings that had branded my nightmares. Asher's hand on my knee was a quiet anchor, but it couldn't douse the inferno in my gut. Nathan's cruelty wasn't a memory—it was a living beast, and I'd slay it.

We left our car a block away from the warehouse, whose massive outline resembled a predator lurking under faint streetlights. Its paint was peeling, windows boarded up, shadows resembling talons—more a grave than a building. The smell of rust, decay, and a chemical sting filled the air, searing my throat. As my boots crunched on the frost-covered asphalt, each step was a deliberate challenge against the darkness. I wasn't here to back down—I was here to prevail.

"Stay close," Asher murmured, but his voice was drowned by the roar in my ears. My hands clenched, knuckles sharp against my coat. This was Nathan's lair, his altar of madness, and I'd tear it down.

Inside, the warehouse looked like a maze of dust-filled tunnels, with the air heavy with long-forgotten screams. Our flashlights pierced the darkness, exposing cracked walls and rusted pipes. A faint hum echoed through the halls, drawing us deeper inside. My chest ached with every step, shadows closing in, but I kept moving. I wasn't the girl who ran away—I was the one who faced the challenge.

We entered the room, and my breath caught—not from fear but from rage. The tall concrete walls were marked by wolf paw prints that gleamed in the light. My heart pounded fiercely—a battle cry—as I brushed my fingers over a claw mark, its jagged edge pulsated. Rhymes twisted across the stone—*"Humpty Dumpty," "Ring around the Rosie"*—their verses warped into signs of death. My sight sharpened, tears driven not by weakness but by anger, burning intensely. He thought he could break me here, in his madness's shrine. I would turn it to ashes.

The stench hit—damp concrete, metallic blood, decay so thick it choked me. My stomach twisted, memories of Sadie's body, Mom's finger, crashed over me. "He kept people here," I growled, voice steel, no longer breaking. "He tortured them. Caged them." The words were a vow, not guilt—I hadn't stopped him then, but I would now.

Asher's hand gripped mine, a lifeline I didn't need but took, his touch grounding my fire. "I feel it too," he said, but his voice was a whisper against the screams I heard in my head—captives, victims, lives Nathan had stolen. Crates lined the walls, some empty, some spilling horrors—torn fabric, rusted chains, a cracked dog collar. Each a story, a soul he'd crushed. I didn't stagger; I stood taller, gripping Asher's arm. "I won't let him," I hissed, teeth bared. "He wanted me here, to feel this. He's wrong—I'm not his bait. I'm his end."

"You're not helping him," Asher said, fierce, but I didn't need his words. I was already moving, my resolve a blade cutting through fear. Cooper and Tanner appeared, flashlights carving the dark, their steps purposeful—Cooper decoding scratches, Tanner tracing rhymes—but I didn't need their answers. My eyes locked on the far wall, where photographs hung like trophies. Us—me, Asher, Cooper, Tanner—in Gold Beach, in Austin, at college, in moments I'd thought were mine. Stolen. Violated. My breath hissed out, a single tear falling, but I wiped it away. "He's been watching us," I snarled, voice a low burn. "Not anymore."

We pushed deeper into the warehouse, the crates heavier with relics—bloodstained rags, a cracked mirror, a child's shoe. The rhymes grew frantic, scrawled in jagged red ink—or blood— Nathan's mind unraveling on the walls. A smaller room opened, a suffocating vault, its walls a gallery of his obsession. More photos, more rhymes, pages torn from his nursery rhyme book—mine, but defiled, bleeding ink. A mannequin loomed in the corner, wearing my jacket from high school, a *"Ladybug, ladybug"* note pinned to its chest. My heart thundered, not with fear but with defiance. I wasn't his doll, his verse, his prey. This was his altar, and I'd shatter it.

Fields stood nearby, his face a grim mask, but he was a shadow to me. This wasn't his fight—it was mine. The warehouse was Nathan's mind, every scratch a scream, every photo a taunt. I wanted to torch it, to erase him, but I wouldn't. Not yet. Within this horror was the key to his downfall, and I'd carve it out with my own hands. I stood, unyielding, the shadows recoiling from my fire. Nathan thought he could pose me, break me. He was wrong. This was my story now, and I'd write his ending in blood.

19
Asher

The plane's engines hummed, a low growl that couldn't drown the fire in Alexis's eyes. She sat beside me, staring out the window at the Oregon clouds fading into dusk, her jaw set, her gaze burning with a fury I hadn't seen since the cave three years ago. The Bandon warehouse—its wolf paws, bloodied rhymes, and that damned mannequin in her jacket—had lit a fuse in her. She wasn't the broken girl, haunted by Sadie's death and her mother's loss. She was a hunter now, forged in pain, her wings of steel carrying her toward Nathan's reckoning. I admired her, hell, I was in awe, but my gut twisted with fear—she was ready to be bait, to walk into the Rhyme Reaper's jaws, and I wasn't sure I could protect her from that blaze.

Gold Beach had gutted us, ripped open old wounds, but the warehouse was worse—a shrine to Nathan's madness, his photos of us pinned, his rhymes a taunt that we'd never escape. I shifted in my seat, the plane's recycled air sharp with jet fuel and tension. Cooper and Tanner sprawled across the aisle, their usual chatter muted, but I caught their glances—worried, restless, like mine. We were the Four Blind Mice, bound by loss, and now we were flying back to Austin, chasing a life we'd thought was safe. But Nathan's shadow followed, his wolf paws carved into my mind as deeply as they were into that warehouse wall.

"You okay?" I asked Alexis, my voice low, rough with the weight of what we'd seen. She didn't turn, just nodded, her fingers gripping the armrest, knuckles white. The fire in her eyes wasn't just anger—it was purpose, a vow to end Nathan. I wanted to hold her, to ground her, but she was a blade now, and I didn't want to dull her edge. "You should talk to Genevieve when we land," I said, keeping it steady. "She's helped before, right? You don't have to carry this alone."

Her lips twitched, not a smile but a flicker of acknowledgment. "Maybe," she said, voice like iron, still staring at the clouds. "But I'm not running, Ash. I couldn't put the pieces together last time to save everyone. I'll do whatever I can to not fail." Her words hit, fierce and unyielding, echoing the defiance she'd shown in the warehouse. She wasn't just fighting Nathan—she was fighting the girl she'd been, the one who'd let guilt and fear cage her.

I leaned back, forcing a grin to lighten the weight. "Hey, Coop," I called across the aisle, "you think Austin's ready for Lex's new badass vibe? She's gonna scare the Longhorns right off campus."

Cooper snorted, raking a hand through his messy hair. "Man, she's scarier than Nathan's creepy rhymes. I'm just hoping she doesn't bench press me to prove a point." His grin was weak, but it was there, a spark of our old rhythm.

Tanner leaned forward, his notebook open to broken rhymes. "Yeah, but I'm betting she takes out Nathan before breakfast. Girl's got fire." He winked at Alexis, his voice lighter than his eyes, which still carried Sadie's ghost.

Alexis's gaze flicked to them, a spark of amusement breaking through her steel. "Keep talking, Tan. I'll make you run laps with me at dawn." Her voice was sharp, playful, but that fire didn't fade—it burned brighter, fueled by their banter.

I laughed, the sound forced but real enough to ease the knot in my chest. "See? We're gonna need a bigger house in Austin to fit her ego now." I nudged her shoulder, hoping to keep that spark alive. She rolled her eyes, but her lips curved, just a fraction, and it was enough to remind me why I'd fight to keep her safe.

The plane dipped, turbulence rattled the cabin, and my mind flashed back to the warehouse—those crates, the bloodstained rags, the child's shoe. Nathan had been watching us, stealing pieces of our lives for three years. My fists clenched, anger surging for Sadie, for Alexis, for the family fracturing under Dad's betrayal. His affair with Alexis's mom had broken us, left Mom's smiles hollow, Cooper and Tanner silent at Christmas dinner. But Nathan? He was the real enemy, the one who'd turned our lives into his twisted nursery rhyme. I wouldn't let him win.

"You're quiet," Alexis said, finally turning to me, her eyes searching, cutting through my mask. "What's going on in there?" She tapped her temple, her voice softer but still edged with that hunter's resolve.

I shrugged, forcing another grin. "Just planning how to keep up with you. You're moving at superhero speed now." It was a dodge, but I couldn't voice the fear—that Nathan's game would swallow her, that being bait would cost her more than she could give. Instead, I said, "Seriously, call Genevieve. She'll help you channel that fire without burning out."

She nodded, her gaze softening, and for a moment, I saw the Alexis I'd fallen in love with—the one who'd danced in Austin's rain, who'd laughed with Sadie under the stars. But this Alexis was stronger, her fire tempered by pain, and I'd be her shield, no matter what. "I will," she said, voice steady. "But I'm ending this, Ash. For all of us."

The plane's descent began, Austin's lights glinting below. Tanner cracked another joke about Texas BBQ curing our nightmares, and Cooper sketched a cartoon of Nathan as a wolf in a Longhorn jersey, making Alexis huff a laugh. I held onto that sound, small but fierce, a reminder of what we were fighting for. Nathan thought he could break us, pose us like his mannequins. He was wrong. Alexis was a hunter, and I'd stand with her, through every rhyme, every shadow, until his game was over.

The plane touched down, the jolt grounding me. Austin wasn't safe—not with Nathan out there—but it was our battleground now. I glanced at Alexis, her eyes still burning, and knew we'd face it together. Her fire was my fire, and we'd burn his world to ash.

20
Alexis

T he Uber driver dropped us off at our two-story house in Austin, its large windows snaring the late afternoon sunlight, casting golden shards that stung my eyes. The warmth sank into my skin as I stood frozen, staring, the heat a cruel tease of safety. Home. This was our sanctuary, where laughter with Asher, Cooper, and Tanner had stitched together a life after Gold Beach's horrors. Late-night study sessions, impromptu dance parties in the kitchen, coffee-fueled dreams under the Texas stars—they'd built a fortress against the past. But the Bandon warehouse, with its pulsing wolf paws, bloodied rhymes, and that mannequin wearing my jacket, had followed me, a shadow hissing Nathan's name. My half-brother. The Rhyme Reaper. The monster I'd failed to kill in that cave three years ago. I wasn't that weak, naïve girl anymore—my wings of steel, forged in pain and guilt, carried me now, and I'd burn his world to ash before he stole this home from me.

I dropped my bags, the thud jarring against the sun-warmed pavement, and ran to the grass, spinning like a child, arms wide, defying the darkness that clawed at my bones. The earthy scent of soil filled my lungs, warm and alive, grounding me in the moment. I collapsed onto the ground, moving my arms and legs as if making a snow angel, grass prickling my skin, daring me to feel free.

Cooper's chuckle rumbled nearby, deep and steady, sketching the scene in his notebook, his pencil feverishly scratching. Tanner's laugh cut through, sharp and bright, his fingers already weaving a poem in his mind, words to cage the ghosts we'd brought from Gold Beach. Asher's soft grin warmed me more than the sun, his eyes searching mine, anchoring me. They were my family, my tether, and I'd fight with every ounce of my soul to protect this—this life, this home, these moments.

"Lex, you're gonna wear out the lawn," Cooper teased, his broad frame casting a shadow as he sketched my sprawl, his pencil capturing the defiance in my spin. His eyes sparkled, but the tightness around them betrayed the warehouse's claw marks, the wolf paws he'd drawn in Bandon still haunting his lines.

Tanner, scribbling in his notebook, smirked. "She's a hurricane now, Coop. I'm writing a poem about it—'Wings of Steel,' maybe." His voice was light, but his fingers trembled, Sadie's ghost lingering in every verse he penned for her. His poetry was his shield, but it couldn't erase the warehouse's rhymes.

Asher stepped closer, his hoodie loose, hair mussed from the flight. His gaze locked on mine, soft but piercing, as if he could see the fire I was stoking inside. "You okay?" he asked, voice low, threaded with worry. He didn't touch me, but his presence was a lifeline, steadying the storm in my chest.

I nodded, forcing a smile, the grass cool against my back. "Just staking my claim," I said, voice a blade honed by resolve. I wasn't ever going to be a girl who would cower, who'd let Nathan's shadow cage her. I was a hunter now, and this house was my ground to defend.

We hauled our bags inside, the front door creaking, the air thick with cedar and coffee, but laced with a metallic tang, as if the warehouse's decay had seeped across state lines. The living room embraced us, its mismatched furniture a patchwork of our lives: the couch where we'd binged horror movies, laughing to drown the fear; the table where Tanner's poems for Sadie piled like offerings; the bookshelf holding my worn copy of nursery rhymes, its pages defiled with secrets of the past.

"Man, I'm starving," Cooper said, rummaging through the kitchen, his sketchpad tucked under his arm. "Pizza run? Extra pepperoni, none of Tan's kale nonsense." His pencil tapped, already drawing the pizza box in his mind, a distraction from the wolf paws he couldn't stop sketching.

Tanner scoffed, his pen pausing mid-verse. "Keep it up, Coop, and I'll write a poem about your grease-stained soul." Their laughter was a balm, but it couldn't erase the chill slithering up my spine, the sense that Nathan's eyes were already here, watching through the cracks.

I climbed the stairs to my bedroom, the wood groaning under my boots, each step heavier as the warehouse's horrors clawed at my mind—wolf paws pulsing, photos bleeding red ink, that mannequin whispering *"Ladybug, ladybug."*

My room was a haven, walls lined with photos of happier times: Sadie's mischievous grin at a beach bonfire, Asher's arm around me at Barton Springs, Cooper and Tanner mid-laugh at a UT game. But the warmth turned to ice as I reached the window, the glass glinting under the fading sun. There, taped to the pane, was a note, its edges curling toward me, red ink seeping across it: *"Goosey Goosey Gander, whither shall I wander? Upstairs and downstairs, your blood I'll squander."* The words hummed faintly, a distorted melody rising from the paper itself, Nathan's malice vibrating through the glass, as if the house itself breathed his threat.

My breath caught, heart pounding, fingers trembling as they brushed the cold pane, the chill biting. He'd been here, in my room, defiling my sanctuary. The room spun, visions of the warehouse crashing over me—mannequins with whispering lips, their painted eyes glinting, Sadie's lifeless gaze blaming me for her death, my mother's finger in that cursed pumpkin. My stomach churned, bile rising, but I clenched my fists, nails digging into palms, grounding my fury. This wasn't fear—it was fire, molten and unyielding. Nathan thought he could cage me, pose me like his mannequins. He was wrong. I was his hunter, and this note was his mistake—a gauntlet I'd pick up with steel.

I ripped the note from the window, the tape tearing with a sharp rip, the hum fading but lingered in my ears. "Guys!" I called, voice steady despite the storm inside. Cooper and Tanner appeared, Cooper, clutching his sketchpad, Tanner his notebook. I held up the note, its ink staining my fingers. "He's here."

Cooper's jaw tightened, his pencil flying across his pad, sketching the note's jagged script, capturing the red ink's bleed. "Bastard's got nerve," he muttered, his lines sharp, as if he could trap Nathan's threat in graphite. "I'm drawing this—every detail. Might be a clue."

Tanner's eyes darkened, his pen scratching a poem, words spilling like a spell. "*Goosey Gander, stalking near, blood and shadow fuel the fear,*" he murmured, voice low, his verse a blade against Nathan's rhyme. "We're going to catch this bastard!" His poetry was defiance, a way to cage the terror we all felt.

Asher stood behind them, his gaze locked on the note, then on me, his eyes burning with the same fire I felt. "We'll get him, Lex," he said, voice fierce. "You're not alone." His words were a vow, his presence a shield, and I clung to it.

I sank onto my bed, the mattress creaking, clutching the note. My eyes darted to the photos on the wall, Sadie's smile cutting into me. I'd failed her, failed to kill Nathan, my blade too shallow, his blood not enough. But I wasn't that girl anymore. I'd built this life—college, friends, these walls—and I'd fight for it. Nightmares would come tonight—mannequins moving, their plastic hands reaching, rhymes echoing screams—but they wouldn't break me. I'd call Genevieve tomorrow, let her help channel this rage, but tonight, I'd anchor myself here, with Asher's steady gaze, Cooper's sketches, Tanner's poems. I stood, shoving the note into my pocket, its weight a challenge I'd meet head-on. The window reflected my face, eyes blazing with fire, not fear.

Somewhere beneath the roar in my ears, things started happening.

Lights flickered outside—red, then blue, then white—but they felt distant, as if the world beyond my window belonged to someone else. Shadows moved across the front yard. Boots on gravel. Low voices I couldn't quite separate from the blood rushing through my head.

Cooper said something. Tanner answered. Asher's voice cut through once, sharp, controlled. Words like *evidence* and *interstate* floated up and dissolved before I could catch them.

The note left my hand at some point.

I watched from the top of the stairs as figures moved through the house—dark jackets, gloved hands, small flashlights slicing through corners of rooms. One of them stood in my doorway, the beam hovering over the windowpane where the tape had clung. Another crouched near the baseboards. A camera shutter clicked. Soft. Repetitive. Clinical.

It all felt underwater.

They carried the note away in a clear bag, red ink glaring under sterile light. Someone dusted the glass. Someone photographed the floor. Someone asked questions I couldn't remember answering.

Federal. I heard that word.

I heard *task force.*

I heard *he crossed state lines.*

But it didn't land.

None of it felt real.

It felt like watching strangers document a crime scene in someone else's life.

Like I was already a case file again.

The house breathed differently after they left—quieter, but heavier. Marked. Cataloged. No longer just ours.

And still, beneath it all, the fire in me didn't dim.

It sharpened.

A faint whistling drifted from outside, distorted and chilling, twisting into "Goosey Goosey Gander." My heart skipped, but I straightened, wings of steel gleaming. Nathan was coming, but so was I, and I'd write his end in blood.

21
Nathan - The Wolf

The Lockhart Veterinarian Hospital squatted on Austin's outskirts, brick walls cracked and bleeding moss, the air thick with ammonia and old animal blood. I slipped through the shattered glass doors, shards crunching under my boots, my cat slinking at my heels, yellow eyes glinting in the dim light leaking through boarded windows.

This was my new den—a place once meant for healing, now mine to twist. The scar on my side throbbed as I stepped deeper inside, burning hotter the closer I drew to Alexis. I saw it again—her eyes as she drove the blade into me. She thought I'd died.

But I'd risen.

The Wolf breathed. He hunted. And in this decayed sanctuary, I would carve my verses into Austin's heart—and then into hers.

I dragged the crates into the main operating room, metal shrieking across tile. Becca and William slumped inside, drugged, breaths shallow. I popped Becca's crate first. Her head lolled, blonde hair matted.

"Time to wake up."

The syringe gleamed. My formula was precise—enough to chain their wills, not enough to ruin them before the show. I injected her. She jerked, a moan slipping free as the drug burned through her veins.

William was next, his broad frame pressing against plastic walls. His snores turned to gasps as the needle bit.

They clung to the drugs. Becca drowning the memory of her son Trevor's melting skin in my fire. William enslaved by threats to his ex and boy. I made them need me. Freedom would mean withdrawal, convulsions, death in a gutter.

Kaitlyn huddled in the corner crate. Her thin fingers clutched through the bars toward Benji, whose leukemia-ravaged body curled tight, coughs weak and wet.

"Up, my puppets."

Becca blinked, terror sharpening her fogged gaze. William staggered upright, sweat slicking his pale face.

Kaitlyn's voice rasped. "Benji needs me. Let him come."

I laughed. "Your brother stays. He's no use out there." The police had been sniffing since Gold Beach. She'd run if given the chance. I couldn't allow that. Not when the gander's path was set.

"Barton Springs," I said. "Find me a jogger. Alone. Whither shall they go? Into the gander's grasp. Kaitlyn, you'll make sure they don't stray."

Her face crumpled, but she nodded, eyes flicking to Benji as he coughed against the crumbling walls.

Becca reached for the syringe. I slid it into my cargo pocket.

"You get more when you return."

William eyed my cat, who arched her back, purring low. "What if someone sees us?"

"They'll see junkies. People look away." I tossed him a mannequin arm, plastic fingers curled. "Pose them later. Eyes wide. Mouths open. Singing."

The mannequins were my silent choir—plastic witnesses I could bend into verses. I'd scavenged more from a deserted department store. Tonight they would wander Barton Springs with my puppets, luring the jogger into mist.

They stumbled out. Kaitlyn cast one last glance at Benji. The cat followed them, tail flicking in steady rhythm.

Silence swallowed the hospital, broken only by the drip of a faucet. Each drop counted down to Alexis.

My half-sister. My ladybug.

Ronny's confession in that prison cell had sealed it—Alexis was my blood, the missing verse. Not to destroy. To claim.

The local paper lay crumpled on the exam table. I smoothed it flat.

There she was—Alexis at the UT Austin welcome event, smile tight, eyes defiant. *Victim Advocacy Interns Shine at Orientation.*

Beside her stood a tall girl with strawberry-blonde hair—Lila, the caption read—arm linked with Alexis, unaware of my shadow. Alexis's posture was rigid, pulling back. Fear.

Asher hovered in the background, jaw tight, guarding her as always.

Perfect.

I traced her photo until the paper tore.

"She's close," I whispered. "She will be mine."

The Austin sun dipped, shadows stretching long across the hospital floor. Becca and the others would return soon, the jogger's routine mapped.

The kill would be poetry: a lone runner on the south trail, strangled in fog. The rhyme carved into flesh—

> *Goosey Goosey Gander,*
> *Whither shall I wander?*
> *Upstairs and downstairs,*
> *Your blood I'll squander.*

Mannequins scattered. A hidden speaker humming the verse. A stage for Alexis to find.

I gathered syringes and rope from a rusted cabinet. Trevor's screams still echoed in memory. William's turn would come.

A weak cough broke the silence.

Benji.

I smiled. "Patience, little lamb."

The door creaked.

Becca returned first, pale and hollow. "Female. Early twenties. South trail at dawn."

Kaitlyn followed, eyes red but obedient. William trailed behind, shaking.

Perfect.

"Let's go pose the geese."

Night fell heavy and wet over Barton Springs. Fog rolled in low, swallowing the south trail in a damp hush.

The jogger moved through it alone. Ponytail swinging. Breath steady.

I followed.

When she slowed, hands braced on her knees, I stepped from the mist.

My arm wrapped around her throat before she could scream.

Her skin was warm. Alive.

She clawed at my forearm, nails biting deep, tearing skin. I felt blood bead and run. I tightened my grip.

Her airway collapsed with a wet choke. Cartilage shifted beneath my forearm. A soft pop.

"Goosey Goosey Gander..." I breathed into her ear.

Her heels dug into gravel, kicking wildly. One shoe slipped off. Her body spasmed harder, oxygen starving her brain. Her face darkened—red to purple to a mottled gray. Veins bulged at her temples.

Her eyes.

They widened until the whites swallowed everything. Tiny red vessels burst across the sclera in spiderweb fractures.

I squeezed until her movements turned erratic, then weak. A tremor. A final shudder.

Her bladder released.

Warmth soaked through her leggings, mixing with the damp fog.

Then stillness.

I lowered her to the trail.

My knife slid free with a soft metallic whisper.

I carved slowly.

The blade split skin with a delicate resistance, then parted it cleanly. Blood welled thick and dark, spilling down her forearm, pooling in the grooves of her palm. I etched each word deep enough to scar bone.

Whither shall you wander?

When I finished, her arm was a ruin of opened flesh, letters swelling, edges ragged.

I posed the mannequins around her.

One knelt too close, its plastic hand resting in her hair. Another leaned back, jaw wrenched open wide enough to crack. I pinned photos to their hollow chests—Alexis. Asher. Cooper. Tanner.

Alexis's scarf draped over the nearest mannequin's shoulder, soaked in fresh blood until it clung dark and heavy.

I pressed play.

The hidden speaker crackled.

Goosey Goosey Gander...

The rhyme drifted through fog, thin and childish.

Dawn began to bleed across the sky.

I stepped back.

The jogger's eyes still stared upward, frozen wide, reflecting pale morning light.

The stage was set.

A body for the trail.

A message for my ladybug.

22
Asher

T he UT Austin campus buzzed with morning energy, students spilling across the quad, their laughter a stark contrast to the shadows clawing at my mind. The Tower loomed overhead, its clock ticking loudly, but all I could hear was the faint, distorted hum of *"Goosey Goosey Gander"* from Alexis's note she'd found last night. Her eyes had blazed with fire when she showed it to us, but I saw the cracks—fear beneath her defiance, the same haunted look she'd worn after losing so much three years ago and now still haunted by Sadie's ghost. Now, it was my turn. The wolf paws from the warehouse and the tree by our Oregon home pulsed in my vision, mannequins' painted eyes glinting in corners, Sadie's voice echoing rhymes in the wind. I shook my head, trying to banish the hallucinations, but they clung, mirroring the nightmares that had gripped Alexis three years ago. With Nathan's return, I felt as though he was tearing us apart from the inside.

We were at the victim advocacy center for our internships, the office a sterile box of fluorescent lights and coffee-stained desks, but the air felt heavy, laced with the metallic tang of dread from Gold Beach. Alexis sat across from me, her fingers tapping restlessly, her friend Lila beside her, chatting about track practice at Mike A. Myers Stadium. Lila's smile was bright, her energy infectious, but Alexis's posture was stiff, her answers clipped, as if she was afraid to let her get too close. I got it—Nathan's shadow made trust a luxury we couldn't afford. Lila had been her friend since freshman year, running laps together, sharing late-night study sessions, but Alexis kept her at arm's length, her fear of losing another Sadie a wall between them. I wanted to tell her to let Lila in, that she couldn't fight alone, but my own mind was fracturing, Sadie's laugh ringing in my ears, the cave's blood dripping from the ceiling in flashes I couldn't shake.

"Earth to Asher," Cooper said, nudging my shoulder, his sketchpad open on his lap. He was drawing the office, the lines sharp, capturing the tension in Alexis's jaw, the way Lila leaned in, oblivious to the distance. "You zoning out on us again?"

I forced a grin, my throat tight. "Just planning how to survive your cooking, Coop." His laugh was a low rumble, but his pencil didn't stop, sketching a wolf paw in the margin, a sign he was haunted, too.

Tanner sat nearby, scribbling poetry in his notebook. *"Shadows hum, the gander's near, verses carve our deepest fear,"* he murmured, his voice soft but heavy—a poem for Sadie, for all of us. His words were a shield, but his eyes were clouded, mirroring mine, mirroring Alexis's. Every so often, I caught him staring at Lila. It brought a quiet smile to my face. He'd never looked at anyone that way before—not even Sadie.

Lila glanced at Alexis, her strawberry blonde hair catching the light, her smile faltering as Alexis pulled back. "You okay, Lex? You've been quiet since track practice." Her voice was warm, but Alexis's nod was curt, her eyes flicking to the window, as if expecting Nathan to stare back.

"Yeah, just... tired," Alexis said, her voice a blade, sharp but brittle. She was lying, and I heard why—Nathan's note, his rhyme, his violation of our home. We didn't think he'd come so quickly for us, for her. Lila's concern was genuine, but Alexis's hesitation kept her at bay. Cooper's pencil paused, Tanner's pen stopped, both watching the exchange with subtle worry.

"I'm grabbing coffee," I said, standing abruptly, needing air. "Anyone want some?" Cooper waved me off, still sketching, and Tanner shook his head, lost in his poem. Alexis met my eyes, her fire flickering, and I nodded slightly, a silent promise: *I'm here.* Lila started to speak, but Alexis cut her off with a forced smile, keeping that wall up.

In the hallway, I leaned against the wall, the cold tile grounding me as Sadie's voice faded. My phone buzzed—Genevieve, Alexis's therapist, confirming a video call for her this afternoon. Good. Alexis needed to talk, to channel that fire before it burned her out. I'd pushed her to call Genevieve on the flight from Gold Beach, knowing she couldn't carry Nathan's weight alone. But who was I to talk? The mannequins haunted me, their whispering mouths echoing "Ladybug, ladybug," Sadie's face flickering in their plastic features. I rubbed my eyes, willing the images away, but they lingered, a reminder that Nathan wasn't just after Alexis—he was hunting in Austin.

Back in the office, Alexis was on her phone, her face pale, fingers gripping the edge of the desk. Lila hovered nearby, concern etched in her features, but Alexis's distance kept her at a distance. "Fields," Alexis said, her voice low, urgent, as she put the call on speaker. The room froze, Cooper's pencil pausing, Tanner's pen stopping mid-verse.

"Are all of you there?" Fields' voice crackled, sharp with tension.

In unison we all said, "Yes!"

Lila stood up to go, but I mouthed "It's okay," knowing Alexis could use her. She gave me a tight smile and sat back down.

"Barton Springs. We've got a body. Female, early twenties, jogger. Found at dawn on the south trail."

My stomach dropped, the hallucinations surging—Trevor's scorched body, mannequins in the mist, their mouths humming *"Jack Be Nimble."* I gripped the chair, forcing myself to focus. "Details?" I asked, voice steady despite the dread.

Fields' pause was heavy, the line hissing with static. "Strangled. Rhyme carved into her arm: *'Goosey Goosey Gander, whither shall I wander? Upstairs and downstairs, your blood I'll squander.'* Mannequins posed around her, eyes wide, mouths open like they're singing. And... photos. Of you all. Pinned to the mannequins. One's got Alexis's scarf."

The room spun, Sadie's voice louder now, chanting the rhyme in my head. Alexis's face hardened, her voice unyielding, but her hands trembled, betraying the fear beneath her steel. Lila's eyes were wide, her hand reaching for Alexis, but Alexis pulled back, her wall higher than ever. Cooper's jaw tightened, his pencil scratching furiously, sketching the scene from Fields' words, a mannequin with Alexis's scarf taking shape. Tanner's poem spilled faster, *"Blood on the trail, the gander's call, shadows rise to make us fall."*

"We're on our way," Alexis said, standing before I could stop her. "He knows we're watching." Her voice was fierce, but I saw the ghost of her old self—Nicole's death, Sadie's murder, the nightmares that had torn her apart. Lila started to speak, but Alexis cut her off with a forced smile, keeping that wall up.

"Lex, wait," I said, stepping closer, my voice low. "You need to talk to Genevieve first. This is...it's too much." I glanced at Lila, her concern palpable, but Alexis's hesitation kept her at a distance. Cooper's jaw tightened, his sketchpad clutched—shielding him, and Tanner's eyes darkened, his poem a quiet vow.

"I'm not alone," Alexis snapped, but her gaze softened, flicking to Cooper, Tanner, then me. "But I'm not letting him take anyone else." She paused, glancing at Lila, her voice quieter. "I'm sorry, Lila. I just... I can't lose you, too."

Lila's lips pressed into a line, her strawberry blonde hair falling over her shoulder as she nodded. "I get it, Lex. But I'm tougher than I look. Track teammates, remember? I can keep up." Her words were light, but her eyes held a quiet strength, as if she knew more than she let on. I wondered if she sensed the danger, but Alexis's fear of closeness—Nathan's doing—kept her from asking.

We piled into Cooper's truck, the air thick with tension, the Austin skyline blurring past as we headed to Barton Springs. The trail was cordoned off, police lights flashing, the mist heavy with the stench of decay and wet earth. The jogger's body lay under a tarp, but the mannequins stood, their eyes wide, mouths agape, a faint hum of *"Goosey Goosey Gander"* drifting from a hidden speaker in one. My vision flickered, Sadie's face on a mannequin, her lips moving with the rhyme. I blinked hard, heart pounding, the hallucination fading but leaving my hands shaking.

As we approached, Alexis froze, her face draining of color. "No... that's Nina," she whispered, her voice breaking, the fire in her eyes dimming to shock. Nina—our track team acquaintance, always running the south trail at dawn, her ponytail bobbing back and forth. She lay twisted, neck bruised purple, the rhyme carved into her arm in jagged lines, the blood congealed. Mannequins encircled her, posed with limbs splayed like fleeing geese, eyes wide and unblinking, mouths open in silent screams, photos of us pinned to their chests—me at the internship, Cooper sketching, Tanner writing, Alexis running with Lila. Alexis's scarf draped one mannequin's neck, stained with Nina's blood, the fabric whispering in the breeze.

Alexis staggered, her breath hitching, tears welling as she dropped to her knees, the mist soaking her jeans. "Nina... she was just... she was so good," she choked, her voice raw, guilt crashing over her. Her hands trembled, reaching toward the body but pulling back. Lila knelt beside her, her hair damp in the mist, her face pale, eyes wide with horror, but her hand steady on Alexis's shoulder. "Oh God, Lex...," Lila murmured, her voice breaking, tears streaming, but there was a steel in her eyes, a quiet resolve that seemed too composed for the chaos. Alexis leaned into her slightly, her hesitation crumbling in the moment, but I saw the fear—Nathan had struck close, turning their track team bond into a grave.

I stood frozen, the hallucinations surging—Sadie's face on Nina's body, her lips humming the rhyme, the cave's blood dripping from the mannequins. My heart hammered, Sadie's voice louder: *"Goosey goosey, whither shall you wander?"* I gripped Alexis's arm, pulling her up, my voice fierce despite the dread. "We can't stay here," I said, my throat tight. "He's doing this to get to you." But inside, the whispers grew, Sadie's laugh twisting with the hum, Nathan's shadow closing in.

Fields approached, his face grim, handing me the scarf. "He's escalating," he said, voice low. "And he's watching." Cooper sketched the scene, his lines frantic, capturing Nina's carved arm and the mannequins' gaping mouths. Tanner muttered the poem: *"Goosey gander, blood on the ground, shadows sing where the lost are found."* I looked at Alexis, her fire flickering back, but her eyes haunted, Lila's arm around her a fragile tether. Nathan wasn't just killing—he was breaking us, one rhyme at a time.

The mannequin moved slightly, or maybe it was my mind, but its hum grew louder, a chorus of doom.

23
The Captive

I couldn't bear the aches in my bones any longer as they pressed against the rusted bars of the dog crate in the Lockhart Veterinarian Hospital. My papery thin skin on my knees and elbows had turned dark purple, bruised from the unyielding metal that trapped me. Time had meant nothing there, and I had wondered if there'd be a day I'd never wake up, when the pain would finally stop. When I moved my hand to my head, I caught a whiff of something rotten. At first, I thought it was the stench of animal decay that had seeped into the hospital's walls, but then I realized it came from me. An oozing green and red sore had festered in my armpit, born from sweat and weeks without washing. Moving made me regret it, the pain and stink a cruel reminder of my body's decay, caged in The Wolf's prison.

The crate's air was thick with ammonia and mold, burning my lungs with every shallow breath. The ropes around my wrists had been raw, biting, each twist sending jolts of pain that mixed with the hunger gnawing at my gut. My mind had frayed, teetering on madness, and hallucinations crept in—a girl's face, her emerald eyes glinting through the crate's slats, her lips whispering rhymes like a prayer I couldn't answer. I clutched the frayed red ribbon in my hand, its faded fibers a lifeline to a life stolen by fear and torture. Three years in the Bandon warehouse's concrete walls had shattered me, but that crate in Lockhart was a fresh verse in his twisted rhyme, and I remained his pet.

With a jagged nail, I scratched a wolf's paw into the crate's splintered wooden base, the rough grain tearing my skin, blood welling into the grooves as ink.. Each mark was a scream, a defiance against the darkness holding me, a map of my torment etched in shadow. The Bandon warehouse had been my first prison, but I had never seen the others—the pack he'd forged. I'd heard their whispers through the tunnels, their footsteps echoing as if they were wolves circling prey, but The Wolf had kept me hidden, a secret even from them. They had known I existed, a ghost in their midst, but never saw my face, never heard my voice—until then.

Muffled voices pierced the crate, sharp and urgent, cutting through the hospital's eerie silence. Becca's voice, raw and hollow, sounding half-dead. "She's here, isn't she? The one he kept in Bandon. I heard her scratching, she's... familiar, somehow." Her words had trembled, laced with the apathy of a mother who'd lost her son—Trevor, burned in The Wolf's fire at Cape Sebastian. I'd heard his screams through the warehouse walls, a melody The Wolf had hummed, and it had broken Becca, leaving her a husk tethered to his drugs. She wouldn't run to the police; her soul was ash, her body craving the next hit he dangled, a false promise of relief.

William's voice followed, low and venomous, thick with disgust. "Really, Becca? I don't believe you. For all I know, you helped Nathan burn our son!" His tone burned with blame, his anger aimed at Becca's complicity in Trevor's death, her willingness to follow The Wolf's orders. He wasn't part of the pack—his presence there was forced, bound by fear for his sister and nephew, their lives a leash The Wolf held tight. He'd tried to find Trevor three years before, searching for police help, but no one could trace him, and now his fear kept him silent, his disgust at Becca's cruelty seething.

Becca sobbed, her voice choked. "Will, you know I loved him. I'm so sorry. If I could, I'd go back and fix it, but I can't." They shared a large crate with a divider, their voices close, raw. My mind spun, confused at first why The Wolf had caged them together, but then I saw his sick game—he hoped they'd tear each other apart.

William fell silent for a moment, then his voice softened, bitter but resigned. "I know, Becca. But... I'm serious. Who is she?" The question hung, heavy with dread, his fear for his family warring with his revulsion.

My heart lurched, my nail pausing mid-scratch, blood dripped onto the crate's base. Becca knew me—or of me—but The Wolf's rules had kept us apart, my existence a whispered myth in the Bandon tunnels. I wanted to scream, to call out, but my throat was raw, my voice a ghost. What would I say? My name was gone, erased by years of torment, a blank where memory should be. Instead, I scratched harder, the wolf paw deepening, a silent plea they'd never see. My mind flickered to the girl with emerald eyes—someone vital, someone he hunted. The ribbon trembled in my grip. I needed to remember.

A scream tore through the air—William's, raw and guttural, as if he was an animal caught in a trap. I froze, my breath catching, the sound sliced through me. "No, please!" he gasped, his voice muffled but desperate, followed by a thud, as if he'd collapsed against the crate's divider. Becca's voice came next, a low sob, barely audible. "We did what you asked... let him go." The Wolf's presence loomed, unspoken but heavy, his silence a threat more chilling than words.

My mind reeled, memories of Bandon flooding back—the dog crate's rusted bars, the wolf paws I'd scratched until my nails bled, the boat's hum signaling his return. I'd tried to fake my death to escape, but The Wolf wasn't fooled; his beating was a lesson never to lie again. Then, in that Lockhart crate, I was closer to his captives, their voices confirming my myth. "She sounds like someone I knew," Becca whispered, her voice cracking. "Before all this... before Trevor. But how? Nathan never let us near her." The words were a knife, twisting in my chest. I'd been a mother, a wife, before his chains, but that life was ash, burned away.

The crate's bars pulsed, the ammonia sting burning my lungs, mingling with the rot from my armpit sore. I scratched another paw, my fingers trembled as blood smeared on the wood. My hallucinations surged—the girl's face in the bars, her emerald eyes pleading, her voice chanting "Goosey Goosey Gander," the rhyme The Wolf had left in Austin, the one that claimed Nina, a track teammate, on Barton Springs' trail. My heart pounded, the ribbon slipping from my grip, falling to the crate's floor like a dead leaf. I reached for it, my fingers brushing the wood, and saw a man's face instead—my husband, perhaps, murdered in that cave, his eyes accusing. "You lied," his ghost whispered, his voice blending with the hospital's hum, the crate's creak, the distant city's drone.

"About what? Who are you?" I rasped, my voice barely audible, tears burning my raw cheeks. I clutched my chest, my heart aching, my scratches faltering, my nail snapping under the strain. I was close to some memories, yet unreachable, my existence a secret The Wolf wielded.

A new sound cut through—a faint hum, distorted and chilling, rising from the hospital's darkness. "Goosey Goosey Gander, whither shall I wander?" The Wolf's voice, low and mocking, twisted the rhyme into a hymn of malice. The crate shrank, the bars closed in, the hum echoed in my skull. My hallucinations surged—the girl's emerald eyes, the man's accusing face, wolf paws pulsing on the wood. I scratched harder, blood pooling, my defiance a fading spark. The Wolf knew who I was, and I had to find a way to get that truth from him.

24
Alexis

The mist at Barton Springs hung heavy, curling through the air and carrying the stench of decay and wet earth that clung to my throat. Cooper's truck screeched to a stop at the trailhead, police lights flashing red and blue through the fog, their strobes slicing the dawn—a warning. My heart pounded, the "Goosey Goosey Gander" note from my bedroom window burning in my pocket. Nathan was here in Austin, turning our sanctuary into his stage, and Nina—our track teammate, always running the south trail at dawn—was his latest verse. Fields' call had gutted me, but the crime-scene cordon and the officers' grim faces made it real. My jacket, damp from the mist, clung to my shoulders like a shroud, heavy with what I'd find. I stepped out, Asher at my side, his hand brushing mine, a lifeline I clung to despite the fear clawing at my chest.

Lila was right behind me, her track jacket zipped tight, hiding a tension that matched her steady gaze. Her usual team energy was gone, replaced by a quiet focus, her strawberry blonde hair damp in the fog. She'd been my friend since freshman year, running laps at Mike A. Myers Stadium and sharing late-night study sessions, but I kept her at arm's length, Nathan's shadow making every bond a risk. Sadie's death, my mom's murder—they'd taught me loss was a blade, and I couldn't let Lila close, no matter how much I wanted to. Asher's gaze flickered to her, then to me, his worry palpable, his own hallucinations of Sadie haunting him as mine once had. Cooper and Tanner followed, Cooper's sketchpad open, his pencil scratching the outline of the cordoned trail, Tanner muttering a poem, *"Mist and blood, the gander's call, shadows rise to make us fall."*

Fields met us at the tape, his face carved with exhaustion, his voice low. "It's bad, Alexis. Brace yourself." He lifted the cordon, and we stepped onto the south trail. The mist thickened, the air rancid with decay. Mannequins loomed in the fog, their eyes wide, mouths agape, a faint hum of *"Goosey Goosey Gander"* drifting from a hidden speaker in one. My breath caught. The rhyme echoed the note in my pocket, and Nathan's malice vibrated through the air. Photos were pinned to the mannequins' chests—Asher at our pre-internship, Cooper sketching, Tanner writing, me running with Lila. My scarf, bloodied, draped one mannequin's neck, a taunt that twisted my gut.

Then I saw her—Nina, our teammate from track, her ponytail still in place, her body twisted beneath a tarp. When I noticed her bloodied arm, a lightning bolt seemed to strike—Nathan's hands, not mine, were grabbing her neck, holding her down, and a rush of adrenaline surged through me. I froze, my knees buckling, a sob escaping from my throat. "No... Nina," I whispered, my anger and fear flickering like dying embers. Lila gasped, reaching for my hand, but I flinched, paralyzed by my fear of losing her—a barrier I couldn't lower.

"She was with us...yesterday," Lila choked out, tears falling, her eyes glaring with a strange steadiness—as if trying to remember every detail. We had run with Nina, laughed with her, her quick smile brightening the track, and now Nathan had carved his mark into her arm, her blood, her life taken to get to me.

Asher's hand on my shoulder snapped me back. The thrill vanished, leaving nausea. Lila grabbed my arm, helping me up, both giving me questioning looks. I couldn't tell them I'd felt Nathan's madness—it was too close to his blood in me. I pulled my jacket tighter, as if it could trap the image inside. "I'm okay," I lied, pressing cold fingers to my temples and willing the vision away. The thrill lingered, a sick echo of Nathan's malice whispering that I might become him. I pushed it down, my fire flaring—Nathan wouldn't break me. Nina's death wasn't my fault, but the guilt clawed deeper. Her laughter from yesterday's practice was now a ghost in my ears.

Fields approached, his face grim. "How are you holding up?" His eyes tightened, searching mine. I looked away, hiding the hallucination, my nails digging into my palms as green paint flaked off—a nervous tic I couldn't stop.

"As good as can be," Asher said, wrapping his arm around me, his gaze on Nina's tarp, her bloody fingertips peeking out, a silent accusation. Cooper's pencil scratched faster, capturing the mannequins' gaping mouths, Nina's carved arm, his lines sharp with fury. Tanner's poem grew darker: *"Blood on the trail, the gander's song, shadows weave where we belong."*

"We've logged these, but look through them," Fields said, offering a gloved hand with Polaroids. Cooper and Tanner crowded in, curiosity bubbling despite the horror. We sat at a wooden picnic table near the scene, passing the photos, the mist hovering around us. My hand shook, green paint flaking from my nails. The last Polaroid, from Lila, showed Nina running, her clothes different from her death, but a figure in the distance, half-hidden by a tree, caught my eye.

"Guys, didn't you see this?" I asked, spinning the Polaroid. Cooper squinted, and Asher sucked in a breath.

Tanner's eyes widened, his forehead wrinkling into his dirty-blond hairline. "Kaitlyn," he said, his voice low. Her face, caught in the shadows, was tied to Nathan's grip, and her fear for Benji—her sick brother—was now a blade in my heart. She'd fled Gold Beach, but Nathan had her, and this photo—her watching Nina—proved she was his pawn.

Fields' eyes met mine, heavy with purpose. "We need you to draw him out, Alexis. A campus event—be his bait." My stomach twisted, Nina's death a weight, Kaitlyn's face a warning, but my fire flared—Nathan wouldn't take anyone else. I nodded, my chest burning, as the mist tightened and the mannequin's hum grew louder, as if Nathan watched.

The tarp was lifted briefly, revealing Nina's body—her neck bruised purple, the rhyme carved in jagged lines across her arm, blood dried like ink in the morning chill. Her running shoes, scuffed and muddy, lay askew, one lace undone, a detail that broke me. She'd been alive, laughing yesterday, and now she was a message, Nathan's verse meant to pull me closer. I turned away, bile rising, the hallucination surging—Nathan's hands, his thrill, my blood. Asher's arm tightened around me, his breath uneven, his own visions of Sadie haunting him. "Lex, we need to move," he whispered, his voice a tether, but I couldn't look at him, not with Nina's blood on my scarf.

Lila's hand grazed mine, her touch steady despite her tears. "We'll get him," she said, her voice low, her resolve cutting through the fog. I wanted to believe her, but my fear of losing her—of losing anyone—kept me silent. Cooper's sketchpad trembled as his lines captured the mannequins' eerie poses, their plastic limbs splayed like fleeing geese. Tanner's pen scratched faster, *"Geese in the mist, their song a blade, shadows carve where hope will fade."*

Fields handed me another Polaroid, this one different—Kaitlyn, her eyes wide with fear, holding a note that read: *"Help us."* My heart sank as Benji's leukemia-ridden face flashed in my mind, and Kaitlyn's desperation mirrored my own. "She's with him," I said, my voice shaking. "She's alive, but not for long." The group fell silent, the weight of her plea crushing us. Nathan was weaving his web, and I was the fly he wanted.

I stood as the mist swirled and my fire burned hotter. "I'll do it," I said to Fields, my voice steady despite the nausea. "The campus rally—I'll be his bait." Asher's jaw tightened, his hand gripping mine, but he nodded, his protectiveness a shield I needed. Lila's eyes met mine, her steel unwavering. I wondered what drove her, but I couldn't ask—not now.

Cooper and Tanner exchanged looks, their sketches and poems a vow to fight with me.

The mannequins' hum grew louder as the fog thickened, and a shadow shifted in the mist, too quick to catch, whispering "goose" like a taunt from Nathan's rhyme. My heart skipped, and the hallucination flared—Nathan's face, grinning, his eyes my own. I blinked, and it was gone, but the mist felt alive, watching, waiting.

25
Nathan - The Wolf

Laughter and conversation cut through the cool, crisp evening as I jogged around the UT campus, the air sharp with damp grass, fryer grease, and something metallic beneath it all. Students moved in loose clusters, faces washed blue by laptop screens, oblivious to the way the night pressed closer than usual. Some frat boys flirted with girls who brushed them off with practiced disdain, their laughter a little too loud, a little too brittle. Patrol lights flashed intermittently across brick buildings—more cops prowling, drawn by my handiwork like flies to rot.

I tightened my black hoodie around my face, the rough fabric scraping my jaw, swallowing my profile in shadow. No one looked twice. Their blindness thrilled me. A wolf threading through lambs, unseen and unchallenged.

I chuckled under my breath, tasting anticipation—bitter, electric.

"You can't catch me, I'm the gingerbread man," I whistled softly, the childish tune fraying at the edges in the dark.

As I rounded toward Lady Bird Lake, excitement surged through me, bright and feverish. The water rippled under the city lights, fractured reflections trembling like something alive beneath the surface. *Ladybug, Ladybug, Fly Away Home.* The lake would carry the echo perfectly.

I slipped beneath a gnarled willow, bark biting into my palm, the lake's fish-stink thick and damp in my lungs. The air felt heavier here. Quieter.

Then I saw her.

Kaitlyn.

The red dress clung to her like wet paint; every curve sharpened beneath the moonlight. She didn't look at me as she passed. She didn't need to. I slid the poison vial into her trembling hand, the glass slick with condensation, cold as a corpse.

Her pulse thudded visibly in her throat.

I licked salt from my lips as her heels clicked softly on pavement, the rhythm unsteady. She reached into her cleavage, withdrew red lipstick, and with shaking fingers applied the poisoned balm. The scent drifted faintly—sweet, almost creamy beneath the lake's rot.

Backup plan.

Women—fragile yet calculating. They could manipulate softness into power. But tonight, she was only a vessel.

Her punishment for the Polaroid stunt would bind her tighter. Benji's leukemia medicine remained my leash. Zane's failed heroics left him chained in Lockhart, alone in the dark with nothing but his own breathing for company.

"He's coming," Kaitlyn whispered, her voice thin as thread.

Gideon approached, phone light illuminating his face from below, casting hollow shadows beneath his eyes. He walked with careless confidence, unaware of how easily bodies failed.

Kaitlyn leaned against the fence, metal cold beneath her palms. The lake lapped softly behind her—slow, patient.

She released her blonde hair from its bun. It spilled down her back like something cut loose.

"Hey, want some bread?" she asked, holding out the poisoned snack. Crumbs caught in the moonlight like flecks of bone.

Gideon smirked. "Nah, sweetheart. Not into random snacks."

Her jaw tightened.

He stepped closer anyway.

"Well, aren't you a sight on this beautiful night?" Beer breath washed over her. "Lost?"

He was too close now.

"I... I'm sorry," Kaitlyn murmured.

The apology felt wrong in the air.

"Sorry for what?" His hand brushed her arm. His skin lingered.

"Just... let me make it up to you."

She leaned in.

The kiss was slow. Lingering.

I watched carefully.

Her poisoned lips pressed against his. The balm transferred in the warmth of their mouths. Tears slid down her cheeks, salt mixing with the chemical sweetness between them.

For a second, nothing happened.

Then his breath hitched.

A small, confused sound escaped him. He pulled back, blinking rapidly.

The first tremor rippled through his shoulders.

"What—"

His throat constricted mid-word. Fingers flew to his neck. His knees buckled violently, shoes scraping against pavement. A wet choking noise clawed out of him as his airway spasmed shut.

His eyes widened in dawning horror.

Foam bubbled at the corners of his mouth.

His body convulsed harder—muscles seizing in grotesque jerks. Tendons strained visibly beneath skin. His jaw snapped shut so hard I heard the crack of teeth grinding together.

He collapsed to his side, limbs twitching erratically, heels drumming against gravel.

The lake's damp smell thickened.

I stepped from the shadows.

His lips had already begun to turn blue; veins dark beneath his skin. His eyes rolled upward, whites showing, red capillaries bursting in spiderweb fractures.

He tried once more to inhale.

Nothing came.

I crouched and tilted his chin, feeling the faint flutter of a dying pulse against my fingertips.

Then stillness.

I dragged him beneath the willow. Gravel grated against his cheek, skin tearing slightly as I positioned him upright. I arranged his hands carefully; fingers curved like he was still reaching for her.

Pie-crust crumbs clung to his lips.

Mannequins stood waiting.

I positioned them slowly, deliberately. One leaned forward too far, its neck twisted sharply to one side. Another knelt as if mourning, painted tears streaking its face. Their hollow eyes reflected moonlight.

The hidden speaker crackled.

"Georgie Porgie, pudding and pie..."

The nursery rhyme floated softly over the water.

I pinned the photos one by one—Asher, Cooper, Tanner. Alexis running with Lila. And the extra-special one, placed dead center.

Alexis's scarf hung from a mannequin's stiff shoulder, soaked dark and heavy.

A note beneath:

Georgie kissed, now run away,
Your ladybug's next in my play.

Kaitlyn stumbled back, her dress catching on a branch. The rip tore loud in the night. Her sobs trembled through the humid air.

She turned to flee.

I caught her wrist.

Her pulse hammered wildly beneath my grip.

"Benji's medicine stops if you run."

Her face drained of color. Her eyes darted instinctively toward Lockhart—as if she could see her brother coughing alone in the dark.

Becca and William emerged from shadow, drugged and shaking, hands unsteady as they adjusted mannequins into place. The air thickened with fear-sweat and lake rot.

William's disgust flickered at Becca, but my threats kept him compliant.

Leashed.

I stepped back beneath the willow, its damp leaves brushing my cheek like fingers. Mist curled low around Gideon's body, weaving through mannequin legs, pooling at his unmoving feet.

The hum grew louder.

The lake whispered against the shore.

I hummed along, pressing my knife's edge lightly against my thumb until a bead of blood surfaced, bright and clean.

Kaitlyn would pay more.

Benji would suffer for every flicker of rebellion.

I imagined Alexis standing here at dawn. Her breath catching. Her fire igniting.

McKinney Falls next.

The thought sharpened everything inside me.

My scar throbbed violently as if her emerald gaze pierced straight through the dark and into me.

The lake water lapped softly, algae thick on the breeze.

I slipped into the fog, letting the mist swallow my outline, the rhyme fading behind me.

"Georgie Porgie..." the speaker whispered.

I left the note for Alexis.

Whispered her name once into the dark.

The city hummed in the distance.

The lake answered.

And somewhere, without knowing why—

She would feel it.

26
Alexis

The New Year's Eve Marathon started at dawn, a festive event Asher and I once enjoyed organizing. However, recent tragedies—Nina's death and Nathan's return—turned joy into a cruel illusion. Winter Break freed us from classes, a supposed respite, yet I found myself at Lady Bird Lake, the air thick with algae and morning dew, searching the crowd for Nathan's shadow. The lake's ripples shimmered in the rising sun, reflecting his rhymes, while the runners' chatter blended with city traffic noise. My track hoodie was damp and rough against my skin, carrying tastes of salt and dread as I inhaled the cold air. Something in the dense shelter of trees—willows and oaks forming a canopy—called to me, like a whisper from Nathan's voice, drawing me closer to the shadows.

The crowd blurred, and the lake's reflection stung my eyes. I closed them, assaulted by a flash of Nathan's hands choking Nina, the thrill surging through me. Was his blood in my veins pulling me into his madness? I rubbed my eyes, the pressure sharp, then blinked open and spotted Asher near the start line, his gaze worried. My bait role twisted my gut—I was drawing Nathan out, but what if I was becoming him? The thought gnawed, confusion coiling like the mist.

Tanner stood nearby, his dirty blond hair catching the faint sunlight as he flirted with Lila, his smile warm but his eyes sharp. "You're always so calm, Lila," he said, voice probing. "How do you hold it together after Nina?"

Lila's blue eyes squinted at him, and her reply was smooth: "Just focus on the run, Tan." Her steady gaze unnerved me, too controlled for grief, but I couldn't focus—Tanner's poet's heart masked suspicion, and I wondered what he saw.

Cooper sketched the crowd, his pencil scratching like a pulse as he muttered, "This lake reeks of death, Lex." His words echoed my dread, the algae stench choking my throat.

Fields approached, blending in as an undercover runner, his windbreaker loose, his badge hidden. Other FBI agents, dressed as civilians, mingled, their eyes scanning for Nathan, their movements a silent hum beneath the marathon's noise. "Alexis, stay sharp," he whispered, the lake's fishy stench clinging to his breath. "We're watching for him." My heart raced, the "Goosey Goosey Gander" note from my window burning in my pocket. The trees pulled harder, their shadows whispering, urging me forward.

Honestly, I didn't know what we were doing because if I were him, I wouldn't be out in the daylight.

Wait.

If I were him?

I shook my head and broke from the start line, drawn to the dense park, where willows and oaks hid the trail in a thick, leafy shroud. I pressed a hand to my chest as I struggled to breathe. The trees were closing in on me.

"Lex, wait!" Asher called, his running shoes crunching on gravel, but I couldn't stop. The air grew heavier, thick with wet earth and decay, as the lake's ripples lapped softly, a sinister lullaby.

"Asher, not right now," I gasped. "This is too much." I knew I'd sound really crazy if I told him that being paid paled in comparison to feeling like I was becoming like Nathan.

I reached a gnarled willow, its branches drooping like skeletal fingers, and froze—piles of garbage bags heaped around its base, their plastic slick with dew and reeking of rot and metallic blood.

Asher caught up to me, his arm covering his nose. "What in the hell is that smell?"

I took a step toward the willow, but Asher stopped me.

"If that's a crime scene, which I think is obvious, we can't touch it. Let's get Fields over here," he said, pulling his phone out of his shorts.

He started talking to Fields, but I couldn't make out what he was saying as a loud buzz filled my ear, and the world around me vibrated in and out before going dark.

When I came to, I was in Asher's arms, and my head still felt cloudy. His eyes held worry and shock as he scanned the willow trees. I stayed still, watching his features crease and relax. Guilt wrapped its ugly tentacles around me. Since I had entered his life, it had been difficult, to say the least, yet he refused to leave my side.

Asher looked down at me, and a small, sympathetic smile formed. "Hey, you okay? What happened?"

I started to sit up slowly, and Asher handed me a bottle of water. "I'm fine. I just haven't been able to eat lately." I didn't want to admit I had a problem I'd started after Luke and Sadie's death. I hadn't ignored it, but Genevieve had been helping me try to overcome it. And admitting I was bulimic to Asher was another thing I'd have to work up the courage to tell him.

As my head began to clear, I noticed all the commotion around us. FBI agents now wore their labeled vests and hats, and yellow numbered plastic cards were scattered across the area, effectively marking the crime scene's evidence.

Asher spoke up. "I'll go see if I can find you something to eat." Then he took off toward the lake, where food stands were set up for the marathon.

Fields came up and gave me a look that said, 'you don't look so good,' but I knew he thought it better not to say it to me. "I need you to come take a look."

I followed him as we wove around the crime scene, crunching on the crispy leaves and avoiding any obstruction of evidence. My hands trembled as we got closer to the willow tree. The garbage bags were set aside, revealing what lay beneath them.

I recognized the body right away. Gideon. He was part of our advocacy class and was going to start the internship with us.

His almost naked body lay propped against the tree as if he had been thrown there. His lips, as blue as his boxers, were cracked and bleeding. *"Georgie Porgie"* was carved in jagged, oozing wounds across his bare chest, the flesh torn and puckered, blood congealed like black ink. Pie crumbs clung to his chest, stuck in the gore, a mockery of his cocky grin now frozen in a grimace of pain. This couldn't be real, and what good was it doing to have me here? I was certain things like this fed my bulimia—how ironic.

"That's not all," Fields said, turning around.

I hesitated. Scattered through the trees were mannequins dressed as crying women.

However, one was flesh and blood—human.

Another body lay posed like a mannequin—rigid as plastic, eyes wide and glassy, skin gray, throat slashed open, the gash gaping like a second mouth, blood pooling in the dirt. I gasped, recognizing him from the night my mother was murdered—Trevor's dad, Becca's ex, and the one accused of my mother's murder. His frozen stare, a ghost from that blood-soaked memory.

A sob ripped from my throat as my knees buckled, the ground cold and gritty beneath me. "Gideon... William," I whispered, the fire in my chest dimming to ash. The thrill surged again—Nathan's hands, my blood, choking them both, their torn flesh under my fingers. My stomach churned, the metallic stench of blood mingling with the sight of Gideon's oozing wounds and William's gaping throat. A bitter taste of bile rose as Nathan's thrill flickered in me, whispering that I could be him. Asher's face paled, his trembling hands gripping mine. The gore's horror cut through him as deeply as it shook me.

"So it continues. He's killing people you know. The ones he let get away." Fields spoke with certainty.

"He's cleaning up his mess." Asher grabbed my hand.

"No," I gasped, confusion gnawing. Why had the trees called me to this horror? Was it his blood, his rhyme, pulling me like a puppet? Asher reached me, his arm pulling me close, his warmth grounding me, but not enough. "And I'm part of that mess."

"We all are," he said, his breath shaky against my hair, faintly peppermint-scented. But his eyes held pain, Gideon's gore and William's rigid pose shaking him. His face was pale as he stared at the bodies. "But we won't end up like this," his voice cracked, the lake's fishy stench choking us both.

"His blood's in me," I murmured, my lips trembling, tasting tears. "It drew me here, to this... slaughter. It's pulling me into his madness, like that night Mom died."

Asher's grip tightened, his hands trembling as the sight of William's slashed throat and Gideon's carved arm burned into him. "You're the opposite of him. We'll stop him, Lex," he said, but his voice wavered, the weight of the gore heavy in his eyes. I leaned into him, my heart racing, confusion surging—how did the trees know? Was Nathan's thrill in me guiding my steps, or was it something else, a warning?

Tanner knelt by the bags, his fingers brushing the crumpled plastic as he examined a Polaroid. "Kaitlyn," he said, his voice low, pointing to her in a red dress, her eyes screaming with fear. "She watched Gideon, like Nina."

My heart sank. Her fear for Benji was a blade in my chest. "She's his pawn," I whispered, worry surging—Nathan's blood sang in me, a rhyme I couldn't silence.

Cooper's pencil scratched faster, capturing the mannequins' gaping mouths and tear-streaked faces like "crying girls," while a hidden speaker hummed *"Georgie Porgie, pudding and pie, kissed the girls and made them cry."* Photos of us—Asher, Cooper, Tanner, and me with Lila—were pinned to their chests, my scarf bloodied, with a note reading: *"Georgie kissed, now run away, your ladybug's next in my play."*

Lila scanned the scene, her gaze too sharp, as if memorizing details for a report. Tanner watched her, flirtation fading, suspicion clear. "You see something, Lila?" he asked, his tone sharp. She shook her head, deflecting, but I caught her glance at Fields, a silent signal. Was she hiding something? The crowd's cheers faded, the lake's ripples pulsing to Nathan's rhythm, the damp taste sharp on my tongue.

A scuffle broke out nearby—a drugged man, eyes wild, lunging at runners. Asher tackled him. His grunt echoed as fists grazed his jaw, the sting of the impact hanging in the air. "He's near!" the man gasped, collapsing. A clue was scratched, a wolf and a ladybug merging on a willow: *"Wolves circle, ladybug's next."*

My pulse spiked, the thrill flaring—Nathan's hands, my hands, tearing at William's throat, carving Gideon's arm. "He's close," I whispered to Asher, my voice barely audible. "I feel him."

Confusion tore at me, and the fear of becoming Nathan was a weight I couldn't shake. William's gaping wound and Gideon's oozing arm tied me to that murderous night. Why had I been drawn here? Was it Nathan's blood or his rhyme whispering my name?

Fields and his agents closed in, their undercover movements urgent as they scanned for Nathan. "We need to move," Fields said, his voice low, drowned out by the marathon's buzz. "Alexis, your bait role starts now." I nodded, but worry choked me—Nathan's blood haunted my veins, William's slashed throat and Gideon's carved flesh burning in my mind. Asher held me tighter, his face pale. The gore shook him as much as it did me. The lake's mist curled around us, its algae stench stinging my nose. The crowd's noise faded, replaced by a faint hum from a rally poster—a wolf paw scratched on it, pulsing with "Georgie Porgie." My heart skipped, the thrill flashing again—Nathan's face, grinning, his eyes mine. I blinked, and it was gone, but the mist felt alive, watching, waiting.

27
Asher

It's been twenty-four hours since the New Year's Eve Marathon, and I'm livid. Not only did Nathan's latest horror derail our holiday plans, but Alexis has been catatonic, a moving statue pacing from her bed to her reading nook by the living room picture window. The taste of salt and dread lingers on my lips. I'm no better off, but at least I'm eating—unlike Alexis, who's barely keeping food down, her bulimia flaring since the marathon. I've tried to convince her to talk to Genevieve, but she just stares—no, stares right through me, as if I'm the ghost.

Cooper and Tanner have spent hours in the small den, poring over evidence photos Fields let them take—Gideon's carved chest and William's rigid pose, like a bloodied mannequin. The air smells of burnt Starbucks, and the sound of Cooper's pencil scratching is a constant drone. They only emerge to refill their coffee mugs.

Tanner's suspicion of Lila has grown, his voice low: "She was too calm at the lake, like she's seen gore before." I nod, my throat dry, the memory of Lila's sharp glance at Fields nagging me.

I stand at the back window, watching thin fog roll in, its damp chill seeping through the glass and tasting faintly of algae from Lady Bird Lake. Alexis appears beside me, her green, silky bathrobe loose, her hair in a messy bun, her cheeks sunken in a way that twists my heart. She's still beautiful, but the marathon's horror has drained her. I reach out, tucking a stray strand of hair behind her ear, the touch soft against her cold skin. Her eyes meet mine, shadowed with fear.

"You're warm," she whispered, barely audible, her lips curling into the faintest smile. "You always are."

"Happy New Year," I replied, forcing a beaming smile and grabbing a plate from the kitchen table, a cinnamon roll on it. I held it out, hoping she'd eat and keep it down. Making cinnamon rolls on New Year's was our tradition, but this year, with her lost in Nathan's shadow, I made them alone using her recipe. The dough's sweet scent mixed with my frustration.

Alexis pulled out a chair and sat with her knees to her chest, not caring that her robe rode up, revealing her underwear. She picked at the cinnamon roll, taking small bites, the icing sticky on her fingers. I watched, relief flickering—she's eating, at least. "Want some hot chocolate?" I asked, my voice soft, happy she's trying.

She licked her lips, shivering. Goosebumps rose on her legs. I touched her knee, the skin icy. "Alexis, you're freezing," I said, stating the obvious, but she didn't react, lost in her thoughts. I grabbed the fleece blanket from the couch, its softness warm, and wrapped it around her, the fabric brushing my hands. She didn't answer about the hot chocolate, but I made one anyway. The cocoa's rich smell cut through the burnt coffee, steam curling like the lake's mist. She needed any warmth she could get.

"Lex, I need you to talk to me or... talk to Genevieve," I said, setting the mug down. Its heat warmed my fingers. She pulled the mug toward her mouth, then paused, steam floating before her eyes, her silence heavy. "Please," I added, my voice cracking. The memory of her collapse at the marathon flashed—her buzzing ears, her whispered fear of Nathan's blood.

She shook her head, her eyes distant. The mug trembled in her hands. "I can't, Asher," she murmured, her voice barely audible, tasting of cocoa and tears. "The trees called me to that slaughter—Gideon... William... like Mom's night. His blood's in me, pulling me to his madness." Her words cut, and the image of the gore burned in my mind.

I knelt beside her, my hands over hers, the blanket's fleece soft while her fingers were cold. "You're not him," I said, my throat tight, tasting bile as the crime scene flickered in my memory. "But you can't keep hiding this—those dark thoughts, the thrill you feel. Genevieve can help." Her eyes twitched, fear and defiance warring.

The phone rang. Genevieve's voice was calm but firm through the static. "Asher, bring her in today," she said. "She needs all the support she can get. She's not taking my calls, and I fear it's breaking her. She can't keep bottling it."

I glanced at Alexis, her gaze fixed on the window. "She doesn't want me there," I said in a low voice.

"She may not want it, but she needs you," Genevieve insisted. "I'll find out what's going on. She can't hide. She needs to face it." I nodded, though she couldn't see, the phone's plastic cool against my ear.

"Lex, Genevieve wants to see you today," I said, sitting across from her. "I'll come, but I can stay outside if you want."

She stiffened, her mug clinking on the table, the sound sharp. "No," she whispered, her eyes meeting mine, haunted. "I don't want you hearing... what I feel." Her voice cracked, and I almost caved.

"I'm here, no matter what," I said, my voice steady despite the weight of her fear and the cinnamon roll's sweetness fading in the air.

Cooper emerged, his sketchpad open, showing Gideon's oozing wounds and William's gaping gash. "This wolf-lady-bug clue," he said in a low voice, "is like the carving from Mom and Dad's house."

Tanner follows, his poem darker: *"Mist's call, blood's pull, shadows claim the full."* His eyes flick to his phone, Lila's text unanswered, his suspicion growing: "She's hiding something, Asher."

I looked at Alexis. They weren't helping, and I knew I had to get her out of here, away from their constant research and talk about Nathan.

She didn't protest as I helped her put on a hoodie and track pants. I helped brush her hair, and it was the first time I had seen her relax so completely since yesterday.

As we drove to Genevieve's office, the air was heavy with pine and exhaust, the sound of Austin's traffic a grim echo of Lady Bird Lake's lapping waves. Her office smelled of lavender, a contrast to the lake's fishy stench, and the couch's fabric was soft under my hands.

Alexis hesitated. Her appearance had improved, but her cheeks were still sunken. "I'll go alone," she said, her voice shaky. I nodded and sat outside; the door's click was loud in the silence.

Inside, I heard muffled voices, Alexis's voice breaking: "I felt his thrill again, carving them. What if I'm him?"

Genevieve's reply is steady: "You're not him, but you can't hide this fear—it's feeding your darkness."

My heart ached. She had been doing so well. Her bulimia was a reaction to everything she had been through. I clenched my fists, the chair's wood hard, tasting dread. I wish she had trusted me enough to tell me. Maybe I knew subconsciously, because there were times she was doing too well—like she didn't want to admit it herself. She's fighting the blood of a psychopath, but it's his shadow we couldn't escape.

The session ended. Alexis emerged, her eyes red but clearer. "I'll keep going," she whispered, her hand in mine, the touch grounding. The emotional beat hits—guilt over failing all of Nathan's victims fuels my resolve to shield her, and her dark thoughts are a blade in my chest. "You are amazing," I reassured her, then pulled her closer, knowing my warmth meant something to her.

As we left, a flyer on Genevieve's desk caught my eye—a wolf paw scratched on it, humming faintly with "Little Boy Blue." My pulse spiked. The note read: "Ladybug's next, the blue boy falls." The lavender scent turned sour, the hum sinister, tasting of dread. I pulled Alexis closer—for me this time, her worry mirrored my fear—would I have to give her up to stop Nathan's madness?

28
The Captive

The waiting room's ammonia stench seared my lungs. The air was thick with mold and rust, metallic on my tongue, like swallowing my own decay. Chains bit into my wrists, their cold iron digging through my tattered shirt and pinning me to a rusted chair bolted to the concrete floor. My bruised knees pressed against the chair's edge, the wood splintered and damp. The sound of my trembling nail scratching a wolf paw into the armrest was a desperate scream in the silence. The Wolf had us all chained here—me, Kaitlyn, Benji, Becca, and Zane—to watch what happened to those who defied him, his lesson carved in blood. The gore blended with fleeting shadows of my past—a man's hungry eyes, a woman's angry glare, a child's broken home. Were these real, or hallucinations, like the screams around me? Lady Bird Lake's misty ripples lapped in my mind, a sinister lullaby tying me to something I couldn't grasp.

A thud echoed. Kaitlyn's cry pierced the darkness as The Wolf's fists struck her flesh. Her body was chained to a chair across the room, her ragged dress torn, blood dripping from her split lip, her face swollen, her eyes pleading. "Please, stop!" she gasped, her voice wet with blood, the sound a knife in my chest. I clutched the red ribbon in my hand, its frayed fibers soft yet heavy, my heart pounding, the chains rattling with a metallic clank. Was this real, or another trick of my fractured mind? A flash surged—a man's rough hands, a woman's tears, a family shattered—but no names came, only guilt, sharp and fleeting, like a blade in the dark.

Benji's scream tore through, high and desperate, "Stop! She's all I have!" His coughs rattled, weak, on the brink of death, his leukemia draining him, his skeletal frame slumped in chains, his thin shirt soaked with sweat, eyes wide with terror. I saw him in my mind's eye, pale, shivering, curling in pain as The Wolf loomed, his shadow a wolf's snarl. Another flash hit—a woman's accusing stare, a home I'd ruined, the weight of my selfishness—but who was she? My mind reeled, the images fading, leaving only pain.

Becca, chained beside me, mumbled through a drugged haze, her voice slurred, "Trevor... I didn't mean..." Her sobs mingled with the ammonia's sting, the air reeking of sweat and fear, her tattered jacket stained with grime.

Zane lurched toward Benji, his chains clanking, his voice faint. "Hold on, kid," he said, his hands shaking as he strained against the iron, his shadow flickering like a ghost in my vision. Was he there, or was I imagining him, his body already cold somewhere? The concrete chilled my bare feet, the chains scraping a low groan, my tongue tasting rot as I gasped, confusion swirling. Were these screams real, or echoes of my past, those nameless faces I'd wronged?

I scratched another paw, blood smearing like ink, the effort tearing my skin, the pain sharp yet grounding. The lake's ripples haunted my visions, their lapping waves blending with Kaitlyn's cries, Benji's screams, and Becca's drugged murmurs. Now, in this waiting room, Austin's rot replaced Bandon's damp, the air heavy with decay, tasting of dust and despair. A flash came—a man's whispered promises, a woman's rage, a child's cry—but no names, only fragments. My selfishness was a shadow I couldn't escape. Had I hurt someone vital, a girl I'd wronged? The ribbon trembled, a lifeline to sins I couldn't name.

Kaitlyn's scream spiked. The Wolf's growl was low. "You failed me with the Polaroid!" His fist slammed into her cheek, blood splattering the concrete, the sound wet and final. He turned to us, his eyes cold. "This is what defiance earns."

Benji's coughs weakened, his plea fading to "Stop…" I saw Zane's shadow slump, his effort to save Benji failing, or maybe he'd never been there, a hallucination born of my shattered mind. Becca's sobs grew quieter, her drugged haze a chain I felt in my bones. My heart ached, the ribbon's red a reminder of the pain I'd caused—nameless faces, broken homes, a woman's despair. Was I imagining their pain, or was it real, echoing my own?

The chains rattled as I shifted, the iron biting deeper, the ammonia searing my lungs, the rot's metallic taste mingling with my bloodied fingers. I scratched another paw, my nail snapping, pain flaring, the sound a desperate vow. Gideon's oozing wounds flashed, William's gaping throat a mirror of my guilt, those fleeting faces—men I'd used, women who cursed me—haunting my mind.

"I hurt someone," I murmured, my voice cracking. No names surfaced, only shadows of my sins. Was it my selfishness, my past, linking me to this horror? The lake's ripples surged in my visions, their fishy stench sharp, whispering my guilt.

The air grew heavier as the waiting room shrank, the hum of a distant city drone blending with The Wolf's footsteps. "Goosey Goosey Gander, whither shall I wander?" he hummed, his voice a mocking hymn that twisted into malice. Was it real, or my mind's trick? Benji's coughs faded, Kaitlyn's cries silenced, Becca's mumbles gone. Zane's shadow vanished, dead or imagined, leaving only The Wolf's hum. My hallucinations surged—the men's hungry eyes, the women's angry glares, a child's cry pulsing in the chains. I scratched harder, blood pooling, my defiance fading. The Wolf knew who I was, and I had to find that truth, even if it was all a dream.

A new sound cut through—a faint, distorted hum rising from the darkness. "Little Boy Blue, come blow your horn," The Wolf's voice sang, the rhyme a blade. My pulse spiked as the chains tightened and the hum echoed like a heartbeat. Was I hallucinating, or was he coming for Benji next? I had to hold on, face the shadows of my past, and uncover why I'd hurt them.

29

Nathan - The Wolf

Kaitlyn's blood splattered across the concrete floor of the Lockhart waiting room, each drop landing with a soft, wet patter that echoed like a distant drum in my skull. I stood over her, my fists aching from the blows, the metallic tang of her blood thick on my knuckles, coppery when I licked my lips. Her ragged dress was torn, clinging to her sweat-soaked skin, her face a swollen mess of bruises and cuts, her eyes pleading through the slits.

"Please... Benji..." she gasped, her voice broken, blood bubbling from her mouth. I grabbed her hair, yanking her head back, the greasy strands between my fingers, her scalp warm and pulsing under my grip.

"You failed me with the Polaroid," I growled, my breath hot against her ear as the room's ammonia stench mixed with her fear-sweat, a cocktail that fueled the fire in my veins. One more punch to her ribs. The crack of bone was sharp in the silence. Her body convulsed, and the chains rattled like a prisoner's last breath. The thrill surged, dark and intoxicating, a rush that made my scar throb, reminding me of Alexis's blade—her fire, her defiance. Why did she fight to stay good when this darkness felt so pure?

I stepped back and wiped my hands on my pants; the fabric clung to me, sticky with her blood, that metallic sweetness blooming under my nose like a familiar perfume.

The waiting room was my theater—my chained little audience arranged just so: Kaitlyn slumped in her chair, Benji hacking wetly and weakly from his crate, Becca muttering in a drugged haze, Zane leaning over the boy, his shadow twitching on the wall. "Hold on, kid," Zane croaked once—then nothing. I didn't bother to check.

They mattered only as props. My captive pawed the air like a trapped animal, eyes wide and brilliant with fear—her hallucinations were my favorite scene. Defiance earned pain; pain was my canvas. As Kaitlyn's chest rose and fell in ragged sobs, I slid further into the dark I keep tidy inside myself, where pity is a rumor and only the razor-bright thrill of breaking another counts. I named it for what it was: appetite. I told myself plain, cruel truths—that they were weak, that their cries harmonized with my rhymes—because naming the world a certain way makes it obey. No remorse. Only the cool arithmetic of power and the delicious promise of the next act.

I left the room, the air heavier with blood and fear, the taste of victory bitter on my tongue. But Alexis called to me, my half-sister, my mirror. I needed to watch her closely, stalk her during the day, and understand how she endured so much abuse yet remained "good." I slipped into Austin's shadows, the city's hum a lullaby for my hunt.

Her house was silent as I lurked by the back window, the fog rolling in, its damp chill seeping through my jacket. I climbed the tree in her backyard and shielded myself behind leaves and branches as I watched my beautifully tainted ladybug. I smiled as I watched her flip through her nursery rhyme book while she lay on her bed. A strand of hair fell across her face, making me instantly jealous as it grazed her smooth cheek. A moment later, a tear slipped down her cheek, and then she slammed the book shut and threw it across the room. I froze as her eyes locked onto mine. For a moment, I thought she had seen me, but she blinked and went to her bathroom.

As much as I wanted to stay here and watch her, I knew it wasn't wise with the FBI watching too closely.

I couldn't stand the city, so I went back to Lockhart. The FBI had its teeth in every street; they'd sniff us out soon enough. Benji coughed in the next room—soft, wet, the sound of someone already half-ruled by sickness. I'd read his hospital chart: prognosis terminal. When the future looks like a closed door, you start to see people as pieces on a board. He would not live long. His wasted body would be useful. His pain would do work for me. Watching Kaitlyn unravel would be the payment.

I clapped once, then pressed my fingers to my lips and blew a sharp, businesslike whistle. Chains answered—metal singing, bodies flinching. I pulled them free from the wall, one by one, herded them into the van, and eased them into their crates. Pride rose in me, warm and slow. They were mine—lambs, trembling and tidy, exactly as they should be.

I hoped Benji would hang on for at least a week longer, as I needed time to stage his death.

30
Alexis

Who the hell was I? What was I thinking? A relentless ache clawed at my core, dragging me into a void of despair, its hollow pulse thudding like a storm over Austin's skyline. I despised this feeling, this crushing weight, as Nathan's hands stole lives—their bodies hidden under tarps. Who was I to think I could stop his madness? He was my blood, his darkness a sour sting on my tongue, like tears I couldn't choke down. I'd spent years wondering what shaped him into this monster. My mother, our father—they'd shattered him. The trauma we'd endured from those meant to love us most left scars, their touch as cold as the fog, their voices jagged like shattered glass in the night.

I'd been lying in bed since dawn, sheets twisted around my legs, their cotton rough against my skin, the faint scent of Asher's sandalwood shampoo lingering on the pillow, tethering me to the house's quiet hum. Sleep eluded me; the world outside my window thrummed with distant traffic, a low vibration seeping through the walls, while the taste of stale coffee from last night's mug clung heavy to my breath.

All I could think about was love. Did I know what it was? I doubted I'd been taught. My mother—no. She loved the idea of me, her voice a grating rasp in my memory, her twisted touch icy and calculated, the air thick with cheap perfume masking her neglect. To the men she dated, I was a prop to paint her as a 'good mom.' Their hollow laughter was a distant echo, never reaching me. It seemed like a different life, yet that past life was now intertwining with the present.

Luke almost reached love, holding me warmly and whispering softly, but everything broke apart when he discovered I was Ronny's kin, the revelation hitting me sharply.

"Oh my gosh!" I sat up, the sheets slithering off with a faint rustle, cool air grazing my bare legs and sending shivers up my spine. Nathan and I shared blood, yet a chasm divided us. He'd known a mother's love, her gentle touch, her voice a soothing hum, until my mom and our dad ripped it away, leaving a piercing crack in his childhood's silence.

As a victim's advocate, I'd learned early: without help, trauma could set a child on a path to ruin—drugs, alcohol, self-harm, a litany of shadows whispering through my mind's empty corridors.

I groaned, collapsing back onto the bed as the mattress creaked under my weight. I pulled the sheets over my head with a muffled swish, their fabric stifling yet soft, the faint scent of laundry detergent a fleeting balm. Nathan's trauma birthed a killer; mine birthed bulimia, the acid burn of bile a constant echo, the retching a secret in the bathroom's silence.

My lips curled into a faint smile as dawn's light pierced the sheets, its warmth brushing my face. The distant chirp of birds was a fragile note. I could be the bait, mirroring Nathan's hunger. I'd offer what he craved—love, to be loved. I'd write him a letter, a facade: "I'll go with you, Nathan, if you free them." The plan was a blade's edge, slicing my chest, the air heavy with the scent of rain-soaked earth.

"Lex!" Asher burst through the door, shattering my thoughts. The hinges squeaked as I jolted upright, and the bed groaned. "You okay? I've been up for hours."

I stared blankly, grabbing my phone from the nightstand. Its cold plastic was slick in my hand. My eyes widened—eleven a.m. Where had time gone? "I'm fine," I stammered, standing to smooth Asher's oversized football t-shirt, now mine. Its fabric was soft but heavy. I started toward the bathroom, but he caught my wrist, his touch warm and steady against my chilled skin.

His blue eyes searched mine, as if I were a thousand miles away, then pulled me into a hug, his heartbeat a steady thud against my chest. I hugged him back, knowing I might lose him, but today he was here. When he kissed my neck, his breath warm and the faint peppermint scent grounding, I let him take all of me—one last time, the room's quiet wrapping us in a fragile cocoon.

After showering, I wrapped myself in my towel, its damp fibers clinging to my skin. I pulled jeans and a sweater from drawers, shoved them into my track bag, and the zipper's grating, sharp in the silence. I needed to be ready for what was coming. I'd just started dressing when loud voices crept up the stairs, a harsh clash breaking the house's calm.

I reached the base of the staircase, the wood cool under my bare feet, and saw the Trips locked in a heated argument. Cooper clutched his phone, while Asher's face flushed red, his fists balled at his sides, a sneer twisting his lips. Tanner stood between them, shouting words lost in the chaos, his voice a muffled roar. "She doesn't need his shit right now, Coop!" Asher yelled through gritted teeth, the air thick with tension, the faint smell of coffee lingering.

"You need to let her decide," Cooper snapped, his voice sharp. "She's had enough people controlling her life—she doesn't need her boyfriend to save her."

Asher flinched, eyes flashing. "Someone has to protect her from it. We lost Sadie because we were blind. I won't lose her, too!"

What came next stunned me. Tanner reeled back and landed a punch on Asher's jaw, the crack echoing like a gunshot. Asher stumbled, his head hitting the wall with a dull thud, then collapsed, a reddish bruise blooming on his cheek. I froze, then rushed to his side, my heart pounding, the air tasting of dust and panic. His eyes met mine, squinting at Tanner. "Tan... I'm gonna..." he growled, teeth gritted, trying to stand but falling back, the wall's plaster gritty under his hand.

Tanner's fight drained, tears falling, his bruised hand trembling. "I'm sorry, Ash... but we all failed Sadie," he said, his voice breaking. The room was heavy with guilt.

My head buzzed, a high-pitched whine drowning out my thoughts. "Are you okay?" I asked, glancing between them, their grunts barely audible. "Let's get ice." I moved to the kitchen, the tiles cold under my feet. I grabbed Ziploc bags, the ice clinking sharply, and towels soft but damp in my hands.

Cooper stood in the kitchen doorway, his back to me, speaking in a hushed, firm tone on his phone, his words muffled. He glanced at me, his ice-blue eyes sharp, as I filled the bags. He turned, pushed mute, and his expression tightened. I gave him a questioning smile, the tension thicker than ever, the air heavy with unspoken grief. Asher and Tanner sat on the couch, side by side, their silence heavy.

"Hey... I've got someone on the phone who wants to talk to you," Cooper said, his eyebrows lifting, revealing more of his piercing eyes.

I braced myself, the counter's edge cold beneath my palms. "Who is it?" I asked, his hesitation a warning.

"It's... Ronny," he said, shifting uncomfortably. "An FBI agent is with him, asking about Nathan. He won't talk to them, only to you."

Cooper held out his phone, its weight heavy in my hand. I licked my dry lips, my hand trembling. I didn't want to talk to Ronny, but if it could stop Nathan, I'd try anything. I took a deep breath, the air thick with tension. "Hello."

"Is this Alexis?" a woman's voice asked, firm yet calm.

I slid onto a stool, its wood creaking as the kitchen's dim light cast shadows. "Yes, it is."

"This is Agent Brown. I have Ronny Moore here. He's to talk about Nathan, nothing else. If he deviates, we end the call. Understand?" Laughter rumbled in the background, Ronny's voice mocking. "Mr. Moore, this is your only warning," she snapped. "Sorry, Alexis. Ready?"

I nodded, though she couldn't see, my throat tight, the phone's static hissing like a distant storm. Ronny's chuckle grated like gravel, chilling, as if he found this a game. Was he the root of Nathan's darkness? "Hello, my daughter."

I felt as if someone had punched me in the gut.

Agent Brown snapped, "Mr. Moore, that's your last warning."

"Okay, okay. Geez!" he said, his amusement a cold blade. "Alexis, how are you holding up?"

The Trips sat at the kitchen table, murmurs low, eyes on me, listening. "How do you think, Ronny?" I said, my voice trembling, my body shaking. "Your son's killing people we know, some he grew up with."

A long pause. The static crackled. "Look, Alexis, they helped him, wanted something from him, then betrayed him."

"Are you blaming everyone else?" I snapped, the counter's edge digging into my arm. "I need to know why. What happened to his mom? You were there."

His breath grew heavy, the air thick. "His mom... loved him, soft and warm, until your mom, Nicole, got in her head. Told her she wasn't enough, that I'd never love her as I loved Nicole. She..." His voice cracked, raw. "Nicole pushed her to hang herself, Alexis. I stood there, shocked, in love with Nicole, and would've done anything for her. Still would."

The words struck like a fist. My breath caught as the kitchen's coffee scent soured. Nicole's cruelty, Ronny's blind love, and his mom's hanging—each forged Nathan's darkness and mine. "You watched her die?" I whispered, tears burning, the phone trembling.

"I couldn't stop it. I didn't want to stop it," he said, his voice low, static hissing. "Nathan saw it too. He was never the same."

A flashback to the night in the cave hit me hard, and my head spun. Knowing my trauma from seeing my mother's room splattered with blood and her finger inside that creepy pumpkin, I truly felt sad for that young boy who saw his mother hanging from a rope.

"Ronny, you're not telling me anything new," my voice shook, and the Trips shifted in their chairs, screeching against the floor. I held up a hand and shook my head. Even though this was not what I wanted, I knew I could handle it. "You're wasting my time. I get it. Nathan's been traumatized by you and my mother. As much as I understand, it doesn't erase the people he's killed." My hand gripped the phone tighter, making it cramp.

"Alexis, I'm getting there." He must have moved, and I could hear chains clanking together. I imagined him hand-cuffed to the table.

"Then get to it!" I said, my tone sharpening. My entire body tensed, and I exhaled slowly.

"If you're thinking of being any kind of bait, that's exactly what Nathan wants. You know he's playing a game just like last time. He's pulling you in again," Ronny said with surety in his tone. Surprisingly, he seemed genuinely worried.

I shook my head, and anxiety took over. I needed to purge. To get rid of everything inside me, but I knew no matter how much I'd force myself, I wouldn't be able to rid myself of the pain—of Nathan.

"I have to play the game." I swallowed the acid burning my throat, and tears fell. I turned away and walked out to the porch. I didn't want the Trips to hear me. "Others will die if I don't."

Ronny coughed, then said, "You'll die if you do. He'll kill you this time."

"I know." I hit end on the phone and stuffed Cooper's phone into my pocket, wiping the tears from my eyes.

31
Asher

"We are all completely aware of what Alexis has planned," Cooper said as we were walking to our classes on campus.

This place made me feel as if I were leading two lives: one of normalcy and one of fighting for our lives. Obviously, I would prefer normalcy—something boring and predictable sounded better than all this shit that was going on.

"What do you mean?" Tanner asked, seeming very preoccupied and clueless. Over the last week, he had seemed completely unaware of what any of us were doing, and I couldn't figure out why. However, to be honest, I was more focused on Alexis and her sidekick—bulimia, which had taken up permanent residence in her life.

The three of us hadn't hung out much, so being on campus was a rare occasion. "Dude, where have you been, Tan? Have you not noticed how Alexis has been since her talk with Ronny a few nights ago?" Cooper readjusted his backpack on his shoulder, as if it were full of bricks, though it held only his laptop. Like the rest of us, he hadn't been himself—missing days at the gym and having restless nights trying to help the FBI.

Tanner paused in the middle of the path, causing Cooper and me to stop. He rubbed the back of his head—his nails worn down from stress—or exhaustion. "Sorry, guys. I'm trying to keep up with all my classes and help catch this guy, and..." he hesitated before grabbing both Cooper and me by the arms, pulling us toward a tree. He glanced around nervously, as if worried someone was listening.

"What's going on?" I asked, looking around as well.

Cooper gripped Tanner's shoulder. "Talk to us, man. Whatever it is, we can help."

Tanner shifted his gaze between Cooper and me. "I may be totally wrong here, but I... I don't trust Lila." Cooper and I looked at each other, then at Tanner. "Okay... she never answers her phone when she's around us. She always goes off, and when I see her, she looks like she's having some intense conversations. And don't you find it odd that she seems to have completely ditched Alexis? She doesn't come over as she did before Christmas."

Silence thickens as we just stare at one another.

"Well... come to think of it, Alexis has been trying to talk to Lila, and Lila hasn't been as responsive, which has been unusual. However, it doesn't seem to bother Alexis at all," I said, feeling very curious myself.

Cooper slammed his backpack to the ground, then punched the tree. "If she has any part in this with Nathan, I'm going to...." He let out a loud breath and looked at his knuckles, which were just as purple as the dark circles under his eyes.

"Shit, Coop, you really need to get to the gym to work off your frustrations," I said, wanting to punch something, too. My phone buzzed in my pocket. I groaned, "Well, this conversation will have to wait," then held the phone to my ear. "Hey, Fields, what's up?"

"Asher, sorry to pull you away from your class," he quickly said, sounding out of breath. "We got another tip, and we are here at the scene. It appears to be Nathan's work; however, there are no victims this time."

Cooper and Tanner pulled in closer as I put it on speaker, adjusting the volume so I knew we were the only ones who could hear. We looked at each other. "What do you mean *no* victim? He always leaves something, someone," I said, thinking back to when he had just left Alexis' mom's ring finger.

"Exactly!" he agreed. "Could you guys come down here? We'd like for you to help us look over the scene and see if there's anything familiar. Maybe something you know about Nathan."

No matter how many times we told him we didn't know Nathan that well, he still had it in his head that we used to be buddies in high school.

"Sure," I answered, knowing full well that all three of us were already behind on assignments.

He rattled off the address and said, "Oh… Kaitlyn and Benji's parents got here a couple of nights ago. They wanted to help find their kids." He cleared his throat. "They don't believe we'll find Benji alive."

My stomach dropped. His untreated leukemia would likely take him before Nathan had a chance.

Damn.

As we drove over to the crime scene, I contemplated whether to call Alexis. She was already in class with Lila, which had now become a problem in itself. However, I felt strongly that she was better off there with her than seeing another crime scene. I wasn't so sure how she'd do seeing Kaitlyn's parents.

We stopped outside an old building and went inside. We considered taking the elevator, but it looked like a relic from the 1940s. Seeing that it was many flights up and that we were already so tired, we stepped in and punched the button. The doors creaked and jerked shut before we started to move. At the elevator's pace, we probably would have been better off taking the stairs.

When the doors finally opened, as they had closed, we hesitated to step off. What would we see? What would we find? For once, I was glad we wouldn't be seeing any dead bodies.

The air in the abandoned office building on the twenty-second floor was thick with the smell of mold and something metallic—the copper scent of old blood, poorly masked by a fresh wave of chlorine. Fields and two other agents were already there, moving through the space with grim efficiency.

The scene was exactly as I'd feared. Nathan was adapting.

In the center of the vast, empty room stood a single, beat-up rolltop desk. A flickering emergency light in the hallway cast long, frantic shadows. On the desk, a small, intricate cage of black-painted wire sat empty, its door slightly ajar. Scattered around the desk were hundreds of fake silver coins—cheap, plastic currency—glittering mockingly in the weak light.

"Sing a Song of Sixpence," I murmured, recognizing the lines instantly. "The King was in his counting house, counting out his money... But where's the King?" Nathan's themes were always precise, and a missing element was never an accident.

Fields moved over to me, holding a plastic evidence bag. Inside, a small black, oily feather was pinned to a piece of parchment. "The note was attached to the cage. He calls them 'blackbirds.' He's escalating, Asher. It's psychological coercion."

I read the note, Nathan's familiar, looping script mocking us:

The four and twenty blackbirds, baked in a pie. My beautiful songbirds, they sing when I tell them to.
And the Ladybug will soon realize where she belongs.

"The captives are the 'blackbirds,' " I confirmed, feeling the cold weight of the new reality settle in my gut. "The people he took from Gold Beach. He's forcing them to perform his rhymes. He's shifted from a killer to a Psychological Architect."

I looked pointedly at the cage. "This scene is a warning, Fields. He's telling us he has the leverage to make anyone turn. He wants Alexis to be like him, a 'Black Sheep'—someone corrupted by the secrets and betrayals in her own lineage."

Fields looked at me, understanding dawning in her eyes. "He's not targeting her physically. He's targeting her morality."

"Exactly. He knows her guilt. He knows she sees herself as tainted by her biological father's blood, Ronny. He's trying to convince her that her purpose isn't to stop him but to join him in the darkness."

Cooper and Tanner came over, looking horrified at the scene and listening intently.

"Look at this," Fields said, pulling out another evidence bag. Inside was a small, wooden carving, clearly showing a ladybug, but its spots were elongated, morphing into the distinct, sharp lines of a wolf's paw. It was painted completely black. "We found this pinned to the back of the desk."

My heart hammered. "He's showing Alexis her fate," I whispered, taking the token and tracing the cold, black lacquer. "The Ladybug—Alexis—is meant to be corrupted. He's not interested in just the kill; he's interested in atonement."

I finally said the thought out loud, the one that had been eating me alive since Austin. "She's not just the bait, Fields. She's driven by a desire to be the sacrifice. She's punishing herself for everything—for surviving, for the shared blood, for all the betrayals. She's preparing herself to be the final victim."

My eyes burned with the urgency of that awful truth. The way she had isolated herself, her return to bulimia—it wasn't just stress. It was a self-destructive preparation.

"The leverage," I snapped, looking at the black ladybug-wolf carving. "He's going to use the innocence she desperately wants to protect. He's going to use the parents' presence as the ultimate pressure point. He'll find the person closest to us, the one Alexis feels most responsible for, and force them to hurt her. That emotional betrayal will be the final step in shattering her resolve."

I turned to Fields, my focus absolute. "We need to stop thinking about the next victim he'll kill and start thinking about the next person he'll force to betray someone Alexis cares about. The hunt has changed. It's about saving her soul now."

I placed the token back in the bag and headed for the exit. "We need to get back. I have to find a way to convince Alexis that her survival is the only thing that beats him. Not her death."

We ran for the sluggish elevator, leaving the sterile, mocking scene behind. Outside, the Austin sunshine felt blinding and fake. I knew the hunt had shifted from a manhunt to a desperate psychological defense, and I had to save Alexis's mind before Nathan could claim her soul.

32
Nathan - The Wolf

The Austin heat was a rancid cloak of dust and decay, unlike the sterile salt bite of Gold Beach. I preferred it. The frantic, almost clumsy exit from the veterinary hospital—a place too exposed, too clinical—had been necessary. A professional knows when to cut bait. This barn on this forgotten ranch, twenty miles outside the city proper, smelled of dried manure, rot, and old wood—honest decay. It was private. It was safe.

I ran a clean cloth over the last patch of floorboards, wiping away the small puddle of water I'd used to dissolve the remaining silver dust. The Sing a Song of Sixpence decoy had been a masterpiece of omission. The cage was empty. The silver coins were scattered, cheap pieces of flair. The note, when deciphered, was a psychological grenade: I know the price of your betrayal.

The media—idiots—framed it as a failure, a hasty retreat. The FBI, relying on Asher—the little boy who once idolized me, now merely helping them—would waste weeks looking for a body that didn't exist, chasing shadows. They always looked for the victim. They never looked for the architect's motive.

My motive was simple: the complete and beautiful collapse of Alexis's soul.

I picked up the small, black carving I'd left for her to find later. The wood was polished smooth, transitioning from the delicate shell of the Ladybug to the sharp, predatory profile of the Wolf. She was still clinging to her shell, trying to atone for sins that weren't hers. Soon, the shell would crack, and only the predator I knew was inside would remain. The guilt was merely fuel.

I slipped the carving into my pocket, the wood warm against my palm, then turned my attention to the barn's inhabitants. They were my true, living canvas.

The air in the western wing—a small, enclosed stall I'd reinforced with plywood and metal sheeting—was stale but quiet.

I approached the corner where my Ultimate Prize lay.

She was the woman I needed to complete Alexis's destruction, the most beautiful prize in my sick collection. She wasn't a twist; she was the perfect, conditioned pet, molded over months to obey and fulfill my purpose.

She was curled on a thin, military-grade cot, her face slack, eyes tracking the ceiling beams that crisscrossed above. Her hair was greasy and matted, and her skin, starved of sunlight and proper nutrition, was pale to the point of translucence.

"Hello, pet," I murmured, my voice low and conversational.

She didn't respond, of course. She rarely did anymore. She was well beyond a simple fight-or-flight response; she was in the process of re-creation.

I examined the wall beside her bed. It was covered in her scratch marks. She used her broken, raw fingernails to etch lines into the wood. Where a normal person would draw crosses or tally marks, my pet drew patterns. Repetitive, circular, frantic patterns. They started as simple geometric shapes but always dissolved into the same symbols: the Ladybug in varying states of distress, the Wolf Paw, and lately, a jagged circle with radiating spokes—The Clock.

He broke my clock. I remembered her whispering in a moment of lucidity a week ago.

Her mind was unraveling. That's what I wanted. The trauma I inflicted on her in Bandon, combined with the past month's sensory deprivation, was producing the desired result. She was a blank, fragile slate, ready to absorb the new programming.

When I am done, she will be the perfect vessel to carry the infection into the next stage of my work. She is the bomb I will detonate after I am safely locked away. She is the reason Alexis can never truly heal. She is the ultimate, silent victory.

I left her without a word. The silence of her cell was the sound of a masterpiece curing.

The rest of the barn floor was sectioned off into makeshift cells with chain-link and tarps. Here, the air was thick with the stench of fear, sweat, and cheap synthetic cleaner.

I stopped before Becca's cell first. She was sitting with her back to the wall, knees drawn up, rocking slightly. She was the most pathetic of my collection, but essential nonetheless.

"Becca. How are we doing?"

She flinched violently at my voice, her eyes—red-rimmed and bloodshot—darting up to mine. She didn't have the fire my pet once did. She had only need.

"It's quiet," she rasped, her tongue too thick for her mouth. "I need... my throat is dry."

She meant the opioids. I smiled gently. "Of course, darling. But quiet is a good thing, isn't it? Quiet means no more surprises. No more disappointments like William."

A faint shudder went through her body, a delayed seismic response to the death of Trevor's father. That man was a loose end; he complicated Becca's desperation. Now that William was gone, Becca had nothing left but the small, controlled doses of relief I provided.

I tossed a blister pack through the mesh. She scrambled for it, her dignity dissolving faster than the pill beneath her tongue.

"I know you miss your son, Becca," I said softly. "But William wasn't the answer. I am."

Her eyes glazed over as the drug hit. She was already compliant, secure. The remaining pieces, however, were fragile.

My gaze drifted to the corner, where Kaitlyn, Alexis's old friend, sat hunched, her hands gripping the chain-link as if trying to rip it apart. Next to her, huddled under a blanket despite the heat, was her younger brother, Benji.

Benji was frail. Too frail. He was thinner than he should be, his breathing shallow, his color terrible. Leukemia, the doctors had said. A cruel, slow wasting.

This was the ultimate piece of leverage. This was the dark, beating heart of my next masterwork: Little Boy Blue.

The rhyme was not about finding a boy who was sleeping. It was about finding a boy who was failing and finding the person who should have been guarding him, preoccupied with guilt and fear.

I walked toward their cell. Kaitlyn saw me coming and instantly placed her body between Benji and me. A valiant but ultimately futile maternal defense.

"Don't touch him," she growled, her voice scratchy but infused with genuine venom. She was the strongest fighter left. I appreciated that. It would make the final scene so much more devastating.

"Touch him?" I chuckled, leaning against the chain-link. "My dear Kaitlyn, I have no intention of touching him. I am simply observing. Observing what a terrible, slow thief this disease is."

I lowered my voice, letting it grow intimate, confiding. "And I'm watching how hard your mother is working to find you both."

Kaitlyn's eyes widened, her entire body tensing in raw, unadulterated fear mixed with sudden, desperate hope.

"She—she's here? They're looking?" Kaitlyn whispered, her voice cracking.

I nodded slowly, letting the lie sink in. "They are relentless. Your mother is right outside Austin, working with the police. They will find you... eventually." I watched the hope ignite, knowing it would make the devastation total. "I know everything, Kaitlyn. I know your guilt over being distracted by Alexis and Trevor's drama. I know your sleepless nights, wondering whether you should have stayed home, whether you should have been checking his blood counts instead of chasing a ghost. I know that if Benji dies, you will spend the rest of your life believing you let him slip away, while your mother was risking everything to save you."

I let the silence hang, thick and heavy, until the ragged sound of Benji's shallow cough broke the stillness. Kaitlyn was weeping silently now, the combination of hope and terror shattering her composure.

"That is the beauty of Little Boy Blue," I concluded, tapping the mesh with one finger. "It's the tragedy of negligence. The death of innocence. And the perfect, final weight on Alexis's soul."

I straightened up, turning away before she could scream. She was ready. The guilt was acute, the fear total, and the target—fragile Benji—is perfect. The lie about her mother was the exquisite twist of the knife.

The next step would be confrontation. I would force Kaitlyn to make a choice so morally grotesque that Alexis, upon finding the bodies, would realize my purpose was not murder but coercion into mutual damnation. Alexis craved atonement; this scene would replace that yearning with pure, absolute, necessary rage.

I looked over the rancid, decaying barn. The air hung still. The only sounds were Becca's shallow, drug-induced breathing, my pet's slow scratching against the wall, and the little boy's faint, terrible cough.

My work here was done. The Architect was ready to build the final, catastrophic scene.

33
Alexis

The air in the sterile office smelled of paper and anxiety, a familiar scent that usually felt like a cage. Today, it felt like a bunker. I sat in the plush armchair, the midday Austin sun glaring through the blinds, casting prison stripes across the carpet.

Genevieve sat opposite me, her notepad resting on her knee. She was calm and professional, but her eyes held a deeper, weary concern.

"Alexis, I'm going to shift our focus today," Genevieve began, her voice soft but firm. "I don't want to talk about the nursery rhymes or crime scenes anymore. We've done enough analysis of Nathan's manipulation. I want to talk about you."

I clenched my jaw, the muscle ticking furiously. "There is no 'me' outside of this, Genevieve. It's all connected. The 'Sing a Song of Sixpence' taunt—it's not a clue. It's a statement. He's telling me everyone around me has a price. That I'm the reason people betray each other."

I finally gave voice to the truth I'd been dodging since Gold Beach. Since the beginning.

"I'm the cancer, Genevieve. I attract it. Everything I touch turns to ashes. My father. My best friend. Even Trevor's death—it started because of me. Nathan used my existence to make Luke, Becca, Trevor—the list goes on—to betray everyone. And now he's doing it again."

My voice was a low, desperate confession. I felt the familiar weight of the world pressing down, crushing the air from me. This wasn't grief anymore; it was a calculated, crushing responsibility.

Genevieve leaned forward, setting her pen down. "I hear that crushing sense of responsibility, Alexis. But that's a belief Nathan is actively trying to install in your head, not a truth. Honestly, I'm not happy seeing you this close to the investigation again. I've watched your decline since we first confirmed Nathan was alive. You've lost the ground you gained since moving away from Gold Beach."

She reached for a nearby tissue box, sliding it closer to me. "You're internalizing his narrative, and that's taking a greater toll than the physical danger. So, let's talk about tools. About how you can manage the immense pressure you're under without letting his ideology destroy your core. What is one concrete, self-preserving action you can take right now to reclaim control over your own stability?"

"Reclaim control?" I scoffed, sitting forward. The armchair leather groaned under my sudden movement. "Look at the evidence. Everyone is tied to me somehow... because of my mother. Nathan uses the exact same tactics on everyone I care about—he finds their weakness and uses my name, my connection, to justify their monstrous decisions. I'm the constant. The common denominator. The virus."

I knew I was spiraling. I could feel the cold logic of the Rhyme Reaper bleeding into my own thoughts, justifying his sick ideology. This was exactly what he wanted.

"So, you're saying your only option is to continue playing his game?" Genevieve challenged, her tone now rooted in therapeutic provocation.

The question hit me like a physical blow. I flinched, reeling back against the chair. "No! God, no. I want him to stop using me as the reason for his existence. I want to end the cycle. But I can't if I don't admit the truth. I am the perfect bait."

The silence in the room stretched, filled only by the frantic drumming of my own heart. I was trembling again, but this time it wasn't fear. It was a terrifying, crystallizing clarity.

"You are making a tactical decision, not an emotional one," Genevieve observed, picking up her notepad again. "You believe that if you accept his premise—that you are the bait—you can control the trap. But Alexis, controlling the trap means surviving it. What tools do you have for survival when you face him?"

"It's the only way," I rasped. "He is working through my guilt. People are dying because of who I am—that is his masterpiece. The Humpty Dumpty of it all. He shattered my belief in friendship and loyalty, then showed me the pieces of silver left behind. I have to make myself visible. I have to give him what he wants."

I pushed up from the chair and began pacing the small office, my nervous energy consuming the space. "The FBI, no matter who is helping them, is too slow. They're looking for evidence, for patterns. They're still processing the Goosey Gander mess with Nina. I know Nathan is already setting up the next kill. He's moving faster. He's closing in on someone I care about, someone with a weakness he can exploit for maximum collateral damage."

I stopped pacing and turned back to Genevieve, my eyes burning with a desperate, terrifying resolve.

"I know who it is. He's going to use Kaitlyn to get to me."

Genevieve waited, saying nothing. Her silence was a demand for justification.

"Kaitlyn's always been the weak link in the chain," I explained, the words tumbling out, fueled by cold dread. "She's riddled with guilt, convinced that if she hadn't wanted to save her brother, none of this would have happened. She blamed herself for months. And now, Benji..."

I choked on the boy's name. The leukemia. The slow, relentless disease had already taken so much from their family. The thought of that sweet, fragile child being used as a pawn made the cold, hard lump of rage in my chest solidify. I would not be responsible for Benji's death. Not now. Not ever.

"Nathan doesn't just kill, Genevieve. He coerces. He finds the leverage. What greater leverage is there than a sister who already blames herself and a child who is slowly slipping away? He'll make Kaitlyn believe she can save Benji only by doing something unforgivable—something that ultimately kills Benji and destroys me."

I had the vision clear in my mind: Nathan whispering lies into Kaitlyn's ear, offering a temporary cure or escape, forcing her to choose between her brother and her soul. The betrayal.

"And what will you do when he comes for the bait?" Genevieve asked, her voice calm, cutting through my panic.

I didn't hesitate. "I will give him the bait. But I won't give him the satisfaction."

My focus hardened. I wouldn't let Nathan use Kaitlyn as the final piece of silver. I was willing to sacrifice my sanity, my safety, everything, but I would not let his ideology win through another betrayal.

"If I'm the bait," I said, a dangerous, raw fury tightening my chest, "I'm the only piece I can control. I'm going to make myself an easy target. But when he moves, I'm not going to be the Ladybug anymore."

I looked down at my hands, not seeing the stitches from the sludge pit but seeing the raw, conditioned muscle of a survivor. I was done being prey.

"He wants to break my clock? He wants to turn me into a wolf in sheep's clothing, as he believes I am? Fine. I will show him what the wolf truly looks like."

Just then, my phone buzzed on the coffee table. It was a text from an unknown number. I snatched it up, my heart hammering against my ribs, a terrible premonition washing over me.

The message: Where is the horn, Little Boy Blue? Your sheep are in the meadow.

My blood ran cold. He was already there. Little Boy Blue. The rhyme of negligence and lost innocence. It wasn't a future threat; it was happening right now. He had Benji and Kaitlyn.

I looked at Genevieve, shock and sudden white-hot fury displacing all the fear. "He already has them. I was right. I have to go."

I grabbed my jacket. I was halfway to the door when the phone buzzed again. This time, it was a photo.

It was a blurry, dimly lit image of Kaitlyn, sitting on a concrete floor, her face streaked with tears, holding a pale, unconscious Benji in her arms. In the corner of the frame, a small wooden sign—the logo of an abandoned warehouse on the East Side of Austin, long known for its structural collapse and isolation.

The message beneath the photo was short, personal, and devastating.

Find the horn, Ladybug. Or watch her sound the alarm for you.

Nathan didn't want the FBI. He didn't want Asher. He wanted me. Alone.

I spun back to Genevieve, my eyes locked on hers. All the therapy, all the attempts at recovery, all the guilt—it vanished, replaced by the instinct of a cornered creature.

"This is it. The ultimate coercion," I whispered, my voice metallic and hard. "He's going to force her to choose. I have to stop him. I have to go there now."

"Alexis, you cannot," Genevieve insisted, rising quickly. "This is exactly his trap. You call the FBI, you use the tracker..."

"No! He knew I'd track him! He knew Asher was helping! The minute the FBI moves, he kills them both. He wants me to break protocol. He wants me to face him, knowing I failed to protect them." I was already moving toward the door, my mind racing through escape routes and weapons caches.

"This is not just about guilt anymore, Alexis. This is about rage," Genevieve said, her voice rising as she tried to ground me.

I stopped at the doorway, my hand on the cool metal of the handle. I looked back, a genuine, feral smile touching my lips.

"I know. And he taught me how to use it."

I threw open the door, letting the office's silence crash into the hallway's noise. I didn't run. I walked fast, pulling my jacket up, pulling the wolf over the ladybug. He wanted a monster? He was about to get one. I was no longer interested in solving the riddle. I was only interested in ending the life of the architect who had dared to use my pain as his blueprint. My rage was cold, pure, and ready to burn the whole world down.

I didn't slow down until I hit the stairwell, punching the elevator button before realizing I wouldn't wait. My feet pounded the marble stairs, each step a testament to the adrenaline and fury fueling my escape. I ignored the confused glances of a janitor and a deliveryman as I burst into the lobby. I wasn't a patient anymore. I was a missile.

I hit Send on my phone before I even reached the parking garage. It was a direct line to Asher. He answered on the first ring, his voice tight with the stress of the command center.

"Alexis! I was just about to call you. They've moved. The decoys—they were just to buy time. We think the next scene is set."

"Don't think, Asher. Know," I spat, my voice raw and loud enough to echo in the concrete structure. "He just texted me. He's going to kill Kaitlyn and Benji next. He sent a photo from the old East Side warehouse. I'm going."

The silence that followed was a physical weight, heavier than any of the chains Nathan had used in Gold Beach.

"You're going where, Alexis? No. Absolutely not. The FBI is mobilizing now. We have the area cordoned off. Stay put. We need you as a resource, not a liability."

I slammed my palm against the roof of my car, the sound muffled by my rage. "A resource? Is that what I am to everyone? A walking clue? You know what drives me insane, Asher? The fact that every time one of these scenes happens—every single time—I'm told what to do or not to do. I'm the only one who can breathe the air Nathan breathes, who can understand the sick poetry of his staging, but you treat me like a child who needs to be protected from the harsh reality of her own life!"

My hand tightened around the phone, my knuckles white. "I've seen. You've damn well seen what Nathan can do. What he has already done. No more. I am not going to be responsible for Benji's death because I waited for the FBI to write a goddamn warrant!"

"Alexis, listen to me. This is exactly what he wants. He wants you there. He wants a confrontation."

"Then he'll get a confrontation," I growled, sliding into the driver's seat. I started the engine. The roar of the V8 was momentarily satisfying. "I have known Kaitlyn since before I moved to Ventura. We were friends, Asher. She was a constant, a lifeline when things were dark. We kept in touch even after my mother's murder and before I moved back to Gold Beach. She was a true friend then. But when I moved back? Something in her changed. It was subtle, but it happened fast. She pulled away, became guarded, and I always suspected it had something to do with Nathan, with his cruel, quiet way of getting people to turn against each other. We know he manipulated everyone into believing their lives could be better if I were dead. Kaitlyn knows now of her mistake in trusting him. I want her to believe she can trust me."

The admission hung in the air: the weight of the past, the ghost of the Ladybug, the Ladybug taunt, and the certainty that Nathan had been planning this web of betrayal far longer than anyone realized. It was never just about the body count; it was about the corruption of loyalty.

"Alexis, the address is massive. It's the old Monarch Steel facility. It covers four blocks. You can't go in blind." Asher's voice was strained, a tight mix of exasperation and genuine worry.

"Give me a better location, Asher. I'm less than ten minutes away. I can be a distraction. I can be the bait and give the FBI the time they need to breach the perimeter. But I will not stand by and let Nathan turn that little boy, that sweet, sick child, into his Little Boy Blue statue. I will not be responsible for Benji's death."

I waited, my breath held tight in my chest. I knew I had him. I had used his own rules against him: I'd offered the perfect leverage.

A defeated sigh crackled through the phone line. "Alexis, I love you. I don't want you to do this. Please."

His begging and concern would normally have broken me into submission, but my mind was already made up. "Asher, you're not going to change my mind. This is my decision."

He sighed again. "Okay, let me get Fields."

The phone crackled, and Fields got right to it. "Alexis, listen closely. We scanned the photo's metadata. The light pattern points to the southeast corner of the complex. Look for a partially collapsed grain silo, the closest landmark. But you drive straight past. You do not stop. You wait for the teams."

"Southeast corner. Got it." I ended the call before he could say another word. I didn't want to hear the pleas, the warnings, or the logic. Logic was for therapists and analysts. I was beyond logic. I was fueled by vengeance.

I decided not to drive toward the warehouse yet. I took a sharp detour, cutting through the dense, disorganized streets of East Austin. I knew this city was a sprawling network of forgotten corners and hidden dangers. I also knew it was where I had to prepare.

I pulled into a derelict car wash bay, its concrete walls covered in faded graffiti. I kept the engine running. Reaching under the passenger seat, my fingers brushed the worn leather case. I pulled it out—a small, heavy piece of insurance I had bought and gone to the shooting range when everyone thought I was in class.

It was a Glock 19, cold and heavy in my hand, nestled in a custom holster. It was loud, impersonal, and efficient. I secured the holster against my lower back, pulling my jacket down to conceal the profile. This was not intimate; this was about stopping power.

But as I felt the undeniable weight of the firearm, the adrenaline abruptly crashed, leaving a vacuum of exhaustion and ultimate despair. Nathan's entire sick game revolved around the Ladybug, around the bait that was me. The innocent decoys—all funneled back to my existence, my guilt, my trauma. If I take myself out of the equation, the game stops. No more silver for him to use. No more bodies for me to feel responsible for. It was the only foolproof strategy. The only way to save Benji and stop the cycle of betrayal.

I pulled the pistol out again. The smooth black metal felt immense in my shaking hand. I thumbed the safety off. I brought the muzzle to my temple. The cold steel was a terrifying, immediate comfort. It would be fast. It would be decisive. It would be the final, necessary sacrifice. I closed my eyes, picturing the quiet release, the absolute silence that would descend on Nathan's world when his target vanished.

No.

The rage, which had been simmering, boiled over, scalding the despair away. I wasn't just bait; I was the target, and self-destruction was exactly what Nathan wanted—he wanted me to internalize his victory. He wanted me to break. I lowered the gun and rammed it back into the holster. I would not give him the satisfaction of winning even in my death. I would not let his ideology consume me. Benji was still alive. Kaitlyn was still fighting. I had to choose life, if only to take his.

I looked at my reflection in the dusty rearview mirror. The face staring back wasn't the broken, guilt-ridden girl who had started the day. The eyes were cold, calculating, and devoid of fear. I was done dissecting the trauma. I was done asking Genevieve for permission to heal. Healing was a luxury I couldn't afford.

The road ahead was a straight, dark stretch of cracked asphalt, leading directly to the Monarch Steel warehouse. It looked like the mouth of a tomb.

I gripped the steering wheel, the leather warm beneath my hands. The thought of Benji, weak and helpless, was a physical ache, a pain I refused to let paralyze me. Nathan wanted me to feel the crushing weight of my own failures. He wanted me to witness Kaitlyn betraying everything she stood for, all because of my connection to her. He wanted me to carry Benji's death on my shoulders forever.

But Nathan had made one crucial miscalculation. He had spent so long turning others into wolves that he failed to notice the one he truly needed to fear: me.

The Ladybug was gone. The Wolf was driving. I pressed the gas pedal to the floor, the car leaping forward, eating up the distance to the final, necessary confrontation. I was the bait, yes. But the bait had teeth, and Nathan was about to find out exactly how much rage one shattered soul could hold. I was going to find that horn, and I was going to make sure Nathan would never hear another rhyme again.

34
The Captive

The darkness was a constant weight, heavier than the cold seeping into my skin from the concrete floor. My head felt like a shattered glass globe, with thoughts like sharp, useless shards rolling inside. I didn't try to piece them together anymore. There was only the cold, the scent of rust, and the simple, necessary truth: He is the master. I am the pet.

I heard it first—a thin, high-pitched whine, swallowed quickly by the vast emptiness of the facility. It was the sound of a closing door, the click of metal, and the sharp intake of a furious breath.

His Ladybug.

The thought was a jolt; a dangerous spark of clarity the man had conditioned me to expect. The Wolf had always spoken of her as a concept, a psychological force, never a woman of flesh and blood. Yet there she was.

Or maybe she wasn't. Maybe the dust and the fevered cold had conjured her from the rust-colored air. I couldn't find the energy to distinguish reality from the next delusion. All my brain could process was the gnawing, insistent ache in my stomach, the deep, heavy realization that if I could just eat, the world might stop spinning for a minute.

She stepped out of the shadows into a shaft of weak, dusty light filtering from a high window. My breath seized in my chest, a cold, sharp ache. I pressed back against the wall, trying to become invisible.

She was stunning. Her hair, the color of wet earth, fell in a dark wave around a face sculpted by fury. Her eyes—I was close enough to see them—were startling, crystalline green, shining with a dangerous, raw fire. She was beautiful in a way that defied the decay of the warehouse, a creature of pure, destructive clarity.

A primitive, jealous resentment twisted in my stomach. She carried the pain of the world, yes, but she carried it with such furious elegance, such perfect, terrible beauty. The Wolf had made me his pet, but he had made her his obsession.

She moved in straight, uncompromising lines, a gun held low at her side. She was searching, sweeping the vast, empty space. I knew exactly what she was searching for: the silver pieces The Wolf had laid out.

My gaze drifted to the corner where the two figures were held. The little lamb and the desperate sister. They were going to die. The Wolf was a clockmaker, and they were the gears he was about to smash to prove the Ladybug's guilt.

Hush, little pet, the memory of his voice hummed in my mind. *The show is about to start. Watch her break.*

But as I watched the Ladybug step closer, her green eyes ruthless and sharp, I knew The Wolf had miscalculated. She didn't look like she was about to break. She looked like she was about to start the fire.

35
Alexis

The air in the abandoned Monarch Steel facility was a cold, metallic rot, tasting of old blood. I'd killed the engine three blocks out and coasted the last fifty yards, pulling the car into the deep shadow of a defunct concrete loader.

I checked the Glock 19 nestled at my lower back. The weight was familiar now, a cold comfort. I pulled my jacket up, zipping it high. No more Ladybug. Just the Wolf.

I moved along the perimeter fence, the chain links rattling softly with each step. I found the collapsed section at the southeast corner and slipped through the jagged opening. I moved with desperate, animal strength, fueled by pure, unadulterated fury. Nathan wanted me to feel the full, crushing weight of failure. He wanted me to be responsible for Benji's last, desperate breath and for Kaitlyn's soul being destroyed.

Not today, Nathan.

The warehouse interior was a cavern of shadows and decay. I followed a barely-there light source cutting through the dust clouds. It came from a suspended gantry crane high above the main floor. The perfect, isolated stage. I scrambled up a pile of rusted scrap metal, hauling myself up the scaffolding with brute strength.

My breath sawed in my lungs, the adrenaline pushing me past the exhaustion. When I finally reached the scaffold platform, the scene snapped into sickening focus.

Kaitlyn was there, hunched over a pale, motionless Benji. They were tied to the rusted railings, lit by a single bare bulb swinging overhead. The setup was textbook *Little Boy Blue.*

And there was Nathan.

He stood twenty feet away, his back to me, inspecting a syringe he held between his fingers.

"The sheep are in the meadow," Nathan said, his voice echoing, calm and conversational. "And Little Boy Blue is sleeping. Do you know why? Because no one sounded the alarm. No one cared enough to look for the horn."

Kaitlyn lifted her head, her face a mask of terror and shame. "Please, Nathan. He's fading. Just give me the medicine. I'll do whatever you want."

Nathan chuckled—a dry, horrible sound. "You already did, Kaitlyn. You already chose. The medicine is just... an end to the guilt."

He's going to make her feel responsible for his death. I have to save Benji.

"NATHAN!" The sound ripped from my throat.

He slowly turned, a triumphant, sickening smile spreading across his face.

"There she is. My Ladybug. Right on time."

I brought the gun up in a two-handed grip, aiming straight at his chest. "Let them go. Now."

"If you shoot, I drop this," he said, holding the syringe higher. "If you drop this, the FBI storms in, and these two are collateral damage. You lose. You always lose, Ladybug."

My finger tightened on the trigger. I shifted the Glock, aiming it at my own temple.

"I said, let them go." My voice was suddenly calm, terrifyingly clear. "You want to prove I'm the bait? Fine. The game stops when the bait dies. No more silver. No more victims. You'll lose your masterpiece."

Nathan's smile froze. This wasn't in his script. "Don't. Don't you dare."

"Give me the boy. I drop the gun. You take Kaitlyn, you walk away, and you never look back." He wouldn't fall for me taking both of them. I just hoped the FBI would make it here on time.

He cocked his head, questioning my resolve as his mind raced. Benji was a liability. He reached down, untied Benji's bonds, and shoved the boy's frail body toward the edge of the scaffolding.

"The boy is yours," Nathan sneered.

I lowered the gun from my head, aiming at his feet, ready to fire the second Benji was clear.

Then the chaos erupted.

A blinding flash of light hit the gantry. The air was ripped apart by the deafening electronic shriek of a dozen bull-horns.

"FBI! DROP THE WEAPON! GET ON THE GROUND!"

They swarmed in. The FBI tactical teams breached the perimeter, using the distraction of my call to storm the north side. They moved on the image metadata and the timing of the decoy—they didn't wait for my signal; they moved on their own tactical timetable.

Nathan roared, a sound of pure, thwarted animal rage. "NO! YOU CHEATING BITCH!"

He kicked Benji's small body, sending him sliding across the metal floor. Simultaneously, he ripped Kaitlyn's bonds free and shoved her violently ahead of him toward a rear exit staircase. I fired a shot—not at Nathan, but at the cable of the bare bulb swinging above us. The bulb shattered, plunging the gantry into near-total darkness, lit only by the frantic strobes of the tactical lights below.

"Kaitlyn!" I screamed, lunging for Benji.

Nathan threw Kaitlyn down the steps, dragging her by her hair. Just as they vanished, a sudden beam of light revealed one last image: a frail, pale woman, her hand on Nathan's back, guiding him and Kaitlyn into the deeper shadows.

Who was that? I thought I knew everyone he had cap-tured. It didn't look like Becca.

I hauled Benji back from the edge, his fragile weight barely registering. I held him, checking for a pulse—thank God, a weak beat—and screamed for medical help.

The fight was over, but the game was lost. Nathan was gone. Kaitlyn was gone.

Seconds later, Asher, Cooper, and Tanner rushed onto the platform, breathless and stunned by the chaos. Asher was the first to speak, his relief quickly turning to shock when his flashlight revealed the gun on the ground.

"Alexis? What the hell is going on? You have a gun?" Cooper and Tanner moved straight to Benji, immediately assessing his near-death state.

"I had him!" I yelled, my voice cracking, shaking with a devastating mix of adrenaline and betrayal. "I had him! I was going to trade myself! You ruined it! You ruined the only chance we had!"

I slammed my fist onto the gantry railing. I was responsible for saving Benji, but I was furious—furious that my friends and the FBI's intervention had prevented me from making the final sacrifice that would have ended Nathan's game forever. They had saved my life, but in my eyes, they had guaranteed Nathan's continued freedom.

36
Asher

The air in the abandoned warehouse was cold and stagnant, still heavy with the smell of fear and the residue of Nathan's chemical stagecraft. But the sounds from the hospital—the frantic noise, the sterile antiseptic scent—offered no comfort. Nathan's victory was complete, and he used the clinical setting to amplify the psychological harm.

Fields had delivered the official blow minutes earlier. "You three are done," he said to me, Cooper, and Tanner. "The informal consultation is terminated. Your personal history as Nathan's victims and Asher's relationship with Alexis make this arrangement a critical liability. It's our mistake for letting you all get so involved."

Tanner argued about the month we had sacrificed, but I silenced him with a look. I knew the truth. Fields blamed the connection; I blamed Nathan's insanity. The pain, the trauma, the dismissal—it was all a symptom of the cancer Nathan had spread.

I stood beside my brothers, feeling the weight of our dismissal, but my focus remained laser-sharp on Alexis. The discovery of her gun and her secret range practice had shattered the illusion of her recovery. I barely recognized the woman I loved—the trauma had replaced her softness with a dangerous, terminal resolve.

I moved toward her, reaching for her hand. She didn't pull away this time, but her fingers stayed cold and motionless in my grip, offering no reciprocal pressure.

"They're right, Asher," she whispered, her gaze fixed down the hall. "Look at Benji. It's my fault."

"Stop it," I commanded, my voice low and fierce. I pulled her into the partial cover of a nearby privacy screen. "It is not your fault. It's Nathan's. Every agonizing second of our lives since the first time he found you—the capture, the trauma, the dismissals—it is all his insanity. He uses our connections because he is a coward, but he is the cause, Alexis. Never you."

"But he was punishing me," she insisted, her voice hollow.

"He was punishing the world for denying him control," I corrected, fighting to keep her grounded. "And now he's punishing you for having the courage to survive him. I know you have a gun, Alexis. I know you're preparing for a final showdown. You will not walk into that fire alone."

She finally let a single tear fall down her cheek. "I won't be alone. He'll be there. And I'll end it."

"Then we end it together," I insisted. "We find Kaitlyn. We bring him down. But we fight his insanity, not yours."

The need to gather intelligence interrupted the conversation. We sat with the Martins—Kaitlyn and Benji's parents—in the consultation room. Their raw anguish was overwhelming. The mother, consumed by fear and grief, clung to the fact that her children had been taken because of Nathan's vendetta against Alexis.

I stepped in, repeatedly steering the conversation away from blame and toward tactical information. "The blame is Nathan's," I told the Martins, my eyes steady. "But we need to know what he needs from Kaitlyn now. He hasn't killed her. Why?"

The mother could offer little, consumed by the agonizing reality that Benji was barely hanging on.

I stepped away and made the call, my voice tight with urgency. "Mom, it's Asher. Alexis is running out of time. I'm afraid I won't be able to hold her together alone. The FBI cut us off. We need you and Dad to come to Austin. Now."

"Asher, what about Benji?" Tami's voice was sharp with maternal terror.

"He's bad, Mom. Really bad. His leukemia and the lack of treatment. We need you here. Since they know you and Dad, they need support, and we need stability. Please, get the first flight."

As I hung up, a heavy weight lifted—the burden was now shared.

I rejoined Cooper and Tanner near the consultation room. Alexis remained where I'd left her, paralyzed by guilt. Just as I reached her, the sound began: the rapid BEEP... BEEP... BEEP... from the ICU.

Suddenly, the beat stopped, replaced by a harsh, continuous EEEEERRRR.

The sound shattered the silence.

Chaos broke out. Nurses and doctors hurried past us. The Martins let out a unified, guttural cry of pure, agonizing terror.

I pushed through the small crowd toward the sliding glass doors of the ICU. A doctor slammed his hand against the glass, pushing us back.

Through the glass, I saw the frantic movement of blue scrubs. I watched the doctor grab the defibrillator paddles. Above the small bed, the cardiac monitor revealed the terrifying, undeniable truth: the flat, relentless line of sudden, complete heart failure.

Flatline.

The Martins rushed in. Not with dignity. Not with restraint.

With animal terror.

The mother's scream tore at the very fabric of the world. The father sank to his knees beside the bed, wrapping Benji's tiny body in his arms, holding him like a newborn again.

He rocked him.

Slowly.

Desperately.

As if rhythm could restart a stopped heart.

"No… no… no… baby, please—" the mother sobbed, her voice cracking raw, her forehead pressed against Benji's. "Please… please—come back—come back—"

The monitors didn't care. The doctors didn't step in. They knew when a battle was already lost.

Benji was gone.

Benji's body, weakened by leukemia and Nathan's neglect, had finally given out.

I turned, my chest tight with grief, but my focus shifted back to Alexis. She hadn't screamed or moved. She simply stood there, watching the aftermath of Nathan's madness, her face a mask of frozen horror. The FBI escort finally had to physically support her as she swayed slightly, like a statue crumbling from within.

Nathan had just reached his goal. He had destroyed the last piece of innocence Alexis felt responsible for, making sure that when she finally left the hospital, she would be running not just to find him but to end them both.

I grabbed her arm tightly, ignoring the FBI. "No more running," I whispered into her hair, my voice a desperate, silent promise. "We find him. We end this. But we do it together, and we blame him."

She leaned into me, not for comfort, but for the grounding support of my body—a necessary scaffolding for a woman whose world had just been shattered by Nathan's unrelenting madness.

37
Nathan - The Wolf

"**D**ammit all to hell!"

We were back at the farm, and I had been pounding on the van for the last fifteen minutes, to the point that it looked like it had been sideswiped. My knuckles were split, throbbing with a dull, persistent ache, but the rage—that perfect, burning fire of betrayal and frustration—refused to fade.

I could have taken it out on Kaitlyn, who was currently secured in the old barn's basement, but I needed her alive and knew that once I started, I would have killed her. The finale required her presence, intact and terrified.

If Alexis were here, I'd gladly end her.

There was fire in her, that was for sure, but it wasn't the same cleansing, righteous fire that burned inside me. It was weak, messy, and fueled by pathetic human sentiments. I saw something else in her green stare today—fear. I had instilled that in her, and knowing that was a comfort, but it didn't fix the failure.

I will need to teach her and show her that she can be like me.

The air around me smelled of earth as the sunrise threatened to peak. I pulled a joint from the glovebox and lit it. As I took a long, hard drag, calm spread through me. I hadn't had one in years, and now I wished I'd had more because it helped me contain the growing anger. There was no time to be erratic. I had to pull myself together and assess the damage.

My rage stemmed mainly from losing my stage. When I had to escape the warehouse, I couldn't recover half the carefully arranged mannequins. I had lost some of my key staging elements and my audience. The biggest operational loss wasn't Benji; his life was just a disposable tool used solely to break Alexis.

I walked toward the barn, descending the rickety steps into the cool, stone basement. The single dim lightbulb cast long, grotesque shadows over my remaining captives.

Becca was huddled in her cell, a completely useless, whimpering vessel.

Zane was pacing. He was only valuable because his sheer expendability was a statement. His parents never cared where he was, let alone whether he was alive. They treated his life as a minor inconvenience, so his disappearance carried no emotional weight, making him a useful, empty prop to fill space.

And then there was the defiant one.

I approached the cage holding Kaitlyn Martin. She was curled up but not crying. As she lifted her head and blinked at the light, I saw it: a small, irritating smile on her lips.

"Something amusing, little mouse?" I asked, my voice dangerously soft.

Kaitlyn sat up, hugging her knees to her chest. She met my gaze, and her smile grew into a look of pure, challenging conviction.

"I'm glad you had to run away," she said, her voice unexpectedly steady. "You had to escape from Alexis and the FBI. You didn't leave Benji to break her; she forced you to let him go. That means you didn't win."

I threw my head back and let out a burst of cold, mocking laughter that echoed off the stone walls. "You truly believe that pathetic spectacle meant I was defeated? I released him on my terms, a calculated sacrifice to maximize her despair!"

"No," Kaitlyn insisted, shaking her head. "You released him because she fought you. And I know she's not going to stop. I'm happy because Benji got away, and I know Alexis is fighting for me. She hasn't given up, and she's not afraid of you anymore. She's going to find me."

"You think that fire in her eyes was protective? That was the fear of failure! That was the terror that she is exactly like me! She'll collapse under the guilt. She always does!" I snarled.

"No," Kaitlyn whispered, radiating fierce certainty. "She's fighting for herself. And she's fighting for me. You can't break her."

I tore myself away from the bars, the cool metal doing nothing to ease the spike of frustration. Her defiance was a persistent burr, confirming that she had to be central to the grand finale.

My thoughts turned to logistics.

Mannequin Count: Reduced by half.

Time Off: I needed at least a couple of weeks off from killing to restock my collection and scout the perfect final venue. The messy, risky kills could wait.

But then there was her. The only one who truly understood.

I moved deeper into the basement, heading toward a locked, soundproofed door. My main captive wasn't confined in a cage; she was regarded with twisted, possessive reverence. She was my trophy, my ultimate project, my pet.

I unlocked the heavy steel door. Inside, she sat on the pristine white bed, her head bowed. She looked up, her expression completely vacant yet still focused on me. She was talking more now, ever since I started feeding her again—a slow process of rebuilding her physical health while her mind remained painfully fractured.

"Are you upset?" she asked, her voice soft, devoid of inflection.

"Ladybug disappointed me. The little mouse is defiant. I had to abandon the staging," I confessed.

"It doesn't matter," she whispered, slowly rising and walking toward me. "The stage is always you. The audience is always me. She will come to you when you finish breaking her. She is yours."

I reached out, brushing my thumb across her cheekbone. She leaned into the touch, a creature perfectly trained to offer comfort. She was my ideal, loyal pet, a testament to my ultimate, unwavering control.

I laughed, a deeper, more genuine sound this time. The blinding rage had faded, replaced by a sublime, cold confidence.

"You're right, my love," I murmured. "Ladybug will come. She will try to play the hero, and she will walk right into the final lesson."

I took out my phone. My immediate danger was gone.

"In two weeks," I said, a slow, satisfied smile spreading across my face, "we will finish the family reunion."

The cold, controlled feeling of power was absolute. I was finished reacting. Now, I would create the final, perfect ending.

38
The Captive

The Wolf.

He cared for me.
He wanted to take care of me.
I cared for him.
I wanted to take care of him.

39
Alexis

Benji.

I failed him. The weight of that failure clawed at my chest like rusted hooks, tearing deeper with every ragged breath. I couldn't save him. I was too late—watching his light flicker out in that sterile room, his small hand going limp in mine, as if the world had already decided to snuff him out.

Nathan. I didn't kill him. But oh God, the guilt was a venomous echo, a shadow that poisoned every corner of my soul. I failed.

Kaitlyn. I didn't save her. He took her—ripped her from my grasp like a thief in the night, her screams still echoing in my skull like shattering glass. He should've taken me. Let the darkness claim me instead, leave her laughter to fill the empty spaces I'd only widen with my uselessness.

The cool air clawed at my skin like icy talons as I stood on the hospital rooftop, a jagged precipice between the living and the lost. The wind howled through the night, a merciless thief sweeping away tears that burned like acid down my cheeks, relentless rivers carving canyons in my resolve. I gazed over Austin, its sprawl a grotesque stranger below—twisted veins of neon and shadow pulsing with indifferent life, utterly alien, as if the city itself had turned its back on me. If not for the garish lights clawing at the sky tonight, I might have glimpsed the stars, those distant, indifferent diamonds that once felt like fragile promises. I missed that part of Gold Beach—the way the stars blazed like scattered embers of forgotten gods, their cold fire dancing on the restless black mirror of the ocean, whispering secrets of escape. I wished that same ocean would rise now, a vengeful tide crashing over the edge, swallowing me whole in its salty, suffocating embrace—dragging me into lightless depths where the heartache could dissolve into endless nothing, where Benji's absence wouldn't echo like a scream in my veins. Instead, I was chained here, trapped beneath a bruised and bloated sky, a concrete labyrinth stripped of all mercy, all wonder—beauty long fled, taking Benji with it, leaving only this hollowed husk of a world that mocked my grief.

Nathan had snuffed out any fragile thread of Benji's survival, his cruelty a blade that severed hope with surgical precision. The thought ignited a fresh inferno in my gut, and I sobbed harder—gut-wrenching heaves that shattered the night. I crumpled to my knees on the rough gravel, each pebble a needle piercing the raw flesh of my despair. Visions assaulted me: Benji's frail body, once so full of defiant spark, now a battlefield of bruises and betrayal. Every gasp was torture I couldn't spare him, until his heart— that brave, battered engine—finally stuttered to silence. The heartache bloomed like a thorned fist in my chest, squeezing until I thought my ribs would splinter. I clenched my own hand over it, nails digging into skin as if I could claw the agony free, leave it bleeding on the rooftop like an offering to the uncaring gods.

Footsteps scraped behind me, gravel crunching underfoot, freezing me in place—a statue carved from ice and regret. "Ma'am, are you okay?"

I turned, my vision blurred through a veil of salt and sorrow, and looked up at the towering shadow of the man behind me. Agent White loomed like a monolith of unyielding authority, his gaze sweeping the horizon with predatory sharpness, as if threats lurked in the very stars I craved. He was clad in navy-blue jacket and pants that screamed officialdom, the oversized FBI decal glaring like a brand of failure—not subtle, not forgiving. After the reckless inferno

I'd unleashed today, the Bureau's leash had tightened into iron; they couldn't risk my unraveling alone, and I was damn lucky the cuffs hadn't clicked shut around my wrists yet. No autonomy left—I was a ghost escorted through my own nightmare. And beneath the surveillance, a grim chivalry: they figured I'd painted a bigger target on my back, enraging Nathan's viper heart, and they'd be damned if they let him strike again.

In my defense—if defense even existed in this shattered hour—if the FBI had clawed their way out of bureaucratic graves and done their goddamn job, this abyss wouldn't have swallowed us all.

"Don't you have better things to do than babysit me? Like maybe you should try looking for Nathan instead of just standing there watching me cry over something you could have possibly prevented," I was yelling now, surging to my feet, inches from Agent White's impassive face, my voice a fractured whip cracking through the wind. "Benji would be alive right now if you, the FBI, had done your damn job a few years ago!"

"Alexis?" Asher stood in the doorway at the stairs, a wreckage of a man—hair wild as storm-tossed waves, eyes red-rimmed chasms that mirrored my own devastation, as if he'd been weeping rivers of his own unspoken fractures.

Agent White's face remained a mask of granite, unyielding under the assault of my words, but I saw the flicker in his eyes—a microsecond crack, like fault lines spiderwebbing across stone before the avalanche. It only fueled the blaze raging in my veins, grief twisting into something sharper, a serrated blade I wanted to plunge into the heart of every lie they'd fed us. I stepped closer, my breath coming in hot, jagged bursts that fogged the chill air between us, close enough to smell the stale coffee and gun oil clinging to his jacket like accusations.

"You think this is just about today? About my little 'stunt'?" My voice dropped to a venomous hiss, each syllable laced with the rot of years unspoken, the failures they'd buried under red tape and classified files. "Three years ago, Nathan slipped through your fingers like smoke because you were too busy chasing shadows in some other case—some bullshit priority that wasn't a little boy fighting for his life. You had leads, White. Tips from informants, patterns in his kills that screamed his name, but you sat on them. You filed them away in some dusty drawer while he rebuilt his empire, piece by bloody piece. Benji was collateral then—a kid caught in the crossfire of your incompetence, pumped full of whatever poison Nathan cooked up in that lab you never raided. And you let it happen. You let him live long enough to come back and finish what he started."

The words tore out of me like shrapnel, each one embedding deeper into the wound that was Benji's absence—a hollow crater in my chest where his laughter used to echo, now filled only with the ceaseless howl of what-ifs. I could see it all again, unbidden: Benji's tiny frame in that first hospital bed, monitors beeping like accusatory heartbeats, his skin pale as moonlight on a grave, eyes wide with a terror no child should know. The FBI's "investigation" had been a farce—interviews that went nowhere, promises of protection that dissolved like mist at dawn. They'd patted me on the back, murmured sympathies, then vanished into their fortress of bureaucracy, leaving us exposed and vulnerable. Nathan had exploited every gap, every overlooked whisper, turning their negligence into his masterpiece of cruelty. And Benji... God, Benji had paid the price, his body a canvas of their sins, ravaged by drugs that burned him from the inside out until there was nothing left but ash and echoes.

Tears streamed unchecked now, hot brands against my frozen cheeks, but they weren't soft with sorrow—they were furious, scalding comets streaking through the night, carving paths of rage. My fists balled at my sides, knuckles whitening. I shoved against White's chest—not hard enough to topple him, but enough to feel the solid wall of his regret, or whatever facsimile he carried. "He was eight. You failed. Eight! A boy who collected fireflies in jars because he thought their light could chase away nightmares. But your night-mares? Yours are paperwork and press conferences, aren't they? And now? Now he's gone for good—his heart stopped because Nathan's blade went deeper, courtesy of the trail you never followed. Every bruise on his body, every scream I couldn't silence... that's on you. On all of you. If you'd hunted him like the monster he is instead of playing politics, Benji would be here. Laughing. Alive. Not... not this gaping void that swallows me whole every goddamn breath."

White's jaw tightened, a muscle twitching like a live wire, but he didn't retreat—didn't dare. His hands hovered at his sides, not in defense, but as if weighing the anchor of my fury against the chains of his oath. "Alexis," he started, voice low and gravelly, threaded with something that might have been an apology if it weren't so armored in protocol. "We—"

"No!" The word exploded from me, a thunderclap that rattled the silence, sending a fresh gust of wind whipping my hair like Medusa's serpents. "Don't you dare 'we' me. Don't you dare stand there in your starched suit, a decal of hypocrisy, and tell me about protocols or progress. Benji's progress was a flatline on a screen because of you. His future? Erased by the ink you spilled on reports instead of blood on the streets. I trusted you—God help me, I did. Handed over every scrap, every nightmare I clawed from my memory, and you turned it into nothing. So yes, babysit me if you must. Protect me from the monster you helped create. But know this: every shadow Nathan casts? It's yours too. And I'll be damned if I let you forget it."

The rooftop seemed to tilt then, with the city lights below blurring into a smeared watercolor of indifference. My knees threatened to buckle under the seismic weight of it all. Grief and anger warred in my throat, a choking storm leaving me gasping. The heartache was a vise crushing my ribs until I thought they'd shatter like Benji's fragile dreams.

"Alexis?" Asher's voice cut through again, softer this time, filled with a desperation that mirrored my own fractured edges. He stepped forward from the doorway, the stairwell's dim glow casting long shadows that danced like specters across his tear-streaked face. His hand extended as a lifeline in the storm.

Asher's voice hung in the air like a fragile thread, fraying at the edges of my unraveling world. I turned toward him, moving slowly and deliberately, as if the weight of my grief had thickened the night itself, making every shift a struggle against the pull of falling apart. His eyes—those storm-gray, not the blue I was used to, depths I once drowned in willingly—now held the same shattered mosaic of loss, reflecting back the pieces of me I had scattered across hospital floors and bloodstained crime scenes. He reached for me, fingers trembling like leaves in a gale, but I flinched, my raw anger still sparking and unquenched.

"Alexis, please," he whispered, his voice cracking like thin ice underfoot, each word a plea wrapped in the husk of his exhaustion. Disheveled didn't cover it—his shirt untucked and stained with what might have been coffee or tears, his jaw shadowed with stubble that spoke of sleepless vigils at Benji's bedside. "You don't have to do this alone. Not with him. Not with any of it."

But I did. The isolation was a shroud I'd woven thread by thread from failure and fury, and unraveling it now felt like betrayal—to Benji, to Kaitlyn, to the ghost of Nathan's laughter that still slithered through my nightmares. Agent White shifted beside me, a silent sentinel whose presence grated like sand in a wound. His earlier silence was now a dam holding back whatever bureaucratic flood he might unleash. The rooftop air thickened with unspoken accusations, the wind dying to a murmur as if the city itself held its breath, waiting for the next fracture.

I wanted to scream at Asher too—tell him how his gentle hands couldn't close the canyon Nathan had carved through our lives, how his love was a lantern in a hurricane, flickering but ineffective against the encroaching darkness. Instead, the words stuck in my throat, choked by the relentless tide of sobs that threatened to pull me under. My hand—still clenched over the phantom ache in my chest—slipped into my pocket, fumbling for the phone that had become both lifeline and noose. I needed... something. A distraction. A sign. Anything to hold me together before I shattered completely.

The screen lit unexpectedly, a cold glow slicing through the shadows like a scalpel. A notification flickered there, seemingly harmless at first: a message from an unknown number. My breath caught sharply, a gasp tinged with rust and regret, as I opened it with my thumb. The words appeared on the display, stark and venomous against the blue-black void.

Ladybug, tick-tock.

The world shrank to that single line, the rooftop fading into insignificance, the wind's whisper turning into a roar in my ears. Ladybug—a callback to the girl he'd shaped and broken before letting her chase his shadow. Tick-tock. The countdown, the tease, the promise of certainty. Nathan. It was him—sliding through the cracks in the FBI's proud security like the serpent he was, his fingers ghosting over my life from some hidden lair, watching, waiting, relishing the fresh wounds he'd caused.

The phone slipped from my numb fingers, clattering against the gravel like a gunshot in the silence. My knees buckled, and the rooftop rushed up to meet me in a blur of cold stone and colder certainty. Nathan wasn't finished. He never would be. And in that moment, as Asher's arms finally wrapped around me—warm, desperate, a harbor in the chaos—the heartache didn't fade. It intensified, like a blade sharpened on the whetstone of his words, promising that the clock's hands were moving toward Kaitlyn next. Toward me. Toward whatever twisted end he had written in the margins of our destruction.

There was one thing that lingered in my mind that I hadn't told the FBI. I knew I was being a hypocrite, but what would it matter if I told them? It's not like they would do anything about it.

Who was that woman I saw clinging to Nathan in the warehouse as they escaped with Kaitlyn?

40
Nathan - The Wolf

Their failure wasn't merely a mistake—it was confirmation. Proof that the world's self-appointed protectors were as brittle as the porcelain dolls in my mother's curio cabinet. Those wide-eyed cherubs and lace-swaddled debutantes she hoarded like charms against her slipping sanity—each one a substitute for the daughter she never carried, each one staring at her with painted forgiveness she didn't deserve. I destroyed them in a single, incandescent night. Six years old. Hammer in hand. Heels grinding porcelain into powder. Shelves splintering. Faces shattering. It was hours after she swung from the attic rafters—forced there by Nicole and my father, their whispers tightening like invisible wire around her throat until she did the final knotting herself. I remember the slow creak of rope. The pendulum sway in the pale dawn. The way her feet turned gently, as if searching for ground that wasn't coming.

The porcelain shards crunched beneath my shoes like applause.

That was the first time I understood creation required ruin.

Energized? Darling, I was incandescent. A live current under skin. Every nerve a filament ready to burn. That month away from the noise—the blood, the chase—was not exile. It was incubation. I planned. I scavenged estate sales, abandoned theaters, bankrupt prop houses. Twenty mannequins now. Twenty flawless witnesses to replace the nine Alexis and her Bureau lapdogs cost me in that tiresome warehouse skirmish. These weren't placeholders. These were chosen—balanced, symmetrical, eerily serene. Silent partners in the next movement.

And my Shadow—my exquisite familiar—proved indispensable. She carried thread bundles in her delicate jaws up Seaholm's spiral stairs, soft-footed as guilt. Nudged spools into alignment with quiet precision. Her purr vibrated through the iron skeleton of the plant like a blessing. She perched now on a rusted girder, tail swaying in measured rhythm, watching me the way a priestess watches sacrifice.

I whistled softly.

Pop. Goes the weasel.

The melody curled upward through iron beams and broken skylights, threading itself into the bones of the structure. Seaholm became cathedral. Stage. Confessional.

Becca stirred in the mechanism chamber's corner. Duct tape sealed her mouth—a mercy, truly. The belladonna cocktail, softened with a whisper of fentanyl, held her in a drifting limbo between lucidity and oblivion. Her yoga-toned elegance reduced to slack limbs and tremoring fingers. The faint moonlight filtering through shattered windows rendered her almost holy—flushed, glassy-eyed, suspended.

I arranged the scene with deliberate reverence.

The mannequins formed a semicircle around the scarred brass console—fifteen figures clad in the costumes of fallen professions. Nurse. Banker. Schoolmarm. Spectators in a frozen tribunal. Rusted machinery loomed above like an iron leviathan poised to swallow sound.

I adjusted two for emphasis.

A toddler-sized one, echoing Benji's fragile silhouette.

A taller one, Trevor incarnate—hands clasped in plastic prayer.

Both balanced at the catwalk's edge. Thirty feet down waited only steel and silence.

Shadow brushed past their stiff skirts, her fur whispering against polyester as I tilted a mannequin's chin a fraction higher. My whistle rose playfully, almost tender.

The console served as altar.

The monkey's paw—severed, preserved in formaldehyde from my previous errand—floated in its jar at center stage. Its curled fingers twitched faintly with each tremor of the plant's dying systems. Crimson thread spilled outward from it like veins, forming nooses around Becca's wrists and ankles, binding her to the antique chair I'd hauled upward stair by stair.

The rusted pipe rested against her thigh, heavy and patient.

The weasel?

Becca herself.

Her blonde hair braided into a cruel crown. A brass pocket watch nestled against her collarbone, ticking softly—too soft, almost intimate.

I would pop her soon. One precise thrust. Gravity would complete the rest. Her body would tumble through the mechanical gut of Seaholm like an offering, the impact below ringing upward in a final metallic hymn.

But not yet.

Rhyme required pacing.

All around the mulberry bush...

I knelt before her, peeling tape just enough to free sound but not escape.

"Becca," I whispered, breath brushing her ear. "Sweet weasel. The monkey waits. Do you hear the gears turning? The sparks warming in the dark?"

Her lashes fluttered weakly. "Wh... sparks? No... jog... tick... hurts..."

Her pupils drifted, unmoored. The pocket watch glinted. A mannequin arm swayed slightly in a cross-breeze. Shadow's tail flicked once.

Her mind was unraveling in slow spirals.

Exquisite.

I hummed gently, tracing the watch chain along her skin. Her pulse fluttered erratically beneath my touch.

"You thought factory floors were safe," I murmured. "Sing it with me—That's the way the money goes..."

"Mon... no... please..."

Shadow leapt down beside her, nuzzling Becca's ankle with detached curiosity.

"Kit... ty... help?"

"Oh, she helps," I said warmly, scooping Shadow into my arms. "She carried the threads. The nooses. Every step." I replaced the tape slowly. Deliberately. Sealing her murmurs into muffled despair.

Shadow resumed her patrol among the audience.

They watched.

Silent jurors.

The monkey thought 'twas all in fun...

Her eyes darted wildly toward shadows that held no mercy. Seaholm's cavernous interior stretched below us—lights flickering faintly like dying stars.

Fun?

This was communion.

But art requires connection.

Midway through the third verse, I paused.

My phone vibrated against my ribs.

Alexis.

Even from here I felt her fracture. That rooftop unraveling—Agent White's dismissal. The Bureau's condescension. "The Trips." Three hikers left with slit throats and wheels of cheese at their feet. A rhyme embedded so carefully in autopsy notes they dismissed it as coincidence.

Blind mice.

They always blink at the wrong moment.

I thumbed the burner to life.

The glow carved my face into something infernal.

Ladybug, ladybug, fly away home. The Trips were mine—wheels turning, sparks flying—while your shepherds slept. Trip-trap over the girders. Who's alone now?

Send.

The digital whoosh felt intimate.

I pictured her jolt awake. Breath shallow. Asher's arms useless against what hunts in silence. Paranoia blooming like nightshade in her bloodstream. Every creak a warning. Every shadow a silhouette.

Alone.

Yes, my love.

As alone as Becca, bound above Seaholm's mechanical abyss.

The watch ticked in harmony with grinding gears.

I pocketed the phone.

The mannequins leaned closer—or perhaps the shadows only deepened.

Shadow froze, amber eyes fixed.

Becca's muffled keening rose higher. The chair shifted dangerously at the catwalk's edge.

All around the mulberry bush...

I sang louder now. The plant responded. Metal groaned. Steam hissed faintly through unseen veins.

The FBI dismissed me. Alexis doubted herself. The world slept.

The monkey chased the weasel...

The rusted pipe felt heavy in my palm. Cold. Certain.

My whistle rose into a sharp, jubilant trill that sliced through Seaholm's bones.

Pop.

It was time.

41

The Captive

The fog lifted from my mind. The world came into sharp focus. The Wolf's haze had kept me trapped—wrapped in a warmth I didn't question, a safety born of fear. I longed for his voice, his touch, the way his presence filled the empty spaces inside me. He had become an anchor I clung to like breath.

But something inside me clawed at the edges of that obedience—a flicker, an urge to break free, to scream silently.

A deep industrial hum resonated through the walls—low, metallic, vibrating like an ancient beast waking. Just power. A pulse of machinery somewhere deep inside, echoing through rusted metal and concrete. A lost heartbeat, not mine.

Memories surged through me, jagged and bright. For a moment, the fog cleared. Loyalty disappeared. An unfamiliar fire consumed my thoughts, strange, frightening, and wonderfully alive.

My fingers brushed something cold on the ground—a jagged piece of glass, sharp and biting into my skin. I welcomed the cut, for pain was real and meant I was alive.

I tore fabric from my dress and carved shapes into it—the ladybug's wings blending with the wolf's snarl, the colors bleeding together in a trembling declaration. Blood mingled with the threads, staining them with a vow I hadn't spoken aloud.

Not beautiful. But mine. A symbol of betrayal. A symbol of truth.

I draped it across the rusted windowsill where moonlight pooled through a cracked industrial pane—obvious, impossible to miss, bright against the grime.

A message. A plea. A rebellion I scarcely understood.

Wind, carry it to them—to the hunters below, to anyone who still remembers I existed.

For Zane, I would defy him. Even the devil himself.

Somewhere inside the plant, a turbine trembled. The hum grew louder, engulfing the moment. And just like that—the fog returned with the weight of betrayal.

42

Asher

It's been a month since Benji passed away, and we haven't heard from Nathan since then. Our hearts and minds are still heavy with grief. Mom and Dad moved into our house to help as much as they could, cooking meals, assisting us with our studies, and even considering making Austin their second home. They have a way of making us feel like kids again. However, things are still tense between us boys and our dad because of the news of his infidelity.

We were filled with uncertainty about Becca, Zane, and Kaitlyn's well-being, and I was worried about Alexis, too. She seemed almost lost in a haze, caught in a cycle that left little room for joy: get dressed, eat very little, attend class, visit the library, return home, eat a bit more, and then sleep. I could hear her struggling with her eating habits, and it broke my heart. The FBI agents, like Tanner and Cooper, stood by as silent observers.

Today, we decided to keep our spirits up and gather in the library to study together. Lila joined us and made a real effort to support Alexis in her studies, which I appreciated. It did seem a bit odd, though—we rarely caught her actually hitting the books! Tanner was diligently piecing together information about Lila, still hunting for clarity. Despite the challenges, I felt a sense of purpose as I focused on supporting Alexis. Together, we would find a way through this, one day at a time!

We were mostly quiet, but we couldn't shake the feeling of being watched by the other college students, along with the carefully dressed statues looming over us. They kept looking at their phones and whispering, probably trying to figure out who we were.

"What the hell is their problem?" Cooper exclaimed a little too loudly, his voice bouncing off the bookshelves as he slammed his pen onto the table.

Lila was staring blankly at her phone, scrolling with a face that showed a mix of shock and something I couldn't quite identify.

Tanner seemed to notice, too. "Lila, what's going on? Are you alright?"

She paused her scrolling and looked at all of us, her gaze lingering a moment too long on Alexis. Alexis sat statue-still in her oversized hoodie, zipped all the way up to her chin, her leggings crossed under the table like a barrier against the world. Her dark hair fell forward, obscuring the hollows of her cheeks.

Alexis leaned over and checked her phone just as Lila pushed it to the middle of the table. The device skidded across the scarred wood with a rasp that cut the tension like a blade, the screen locked on a breaking news alert:

Rhyme Reaper Rises: *Becca Harper, 45, Slain at Seaholm Power Plant—Presumed-Dead Killer Stages Grisly 'Pop Goes the Weasel' Return, Victim Tied to Past Conspiracy.*

My stomach dropped, a cold plummet like jumping into Barton Springs on a winter dare, the chill seeping bone-deep. Becca—Alexis's brief stepmom, the woman who'd married Luke before his death in that tangled web of lies and had ended up conspiring with him and Nathan to shatter her world, feeding Alexis half-truths over tense family dinners while sharpening the knife behind her back. The article detailed the scene in stark, clinical bursts: mannequins—twenty of them—circling a bloodied tableau amid rusted gears that groaned like accusations, a toddler dummy propped like Benji's cruel echo, its plastic hands frozen in mock prayer, crimson threads binding Becca's body in a marionette's noose, her throat "popped" in a savage slash, a lead pipe clutched like a scepter. And the cloth—smeared with a crude carving of a ladybug morphing into wolf fangs, wings unfurling into snarls, a sigil that screamed Alexis, half-fragile endearment, half-feral threat, etched in what the forensics prelims called "arterial residue." Nathan, back from the grave, the Rhyme Reaper reborn in tabloid ink.

Alexis's breath caught, a raw hitch like tearing silk. Her face drained to the pallor of the library's marble floors as her fingers clamped onto the table's edge, knuckles blanching white, eyes locked on the screen as if it were a portal to hell. "Becca," she whispered, the name a venomous exhale laced with old betrayal—that woman who'd worn a maternal mask while plotting with Luke and Nathan to hand Alexis over as a sacrifice, only for the reaper to discard her now as yesterday's verse.

Whispers erupted around us like ripples on the creek outside, students' heads swiveling, phones tilting for surreptitious shots, the air thickening with that voyeuristic buzz that turned tragedy into campus currency. Cooper swore under his breath, shoving his chair back with a scrape that rattled the stacks; Tanner's jaw tightened, his eyes flicking to Lila with a sharpness that cut through the chaos—Did you know?—because she'd gone still, too still, her hand hovering near the phone as if debating whether to snatch it back. The agents stirred at last, their statuesque poise cracking as radios crackled with clipped evacuation orders—"Perimeter breach, extract now"—hands dropping to holsters concealed under polos, the library's hush shattering into a flurry of footsteps and urgent murmurs.

I reached for Alexis, my palm covering her trembling fist, the warmth of her skin a lifeline amid the storm. She jerked away, eyes wild with a fury I'd only glimpsed in the warehouse's red glow—fury at Nathan, at the feds who'd buried him alive in lies, at Becca for dragging her ghosts back from the grave.

"He's playing us," she rasped, voice low and lethal. "Using her corpse to twist the knife—ladybug to wolf, like I'm his evolution, his heir." The word hung, poisonous, stirring something in me I'd buried deep: Ronny Moore's blood in her veins, the Moore legacy of rhymes and ruin that Nathan wielded like a crown, and me? Just an outsider boyfriend. But in that moment, as sirens wailed closer, converging on the tower's fringe where prickly pear spines guarded the horror like barbed sentinels, resolve hardened in my chest—a vow, silent but steel: no more statues, no more waiting in the wings. I'd protect her, dig into the shadows myself, unravel Lila's secrets or Nathan's web, whatever it took to pull us from this limbo.

I squeezed her hand again, this time holding firm, whispering, "We're getting through this, Lex. Together!" I was shifting from helpless witness to reluctant warrior, the fear of losing her forging something sharper, something willing to bleed.

But as the agents herded us toward the exit, rain spitting fat drops on the quad's bricks outside, Tanner's phone buzzed—a private text from an unknown number. His screen was angled just enough for me to glimpse the words before he palmed it away: *I don't know how much longer I have, but I will fight to the end. Tell Alexis I'm sorry. I could have stopped him years ago. I will do what I can to put an end to all of this now. -Z.*

Zane. Alive? We all suspected he was helping Nathan only because Kaitlyn wanted money for Benji's treatments. Nathan had lied. There was no money. And was there no longer a need for Benji's treatments? A chill slithered down my spine, colder than the creek's murmur, as Lila shot me a glance too knowing, her vine tattoo twisting like a noose.

How was he able to contact us? Where was he?

The hook sank deeper, sirens blending with my pounding pulse. As we spilled into the downpour, Alexis's hand finally slipped into mine, and I wondered if the real wolf wasn't lurking in the pack after all.

43
Alexis

The rain transformed Austin into a watercolor blur, with colors blending so completely you couldn't tell the sky from the street. The live oaks along Congress sagged under it, as if tired of supporting the world. I'd always hated February here—too cool to feel like spring, too damp to pretend it was anything but limbo, with the air thick with the scent of wet creosote and distant barbecue smoke that twisted my stomach into knots.

It's been a month since Benji, and Nathan's silence had been a cruel joke, like a held breath before the gasp. Becca's death broke it open, spilling everything I had buried back into the light, raw and smelling of betrayal. My hope that this was just a really bad nightmare vanished.

I sat in the back of Agent White's unmarked SUV, feeling the leather seats stick to my thighs through my leggings. The windshield wipers slapped a relentless rhythm, trying to wipe away the city blur speeding past. White drove with a stoic grip, his knuckles pale on the wheel, his navy jacket creased at the elbows from long hours in it. The radio murmured softly about perimeter sweeps at the clock tower. Beside me, Asher's hand hovered near mine but didn't touch—wisely, because if he touched me, I might either shatter or lash out, and I wasn't sure which. The grief over Benji had dulled to a steady throb, like a bruise you forget until you bump it. It was slowly healing, the way a storm cloud thins before unleashing more rain: I could now eat a full slice of toast without the urge to vomit it immediately, and I could sleep four hours straight without hearing his cough echo in my dreams. But Becca? She was a fresh wound, tearing open the scar tissue of past losses I had carefully stitched, threads loosening until everything I knew unraveled in my lap.

Becca Harper. Stepmom for just a week—a fleeting moment in the rearview of my Gold Beach childhood, the kind of quick marriage that reeked of desperation and poor choices, like salt spray mixed with the regret of crashing waves.

Luke—my "dad," the detective who patrolled those foggy coastal streets in his worn trench coat, his badge shining under sodium lamps as he pursued smugglers and petty criminals through the dunes—had known her forever, or so it seemed. Becca was intertwined in his life long before she ever entered mine, a constant from his early days married to Nicole, my mother. She was the spirited woman with Ronny Moore's passion in her veins and a laugh capable of drowning out the ocean's roar. Luke and Becca had met in Gold Beach's close-knit community—him working extra hours on cases at the station bar where she served drinks, her with that elegant smile and tweed suits even then, discussing case files over black coffee while Nicole was off storm-chasing with Ronny—an affair that would deeply wound Luke like a hooked salmon.

I embodied Nicole's chaos—dark curls, a sharp jawline, and eyes reflecting my mom's restless hunger. Becca viewed me as an anchor, dragging Luke into pain and causing him to wake from nightmares filled with Nicole's laughter and seagulls' cries, all while chasing ghosts with detective instincts. She collaborated with Luke, hollowed out by betrayal and work that left him smelling of gun oil and rain-streaked streets, and with Nathan—Ronny's golden boy—whose path crossed Becca's through Luke's cases and whispered conversations in the stationhouse where the 'disappearances' of the Moore family were recorded in yellowed files. Their plan wasn't to kill me with Luke's gun but to quietly remove me, since Luke's oath-bound nature saw violence as messy. Luke, distant, nodded—carrying the legacy of Ronny and monsters' blood. Becca kept her hands clean by pushing papers for Luke's undercover operations, covering late nights with Nathan at diners, and replacing my routines with promises of erasure. She smiled, asked about my nights and friends, while her love for Luke blinded her to seeing me as an enemy to be eliminated.

The grief settled like ash on the pile I was sorting—Benji's gone, his tiny body a battleground I couldn't save. Still, that wound was scabbing over, its edges less jagged. I started dreaming again of him laughing and chasing fireflies in Gold Beach meadows, his chubby fists glowing like lanterns at dusk. I would wake crying, but not with the gut-wrenching sobs that once left me curled on the bathroom floor, purging food and survivor's guilt. It was getting better, slowly: Cooper's sketches on the fridge, wildflowers drawn in pencil that I traced in the late-night kitchen, made me linger on their petals. The fridge's hum became white noise, drowning out the ocean's echo in my mind and reminding me of the girl who once believed in simple pleasures like salt-kissed skin and bonfire sparks on the beach.

Mom and Dad—Asher's parents, the steady harbor I had latched onto after Nicole's death—had moved in temporarily, their presence a gentle anchor amid the rental's creaky chaos. Mom's pot roast simmered on Sundays, with rosemary cutting through the stale air like a promise of continuity. Dad's awkward apologies over board games, where he'd let me win at Scrabble, spelled out "resilient" with tiles that clicked like puzzle pieces fitting back into a fractured whole.

Becca's death? It revealed everything—bringing to light timeless memories of loss that shaped me. This includes Benji losing his innocence in that sterile room, Kaitlyn's screams from the darkness where the feds held her, and Zane's silence, lingering like a question mark in the cursed Moore bloodline I carry. It also exposes the betrayals—Luke's so-called "lessons," disguised as tough love from a detective, using his badge to control; Nicole's death, a void like the creaking of a rocking chair on wind-swept decks; and Becca, the temporary stepmother whose brief reign was a poisoned dart, her conspiracy a short yet intense chapter in feeling unwanted. Each memory is a stone in the avalanche, pulling me deeper, the weight pressing down so hard I wonder if I can ever escape—my lungs burning with sand from the Gold Beach dunes where I once ran barefoot and free, before the rhymes began.

My mind felt like a shattered mirror, reflecting different selves: the daughter Nicole discarded, the stepchild Becca tried to erase in seven days of pretended warmth, the sister Benji needed but couldn't save from Nathan's blade, and the woman Asher loved but I couldn't fully love back, my touches hesitant as if affection were a trap. Therapy with Genevieve—held in a sterile, windowless room at the Bureau, smelling of cleaner and stale pretzels—probed my pain like a sore tooth: "The loss keeps building, Alexis. It's a cycle of abandonment, repeating from Nicole to Becca to Benji. Name the pattern to break it." Name it? It was a hydra, with heads multiplying as sirens wailed through Austin's rain-slick streets and shadows pooled beneath streetlamps like ink from Nathan's pen.

Becca's end wasn't about justice; it was a cruel tease, with Nathan using her body as a grim prop to mock the family I never had. The blood ties that bound me to him—the Moore madness, Ronny's reckless fire, Luke's badge-blinded rage—deepened my spiral, making my skin crawl with inherited venom. Benji's grief softened just enough to carve a new hollow, a void where maternal illusions shattered, forcing me to wonder if I am the villain of my own story, the ladybug destined to grow fangs.

The SUV stopped outside the morgue, a low brick building on the city's edge where the Hill Country gives way to strip malls and chain-link fences rattling in the wind, rain streaking the windows like tears we can't afford to cry. White turned off the engine, shifting his bulk as he looked back, his eyes like chipped flint under his cap brim, the dash lights casting sharp shadows on his jacket's decals. "Are you sure about this, Alexis? It's not pretty. Protocol says only family, and even then—"

"Protocol let him slip the noose," I said, my tone flat like the rain-slick pavement outside. My trembling hands unbuckled in the storm of my emotions, fingers cold on the metal clasp. "Becca wasn't family. She symbolized lies. But I need to see her truth—the ending Nathan wrote. Confirm this is real, not some ghost the newspapers spun." Asher's fingers brushed my arm, a tentative question in his touch, warm but careful. I shook it off—not out of anger at him, never that—but because I was fragile, like glass about to break as I faced the uncertain path ahead.

Tanner had reported the text from Zane an hour ago, spilling it to White during the library's frantic evacuation, his phone thrust forward like evidence in one of Luke's old case files.

Zane.

Kaitlyn's boyfriend, the one who was more lost than I was, with drug-addicted parents who couldn't care less if he was dead or alive. The one tangled in sins, the kid who'd played reluctant pawn, feeding Nathan scraps for promises of cash that evaporated like fog off the beach, all to fund Benji's treatments that Nathan had poisoned from the start.

White nodded grimly and recorded it on his tablet with a stylus that clicked like a detective's pen on a notepad, muttering about tracing the burner and pinging towers near the clock tower's shadow. "Could be bait," he said, but his eyes hinted at possibility—an opening in the federal fortress Luke had once navigated as a badge.

Tanner met my gaze, his Longhorns cap damp from the dash to the SUV, jaw clenched as if he were biting into one of Luke's unsolved clues: "He's reaching out, Lex. It indicates a fissure. Like your old man used to say—follow the loose thread." A fissure—that's what I held onto as White led us inside, where the morgue's fluorescent lights greeted us like an old informant. The air was cold and chemical, with the sting of bleach and formaldehyde in my nostrils, as pneumatic doors hissed shut behind us, sealing out the rain's pitter-patter like a withheld confession.

The pathologist was waiting—a woman in storm-cloud-colored scrubs, her gray-streaked ponytail pulled tightly. A mask hung from one ear, and her gloved hands examined a clipboard under harsh lights like those in Gold Beach's stationhouse. "Harper, Rebecca," she called, her voice muffled and echoing. She gestured to the steel slab beneath a sheet that moved with unnatural stillness—no, flat and deceptive. The fabric's drape concealed the horror, and the zipper's teeth gleamed like Luke's badge before it weighed him down.

White cleared his throat, saying, "Limited access, Doc. Visual only. No photos or notes. She's connected." The pathologist nodded, glancing at me with clinical pity Luke disliked in witness statements. Her gloved hands peeled back the sheet, the zipper's rasp echoing like a chalk line at a crime scene. There she was: Becca, mid-40s, but death had stripped her to essentials, a waxen figure in Nathan's tableau of twisted nursery verses. Her skin was the pallor of oyster shells bleached on Gold Beach after a high tide, mottled blue-gray where the blood had settled in the low points, her chestnut hair—once coiled in that professorial bun that hid her calculations—matted and clumped with dried crimson, fanning out on the slab like kelp tangled around a washed-up buoy.

The throat slash dominated, a ragged crescent from ear to ear, the "pop" he'd staged gaping like a second mouth frozen in a silent indictment, edges curled and feathered where the pipe had snagged cartilage and windpipe, flecks of rust embedded like shrapnel from one of Luke's old raid souvenirs, the wound's lips parted in a perpetual gasp that mocked the measured trills of her laughter over those seven days of feigned family.

Crimson threads—silk, scavenged from some weaver's loom in Nathan's fevered mind—still looped her wrists and ankles, loose now in death's slack surrender, the nooses frayed where she'd thrashed in her belladonna delirium, furrows carved into her palms where nails had bitten flesh in futile bids for freedom, the adjunct's manicure chipped to nubs like the edges of case files Luke had pored over in vain. The pipe lay beside her on a stainless tray, lead rusted to the patina of old blood and coastal brine, its mouth crusted with the evidence of her final gurgle, a popped cork spewing silence, the handle wrapped in the same thread that bound her, a bow on the gift Nathan had left for me.

Mannequins hadn't been brought down, but photos pinned nearby showed them in sharp flash: twenty plastic figures in thrift-store clothes—one a nurse in stained whites, another a banker in pinstripes holding an empty briefcase—surrounding the gears where her antique chair had teetered at the catwalk's edge. The toddler mannequin, closest, had glassy eyes fixed in Benji's last gaze from the hospital bed, tiny hands clasped as if in prayer or applause for the finale Nathan had carefully crafted. The cloth, now in an evidence bag under the slab's light, had blood flaking like rust from a detective's badge left too long in salt air. The carving was crude but fierce: ladybug wings merging into wolf jaws, fangs snarling in a face that reflected my own in the steel door's polish. Arterial smears blurred the fragile shell with the beast beneath, forming a transformation that screamed me—the daughter Ronny's heir, the one Becca had tried to drown in whispers and wrong turns.

I leaned in closer, the cold air fogging my breath and raising goosebumps on my arms. The scent hit me—copper and decay, with a faint floral rot from her patchouli perfume tangled in the fibers of her blazer, still buttoned over a blouse stiff with her life's residues. The tweed's weave caught bits of dried foam from her drugged lips. Her eyes, half-lidded and dulled to jade, seemed to stare past nothing. Yet in my mind, they snapped open, accusatory—reminding me of the case files Luke had slammed onto the kitchen table: "You survived the week. I didn't for decades." Betrayal seethed within me—familiar and hot—the woman who once hugged me after my mother's death, her arms stiff yet warm, all while plotting with Nathan and Luke. Her love for Luke was a blindfold, blinding her to seeing me as the enemy she wanted to cut out—the Nicole she had held a grudge against ever since pouring his first post-betrayal whiskey.

"You wanted me gone," I whispered, my voice trembling like the gears in that tower or the static on Luke's old dispatch radio. "For him. For the clean slate you thought I'd already stolen." But I was the slate—cracked, yet still here. And Nathan? He's the chalk that won't wipe off. The pathologist shifted uncomfortably, rustling her scrubs, while White simply watched. His bulk formed a silent barrier at the door, arms crossed over his decal, a badge of his own failures.

Asher's hand settled on my shoulder, steady and firm as an oak tree. His thumb traced a small circle, grounding me. I didn't pull away—couldn't—because waves of grief, salty and regretful, overwhelmed me: Benji's innocence lost to sterile beeps, Kaitlyn's trust broken in Nathan's hidden spaces, Zane's complicity linking us through Ronny's reckless seed, and Becca, the brief stepmom whose short reign was like a poisoned dart dipped in Luke's detective delusions. Her conspiracy was a brutal pause in the saga of being the unwanted remnant. The ongoing loss wasn't a straight line or a ladder out of the dunes; it was a riptide pulling me under with every swell. Benji's grief softened, making space for this new emptiness—an abyss where maternal illusions shattered in a week, leaving me to wonder if I was the villain in my own story, a ladybug doomed to grow fangs from Ronny's blood, Luke's lies, and Becca's brief but bitter strike.

White's radio crackled, pulling me back from the edge of the slab—urgent and clipped, like a detective's wiretap: "Tower follow-up. Partial print on the cloth. It matches the Moore family heirloom ring—Ronny's old signet. And the kid—Zane—traced to a payphone cluster in East Austin. He's moving, but nearby. Possible intercept at the farm site."

Zane. The message Tanner sent, his vow to fight, to end it—a lifeline or a lure from the Moore maze Luke had mapped but never escaped? I straightened, the morgue's cold seeping to my core like the coastal fog that had shrouded Becca's schemes. Her face blurred as the sheet whispered back over her, with a finality that echoed Luke's closed case files.

"Take me there," I commanded, my voice steady as the riptide receded enough for me to swim. The spiral tightened but didn't break me—yet—thanks to Asher's firm grip on my elbow and his warm breath against the cold. "If Zane's breaking the wall, we should go through it. Finish this before Nathan causes us all to fall into graves." White hesitated, jaw working as if chewing on protocol, but Asher nodded, his eyes fierce with a new determination I'd seen in the library—him turning from outsider to warrior confronting my ghosts.

We filed out into the rain, tires hissing on the wet asphalt as the SUV peeled away from the morgue's shadow, city lights fracturing like my reflection in the puddles pooling in the strip mall parking lot. But as my phone buzzed in my pocket—unknown number—a single image loaded slowly through the storm: Kaitlyn, bound in wildflowers twisted like Becca's threads, her eyes pleading through the screen, captioned Your heir's verse awaits. Midnight at Mount Bonnell. Come alone, or the wolf devours the last loose end—Zane. The hook yanked taut. Rain pounded the windows. Nathan understood Zane's reach. It was the bait in a trap snapping shut.

44
Alexis

The wind clawed at Mount Bonnell like a living creature, whipping through the cedars and live oaks that clung to the cliffs, their branches twisting into skeletal fingers against the bruised November sky. Austin sprawled below us, a glittering wound of neon and shadow, oblivious to the horror etched into its highest point—the 775-foot overlook where lovers carved hearts into railings and suicides whispered final goodbyes to the Colorado River's serpentine gleam far below.

Becca's body was still warm, her blood sticky in the gears of the clock tower less than twelve hours after her death. News feeds buzzed with the Rhyme Reaper's resurrection, like vultures circling fresh carrion. Meanwhile, Nathan was already composing his next verse, as busy as a spider in the month since Benji's flatline. He was weaving unseen webs across the city's veins—whispers of vanished joggers in Zilker's scrub, mannequins glimpsed in East Side alleys under sodium light, and rhymes etched in fogged-up car windows that vanished by dawn. He had been like a ghost in overdrive, his silence hiding a frenzied mind.

Now, I had texts burning in my pocket: *"Rock-a-bye baby, in the treetop. When the wind blows, the cradle will rock."* Another read, *"Your heirs wait, ladybug. Come sing them to sleep or watch them fall. Mount Bonnell, midnight. Alone."* Nathan's words, sharp as venom, slithered through the FBI's firewalls like he'd hacked my soul. White had mobilized the raid team—SWAT vans screeched up the winding road, tactical lights cutting through the fog like accusations.

Asher, Tanner, and Cooper had insisted on coming, their faces set in grim masks as they geared up beside me in the trailhead shadows, White's protests drowned by their fury. "He's not getting away this time," Asher had growled, his knuckles white on his borrowed vest, Tanner's jaw clenched like he was already swinging, Cooper's usual quips silenced into a cold, calculating stare. But I'd slipped ahead alone, heart pounding with a song as I hiked the shadowed path, the damp earth pulling at my boots, each step a betrayal of the fragile peace I'd fought to carve from Benji's grave. My grief for him was now a scar—tender but closing—his laughter flickering in dreams, without the gut-wrenching wake of his absence. But Kaitlyn and Zane? They were fresh salt in the wound, the final threads of people I knew in Gold Beach, people who had betrayed me.

Nathan dangled them like a noose, and I couldn't wait for White's perimeter to tighten. Not when I heard faint, rhythmic creaks from the overlook—like a cradle rocking in a gale. Distant sirens wailed at first, their mournful cry swallowed by gusts, but grew louder as the FBI topped the hill, floodlights blazing like sinister stars across the plateau. I reached the final switchback, my breath ragged, the cold seeping through my hoodie like icy fingers along my ribs, and saw it: the scene Nathan had set—a cradle hanging from the gnarled branches of an ancient live oak over the cliff's edge, its ropes frayed and knotted with crimson threads fluttering like bloody ribbons in the wind. The grotesque structure was a makeshift bassinet made from weathered wood and rusted rebar, scavenged from who knows where, swinging thirty feet above jagged rocks that loomed below like bared teeth. Mannequins encircled the tree's base and perched on ledges—twenty silent, thrift-store castoffs with plastic faces tilted upward in eternal judgment: a midwife clutching a burlap swaddling cloth, a father in pinstripes frozen mid-prayer, a nursemaid with askew spectacles and a locket dangling like a noose. One, a child-sized night-mare, hung from a lower branch, its tiny limbs akimbo as if fallen already, glassy eyes reflecting the flashing lights like broken stars. They watched silently as the raid team spread out—White's shouted command piercing the night, "Hale! Federal agents! Stand down!"—their rifles sweeping shadows, boots crunching gravel that scattered over the edge. Asher, Tanner, and Cooper flanked the line, their borrowed vests too big on their frames, eyes locked on the tree like wolves scenting blood, fists clenched with the kind of rage that begged for bare knuckles on bone.

He slipped from the shadows not by stepping out, but by unwinding—like a wolf emerging into the moonlight, lean and shimmering, muscles taut with intent. His yellow eyes flickered with a feral glow that hinted at teeth and throat, flashing in the floodlights. Nathan's coat hung open like a hunt's pelt, soaked in rain and dark stains. His face was partly hidden by messy, wet hair, but his eyes—oh, those eyes—were fixed on me across the plateau. A twisted grin revealed white teeth, and a low growl blended with the wind. Shadow curled at his feet, the form of a cat creeping low, tail flicking like a switch, as if summoning its familiar for a feast. Rage ignited within me, burning away the numbness left by Benji's death; it was hotter than the warehouse fire meant to end him. My half-brother—the monster born from the same poisoned womb, Ronny's twisted gift of blood tying us beyond any badge or book.

How dare he stand there, grinning like we are playthings, Kaitlyn and Zane on his strings, and Becca's body cold in the morgue, her lie-filled week the prelude to this slaughter? I was the ladybug he'd branded, the fragile shell he cracked open to let the wolf inside me howl, and fury flooded over me, trembling hands with the urge to claw his eyes, to make him feel the pain I endured since Gold Beach's salty lies.

"You bastard!" I shouted, words breaking free as I surged forward, gravel biting my palms when I stumbled.

Asher's shout—"Lex, no!"—tangled with Tanner's curse and Cooper's frantic grab, the three of them trying to hold me back, faces twisted in helpless rage.

Tanner snarled, "Let me at him, I'll rip that grin off!"

Cooper muttered, "One shot, that's all I need."

Asher's grip was firm on my arm, eyes promising murder if Nathan so much as twitched. They wanted to beat him bloody, to strip the wolf from him until only the grief-shattered boy remained, but White's team held firm, rifles trained, while Nathan tilted his head and whistled the lullaby's opening bars, his melody drifting through the storm like smoke from a wolf's breath on cold air.

Kaitlyn and Zane were in the cradle, tied back-to-back—her hair soaked in sweat and blood, Zane gaunt with wrists raw from twisting. She looked ghostly, her pale face like moonlight on tide pools, with shallow breaths muffled by a silk gag. Zane had bruises, one eye swollen shut, but his other gleamed with defiance—our Moore fire, Ronny's cursed blood we all share.

"Nathan!" White called out again, his team moving closer in heavy rain, but Nathan tilted his head and whistled the lullaby's opening, the melody floating through the storm like smoke from a wolf's breath. The wind howled like a banshee, rocking the cradle with fierce force, the ropes creaking under the strain.

Nathan's whistle grew into song—his voice velvet and raspy, like a lover's whisper, but edged with a lupine snarl that made my neck hairs stand. "Rock-a-bye baby, on the treetop," he crooned, quietly approaching the trunk, one hand tracing the bark as if scenting prey, the other drawing a slender blade, its edge glinting like fractured moonlight on fangs. "When the wind blows, the cradle will rock."

Zane lunged first, twisting to shield Kaitlyn, shoulder colliding with her as the ropes cut deeper into his skin, snarling through his gag, "Let her go, you bastard—take me!"

Nathan laughed low and guttural, a sound blooming in my chest like thorns uncurling. With a flick of his wrist, he slashed the cradle's far rope, loosening it but not entirely severing it, enough for it to swing wildly, dipping toward the abyss in a pendulum of doom. The mannequins leaned in, their vacant stares expectant, the nursemaid's locket swinging, the child's form swaying mockingly—like a gallery gathered for the alpha's kill.

I broke from the trees, boots pounding gravel as White's shout—"Alexis, stand down! Sniper cover!"—rang behind me. But my focus was on the swinging cradle, Kaitlyn's muffled scream vibrating through the wind, her body pressing against Zane's in futile resistance. Gunfire erupted—FBI rounds hitting the oak, splinters flying like shrapnel from Benji's monitors—yet Nathan moved fluidly, as lean as his wolfish namesake, the blade flashing as he climbed a branch, perching like a gargoyle above the chaos.

"When the bough breaks," he sang, voice rising into the gale, the wind tearing at my hair like rusted hooks dragging me forward. "The cradle will fall."

Zane roared again, struggling with bound hands, clawing at the ropes around Kaitlyn's neck—Nathan had used them earlier, a garrote disguised as swaddling, tightening with each rocking motion. Blood seeped where they bit, crimson beads scattering like venomous rain, staining Zane's shirt as he twisted, muscles strained and screaming, enough to free one arm to grab a hidden shard—his own weapon carved from the cradle's splintered wood. He slashed at the garrote, the silk parting with a wet snap, but Nathan was faster, leaping down the rope ladder, stabbing Zane's shoulder with his knife in a spray of blood that defied gravity, like a comet. The wolf's jaws closed on the pack's weakest link.

The cradle jerked, its anchor rope fraying, Kaitlyn's gag torn away, her ragged sob—"Alexis!"—cutting deeper than Nathan's blade, her voice shard-like in my mind. Zane pushed her up the ladder, bloodied hand shoving her legs away from the edge, but the wind pushed hard, swinging the cradle sideways, the wood cracking against the oak with a thunderous snap that echoed Benji's flatline—splinters exploding outward like a shattered family.

Mannequins fell in sympathy: one midwife tumbling to shatter on rocks, porcelain limbs scattering like fallen fangs under floodlights, another pinstripe figure ripping apart as caught in the wind, briefcase spilling brittle "bones"—twisted chicken wire—clattering like dice in a wolf's den. Nathan now perched on the ladder, knife dripping Zane's blood, face alight with savage joy, veins bulging like rivers of fire, his growl merging into the lullaby's end. "And down will come baby, cradle and all," he finished—the words both blessing and curse—yanking the last anchor rope with a predator's deftness, sealing the trap.

The cradle tumbled down—not a free fall, but a controlled unraveling, the ropes whipping like serpents as the structure swung out over the void. Kaitlyn's scream tore free as she clawed at Zane's shirt, his arm locked around her waist in a vice grip, causing him to gush more blood from his shoulder wound—hot, sticky, and soaking them both in a baptism of brotherhood. They dangled there, suspended in the gale's grip, the cliff's face rushing up—jagged limestone scarred by erosion, mesquite roots snaking like veins thirsty for spill—before the cradle crashed into it mid-drop, wood splintering with a cacophony of cracks that drowned out the sirens. The impact jolted them like a snapped noose, with rebar twisting through the base like claws raking flesh. Zane held on, his body a shield as shards speared upward, one glancing Kaitlyn's thigh in a bloom of red that soaked her jeans like spilled wine, the flesh parting in a ragged tear that exposed bone-white gleam amid the gore, but he took the brunt— a twisted metal brace punching through his side with a wet crunch that sprayed viscera across the rocks, blood bubbling from his lips as he coughed it onto her hair, matting the curls in a crown of gore that dripped in thick rivulets, pooling dark and viscous on the limestone like offerings to the river god below.

"Run... Lex..." he rasped, eyes locking on mine through the chaos, the wind howling the rhyme's echo as if the oaks themselves mocked us with lupine laughter, his free hand fumbling in his pocket, pulling out the bloodied cloth—a ladybug-wolf carve, smeared but defiant.

Nathan dropped to the ledge, knife flashing in a final arc that severed the ladder's last hold, the cradle's remnants plummeting the final twenty feet in a tumble of rope and ruin, bodies entwined in a final, desperate knot that hit the rocks with a sound like thunder cracking bone—Kaitlyn's cry cut short in a gurgle of blood-frothed scream, her thigh wound erupting in a fresh geyser as the impact drove re-bar deeper, shredding muscle and tendon in a spray that painted the cliff red, rivulets snaking down like tears from a weeping wound, her body convulsing in shock's final spasm. Zane crumpled beneath her, his back arching as spines of limestone tore through flesh and fabric, ribs splintering like dry twigs under the wolf's paw, blood fountaining in arcs that arced graceful against the cliff, mingling with rain to form crimson waterfalls that fed the river's maw far be-low, his chest heaving one last, wet rattle before stilling, the Moore fire guttering out in a pool that spread like spilled ink across the stones. The mannequins watched impassively, the nursemaid's spectacles cracked in the fall from her perch, the child's form now dangling limp from its branch like a hanged marionette, its head lolling with a plastic click that echoed Zane's last breath.

White's team swarmed Nathan, tackling him in a frenzy of limbs and shouts—"Federal agent, down!"—cuffs snapping, his laughter bubbling through the scuffle, a velvet rasp that slithered into my ears: "Sleep tight, ladybug. The wind al-ways wins." But I staggered to the cliff's edge, knees buckling on the gravel biting my skin through my jeans, staring down at the wreckage—Kaitlyn stirring faintly, her leg a mangled ruin but chest rising in shallow hitches, Zane crumpled be-neath her, his eyes fluttering open one last time, blood bubbling from his mouth in a froth that caught the floodlights, the cloth clutched in his fist like a talisman turned shroud.

"Lex..." he wheezed, hand twitching toward the rope dangling from the cliff, fingers closing on the bloodied scrap—the cloth with a ladybug-wolf carve, smeared but intact, clutched like a talisman. FBI rappelers were already descending, harnesses whining in the wind, but Zane's gaze held mine, fierce through the pain, the Moore fire undimmed even as his life leaked onto the rocks in thick, pulsing waves that soaked the limestone black. "The... captive... she's alive... he has her locked up.... Tell her... sorry...." His words dissolved into a cough, red spraying the air like mist from the river below, and then his eyes glazed, his hand went limp, the cloth fluttered free to snag on a root, a beacon in the gore that gleamed wet under the strobes.

The image of the woman I saw in the warehouse flashed through my mind. She looked frail and was helping Nathan. She was his captive. We needed to find her.

White pulled me back as medevac choppers roared overhead, blades tearing through the wind in a fury, but the hook sank deep—the captive, hidden. Nathan's last victims were gone, but his screams? They echoed in Zane's dying breath, driving me to find this woman—before she died.

I watched as Nathan was loaded into an armored truck. The predator's sneer was gone. His eyes didn't dull from being finally captured; instead, they gleamed with amusement, and a wide, clown-like smile spread across his face. He knew his game wasn't over. He was holding his last captive somewhere, and his final card was still up his sleeve.

45
Nathan - The Wolf

The room reeked of old coffee, sweat, and something faintly metallic—the kind of smell that stayed under your fingernails. The lights above buzzed and stuttered, too bright for truth but too dim for confession. They wanted me to talk, but light had never made anyone honest.

Agent Fields sat opposite me, sleeves rolled up to his forearms, his shirt once white but now creased and ringed with a day's worth of strain. His tie hung loose, half undone, like even it had given up. His face was marked by years of unanswered questions, the kind that etch themselves in permanent ink. He seemed exhausted, and underneath that fatigue was fear — though he would never admit it. Fear wears so many disguises that it rarely recognizes itself.

He slid a stack of photos across the table. Becca at the clock tower. Kaitlyn and Zane on the rocks. The oak grove. And on, and on... every rhyme, every kill, all the way back to the beginning — the pumpkin shell. I glanced at them, then at him. "You've got your gallery," I said. "Frame it right, and you could almost call it art." I smiled and looked him square in the eyes.

He didn't bite. His voice stayed level, but his collar twitched with every breath. "You call that art? You left blood all up the west coast. Now here in Texas. You want to talk *art*, talk about what you did to them."

I smiled. "I didn't do anything, Agent. I just finished the verse."

His jaw worked. The fabric at his elbows was dark with sweat. "You're not a poet. You're a murderer, a psychopath."

"Same thing," I said, shrugging. "One bleeds words. The other, people. Both leave stains that don't come out."

The rookie in the corner swallowed hard. His suit was the cheap department-store kind—sleeves too long, cuffs unpressed, collar stiff and biting at his neck. He smelled of nerves and aftershave, the kind meant to cover weakness. His pen trembled over the page. I could hear it—the scratch of fear disguised as duty.

Fields leaned forward, the light catching the faint sheen on his temples. "You left someone alive. The woman. Another captive. Where is she?"

"She isn't missing," I said. "She's waiting. There's a difference."

His brow furrowed. "Waiting for what?"

"For the rest of the song," I said.

He rubbed a hand over his face, exhaling like a man trying to keep something inside. The motion pulled his shirt taut across his chest, showing the outline of the badge still clipped to his belt—a piece of authority too worn to shine. "You think this is clever? You're sitting in chains, Nathan. Your father's rotting in Two Rivers. Your sister—"

"Careful," I cut in. "You don't speak her name until you understand the rhyme."

That got him. A flicker in the eyes—the first real crack. "You want to talk about legacy?" he said finally. "Ronny Moore doesn't even remember you exist. He's counting ceiling cracks and pretending the world forgot him."

I let the words hang there, let them rot between us. Then I smiled. "Then bring him to me," I said.

Fields blinked. "Excuse me?"

"I said, *bring...me...my...father*." I leaned forward until the chain bit into my wrists. The orange jumpsuit creased sharply at the elbows, stiff and starched—like they thought fabric could restrain intent. "And bring me the girl. Both of them, together. That's the only way the verses close."

The rookie's pen stilled. "The girl?" he echoed.

"My sister," I said softly. "The one who still hums in her sleep. She doesn't know the words yet, but she will. She always does."

Fields's patience broke clean. His shirt clung to his back now; his voice cracked under its own weight. "You think this is a negotiation?" he snapped. "You give us what we want, or you disappear into a hole."

I laughed, and it startled him. Not loud—quiet, like something you'd hear from behind a wall. "You don't understand, Agent. I'm already in the hole. You're looking down into it."

He stood, scraping the chair back. The metal legs shrieked against the tile. His jacket slid from the chair behind him, collapsing into a heap — a dark, rumpled flag of surrender.

"I'm done talking."

"You are?" I asked. "Then listen instead. Bring me my father and my sister. One carries the curse, the other the cure. When we're all together, our family, the song ends."

He hesitated. Just a second. Long enough for me to see it—that flicker of belief he didn't want to feel.

They led me out a moment later. The lights hummed louder as the door closed behind me. I almost pitied them. They thought the verses belonged to me. They didn't.

They were already singing. The verses were running out.

46

Asher

Grief had settled into the station like dust—light, quiet, and impossible to brush away. It hid in the hum of the fluorescent lights, the faint scent of cleaning chemicals mixed with stale coffee, and the way our rain-damp jackets clung to our arms. Every chair squeaked when someone moved, and every cough echoed too loudly off the walls.

Kaitlyn's parents sat across from us, side-by-side but worlds apart. Mrs. Martin's hands clenched a tissue, crumpled and gray from endless tears. Mr. Martin's shoulders were stiff, jaw clenched, eyes staring into nothing, as if letting go of the tension would make him shatter. Our parents hovered near the room's corners, murmuring soft words of comfort we couldn't quite grasp, their shoes softly scraping the tile, coats damp and heavy, collars pulled up against the cold. They wore muted colors that seemed to try to disappear into the room—dark blues, grays, blacks—as if they could fade away from the sorrow that had overtaken us all.

Cooper and Tanner stood by our parents, trying to keep a steady face and calm breathing, while ignoring the pit in their stomachs that told them it would never feel normal again. Alexis and I huddled near the edge of the table, learning to be victims' advocates we had talked about how we could apply what we've learned into our situation however it was that was easier said than done.

I could feel the rough edge of my notebook against my thigh, smell the faint leather of my jacket, and hear the quiet ticking of the wall clock that made each second feel as if I was suffocating.

Agent Fields leaned against the far wall, dressed sharply in a navy suit that faintly smelled of aftershave and rain. He broke the silence. "Nathan isn't talking about where his last victim is held unless he speaks to Alexis and his father, Ronny Moore."

There was an immediate stir. "That's not smart," Mr. Martin said, voice low but sharp, eyes flicking to Alexis. "You can't just—"

"It's not your decision," Alexis interrupted firmly, her tone sharp and unwavering. She tugged her cardigan tighter around her shoulders, her fingers nervously brushing the soft knit. "I will talk to them if it's necessary."

Fields ran a hand over his face, exhaling as if he carried the weight of every possibility on his shoulders. "We're trying every tactic before we get to this. And we'd have to get Ronny here from Oregon. That's not simple."

Cooper shifted in his chair, the leather creaking beneath him, eyes darting to the floor. Tanner's fingers drummed against his leg, nails leaving shallow marks in the denim. I could feel my stomach tighten into a knot, my pulse pounding in my ears, every sense warning me that this was about to get brutal.

"You're not really offering her a choice," Mr. Martin said softly, almost to himself, "but we all understand it's no longer a true option."

Alexis pulled herself up straight, her chin raised and eyes intense. "This isn't about your comfort. It's about saving a life. If I don't do this, nothing else counts. I have to try. I couldn't save... your children." Tears fell freely, seeming to carry the weight of her guilt.

The room fell silent again, the kind of silence that presses into your chest, cold and heavy. The hum of the fluorescent lights filled the space between us, and the scrape of our chairs against the floor sounded loud in the quiet. We all sat together—our parents, the Martins—a tangle of grief, fear, and determination. The air was thick with it, and I could almost taste it: coppery, metallic, bitter.

I rubbed my palms together, feeling the rough fibers of my jeans and the smooth surface of my jacket buttons, grounding myself. We were going to face it together—every ounce of terror, every sleepless night, every impossible choice. And I knew, even then, that there was no stepping back. Not for us, not for them.

47
The Captive

I didn't know where I was. The walls pressed in—cold, rough, smelling of dust and metal that curled my stomach. A clock ticked somewhere nearby, steady and relentless, measuring time I couldn't grasp. Was it real? Or had I imagined it? My mind wavered like smoke.

I wondered what had happened to The Wolf. I needed him—like my lungs needed air, like my heart needed to beat. I didn't know if I could survive without him.

The others called him Nathan, but that name meant nothing. It tugged at my memory like a loose thread. I only knew him as The Wolf. Once, he hated me. Once, his hands and words left me broken, bruised, and terrified. And yet now... now he was my world. Every scar, every night spent shaking, every meal withheld—all had shaped me into someone who could depend on him. Someone who could... need him. And I believe he needed me.

I hated needing him. Hated how my stomach clenched at the thought of him, how my body yearned for a presence that once terrified me. But I couldn't stop. I couldn't unlearn the suffocating comfort of dependence. He had become the center of my world, the focus of every thought, every heartbeat, every flicker of hope.

My stomach knotted, a cold emptiness twisting like a blade I hadn't felt in years. I had started to eat again when he fed me, gradually regaining strength and slowly trusting the small mercies he offered. Now, it was ripped away, leaving a hollow ache far worse than before. I pressed my hands to my mouth, tasting the bitter tang of hunger and fear.

I clung to the red ribbon like a lifeline. Thin, fragile, yet weighted with all of him. I pressed it to my lips, tasting the fabric, tasting the lie I needed to believe to keep breathing: *The Wolf is my world. Without him, I am nothing.*

The clock ticked again—steady and merciless. Time showed no mercy here. How long until someone found me? Hours? Days? Weeks? I didn't know. Uncertainty tore at my mind. My hands shook as they brushed the rough floor, touched the walls, trying to hold on to anything solid. Cold, metallic, dusty—I didn't care. I only cared that he wasn't here.

Sometimes I wondered if I imagined it all, if my need had twisted me beyond recognition. But then I felt the ribbon in my fingers, heard the cruel tick of the clock, saw the shadows in the corners—and I knew: I could not survive without him.

He once hated me. He shaped me with hate, pain, and fear. And now, somehow, he has become my everything.

My Wolf.

My world.

And I... I could not breathe, could not exist, without him.

48

Alexis

I had lost my mind.

I lost my voice—not in the way that no one could hear me, but in the sense that I no longer expressed my thoughts. The version of me who used to set boundaries and say exactly what she meant had vanished like dust in the wind. All my words were trapped somewhere in the cage of my thick skull, pacing like a caged animal.

I wanted to yell.

I wanted to scream, *Hell no, you've got to be out of your ever-living freaking mind.* I wasn't going to sit down with my father and... what? My brother? Both psychopaths. Both murderers. Both men who had used my life like clay they could mold for their own entertainment.

What—were we supposed to put on a full façade that we were a close-knit family who gathered for holidays and opened presents on Christmas morning?

I could already picture the conversations.

"So, Dad, did you have someone kill another wife of yours?" Or... *"Hey Nathan, run out of friends or mothers to kill lately? Gone back to torturing animals? Oh wow, look at you—really thriving these days!"*

I was starting to think everyone had lost their minds. We were all so close, yet a mountain of granite stood dead center between us. Asher had been extremely clingy—hovering, watching—but he hadn't voiced a single opinion about me being shoved into a room with two people who wanted each other dead. And wanted me dead. Oh yeah, we couldn't forget that.

It had taken three days to ship Ronny from Oregon to Texas—something about legal loopholes—and then two more days later, I was "requested" to return to FBI headquarters in Austin.

Well, *I* was requested.

Everyone else insisted on escorting me like I was some delicate little butterfly who might flutter into danger if left alone for five minutes.

Truth be told, they didn't see the problem the way I did. They were probably just making sure I didn't bail.

The waiting room they stuck us in looked like someone took "government facility décor" as a personal challenge. Concrete walls painted an off-white made everyone look a little sick. American flags stood in each corner as if they were guarding the place. The walls were lined with portraits of past presidents, their eyes glaring down at us in judgment. The overhead fluorescents hummed in a way that made my teeth itch.

The chairs were surprisingly comfy—so much so that Cooper and Keith had fallen asleep. Cooper's head hung forward, his black T-shirt stretched across his broad shoulders, jeans wrinkled as if he'd slept in them. Keith had tilted sideways in his seat, hat pulled low over his eyes, boots crossed at the ankles.

I realized my sense of humor was coming back—but darker. Twisted. Which fits, given the circumstances. I let out a laugh before I could stop it.

Everyone snapped awake.

Asher leaned forward, elbows resting on his knees, his gray hoodie bunching at the wrists. His mom—Tami—stopped rubbing his back as he straightened up. Tanner lowered the magazine he was pretending to read. Cooper blinked himself awake. Keith pushed his hat up an inch so he could see.

"You okay?" Asher asked, half-concerned, half-amused. "What's so funny?"

I raised an eyebrow. "Oh, nothing. Just the hilarious fact that I'm the only one here with an issue about walking into a room with my killer father and my serial killer brother. Truly comedy gold."

Cooper sighed and rubbed his hand down his face. "Lex, it's not that we're not bothered. It's that—"

"It *is* that you're not bothered," I cut in. "You should be bothered. You should be screaming with me. You should be dragging me out the nearest exit."

Tami folded her arms, her cardigan swaying gently. "We're here because you're not alone. That's why it doesn't bother us."

"That—what? That makes no sense!"

Tanner raised his hands defensively. "Look, we don't think it's a good idea. But the FBI believes you might be able to reach them. Especially Nathan."

"Great. Fantastic." I threw up my hands. "Let's just exploit the family trauma. Love that journey for me."

Keith nodded toward the hallway. "Time's up, sweetheart. They're ready."

My stomach dropped.

As I entered the interrogation room, the atmosphere changed dramatically. It felt much heavier, almost like the air had been replaced with wet cement. My lungs fought to breathe, but I pushed myself to inhale slowly and deliberately, following Cooper's instructions and Asher's pleas.

The room was filled with the sharp smell of cold metal and disinfectant, enough to irritate my throat. The fluorescent light overhead buzzed quietly, flickering intermittently as if warning me to go.

Ronny and Nathan sat across from each other at the metal table, wrists chained to heavy iron rings bolted into the surface. Two monsters on display, as if I had to choose which one was mine.

Ronny was dressed in a faded orange jumpsuit, sporting a smug, crooked grin that gave me the creeps. Meanwhile, Nathan seemed almost bored. Sitting slightly leaned forward, his dark, restrained shirt stretched over his body, with reinforced seams indicating that he's learned not to be underestimated—probably by many people. His messy hair hung over his eyes, shadowing the smirk he was barely trying to hide.

My stomach clenched tightly, as if seized by a fist. My legs felt simultaneously too light and too heavy, and the cold metal chair screeched against the floor as I sat down.

Nathan's gaze fixed on me instantly. It felt like being pushed back into the cage he'd made for me without ever touching me. My fingers twitched under the table. I clenched them into fists.

Ronny laughed quietly. "You look like you saw a ghost."

"Yeah," I said. "Two of them."

Nathan tilted his head as if he found that adorable.

I hated that he looked relieved to see me.

I hated even more that my heartbeat quickened at the familiarity of it.

"You look tired," Nathan said, voice smooth like he thought he was comforting me.

My throat tightened, but I kept my gaze steady. "You don't have the right to comment on my well-being."

Ronny gave a theatrical sigh. "You kids love your dramatics."

Nathan snapped his head toward him. "Shut up."

And that—just the tone—made every hair on my arms stand up. Not because he was angry. Because he wasn't pretending. Not for Ronny. Not for me.

For a split second, I saw the same expression he had given me in that cave over three years ago. Detached. Focused. *Mine.*

I swallowed hard.

"So," Ronny drawled, leaning back as far as his chains allowed, "our first family reunion. Such a charming moment. Shame we don't have wine."

"You don't get to play 'Dad,'" I said. "You don't get to play anything in this story."

Something in Nathan's jaw twitched. The chains clinked softly as he straightened.

"You know," Nathan murmured, voice calm—too calm—"we're cut from the same cloth."

My pulse spiked. "Try again."

"You felt it," he continued, eyes locked on mine like he was reading a page he'd memorized. "Every time you got close to the truth. Every time you lose control. You and I—we're built the same. Dad made us this way."

Ronny emitted a harsh laugh. "You can't blame me for—"

"You killed my mother," Nathan snapped sharply, yanking on his chains so forcefully they scraped sparks against the metal. "You killed the one person who cared about me."

Ronny's face tightened. "She was weak."

"And you made me strong," Nathan whispered, turning back to me. "Just like you made her strong. Just like you made Alexis strong. Dealing with her *mother*," he spat out that last word.

I knew what he meant. Understood it.

My hands went cold. My tongue stuck to the roof of my mouth. It felt like the walls were tilting inward, pushing me toward them.

"Damn hypocrite. You killed my mother," I said, but the words came out softer than I meant. More fragile.

Nathan heard the crack in my voice. Of course he did.

He smiled. "We've already established years ago how our mothers were never the same." His eyes bore into mine. And I hated to admit he was right. "You survived things no normal girl could. You survived....*me*," he said, leaning toward me, eyes bright with conviction. "You're not like them. You're like *me*. Why do you think you were able to understand me? Why do you think you could follow the clues? Why do you think you keep seeing—"

"Stop." I pushed up from the chair, my breath shaking. "That's enough."

He smiled. Soft. Almost affectionate. It made bile burn my throat. "You're scared," he whispered. "Not of me. Of the part of you that matches me."

Ronny barked a laugh. "He's good. I'll give him that."

I backed toward the door. The room felt too cramped. The walls seemed too close. The lighting was too bright. The air felt too thin.

Nathan's voice followed me like a hook sinking into my skin.

"Alexis, don't walk away. You know I'm right."

"No," I whispered. "I know you want me to be like you."

I placed my hand on the door.

"That's not the same thing." Nathan surged forward, steel clanging violently, agents shouting behind the two-way glass.

And then he started singing.

Soft at first.

Like a lullaby twisted into a knife.

"Hickory... dickory... dock..."

The nursery rhyme slithered through the room, echoing in that frightening, rhythmic cadence he used when he wanted someone to break before he touched them.

"The mouse ran up the clock..."

My vision blurred for a moment. My ears rang. Panic crawled up my throat like a second heartbeat.

He laughed—short and jagged.

I didn't wait for the last line.

I shoved through the door before the rhyme struck the hour.

Nathan's voice rose behind me, the chains rattling.

"Hickory... dickory... dock..."

Each word struck my spine like a needle. My hand froze on the door. For a split second, the room blurred—the walls, the table, the men chained to it. All I could hear was that rhyme. That damn rhyme. Another rhyme he sang over bodies. Over graves. Over victims he wanted someone to find.

Or never find.

A cold dread crawled into my lungs.

What if he never tells us?

What if this is his victory lap? His last performance?

What if the woman is out there—starving, terrified, alone—and he's just... playing?

My heartbeat fluttered painfully. I suddenly felt the room shrinking around me, pressing me between two evils.

"—the mouse ran up the—"

Why that rhyme?

Why *now*?

Was he using Hickory Dickory Dock to mark time, to signal a countdown... or to mock the idea of running out of it? Every kill, every rhyme had been a message.

My stomach twisted so violently I nearly doubled over. *Is he trying to tell me she's running out of time? Or is he telling me I am?*

I turned back, despite every instinct screaming not to.

Nathan was staring straight at me — eyes bright, unhinged, triumphant — fighting the restraints like he could drag me back with sheer will.

"The clock struck—"

"No," I breathed, stepping back again. "No, no, no—what are you doing? What does that mean? Why are you—"

He grinned, wide and feral.

"—ONE."

He yelled so loudly that the walls shook.

I stumbled through the door as if the room had spit me out.

49

Alexis

The hallway felt like it was closing in on me as I ran away, Nathan's screams fading into the distance, and I was grateful for that. Still, the anxiety I was feeling remained, a tight coil in my chest that squeezed with every ragged breath, the fluorescent lights buzzing overhead like a swarm of angry bees in my skull. I pushed open the bathroom door—feeling the bile rise willingly, sour and burning at the back of my throat—and was about to enter a stall when Lila suddenly burst in, the door swinging wide with a whoosh of stale air that carried the faint, institutional scent of bleach and cheap air freshener.

She looked me up and down with a strange look on her face, her eyes sharp and assessing, like she was scanning for cracks in my armor. I returned the look, my heart still hammering from the interrogation room's echo. I hadn't seen her since Benji died, that hollow day when everything had fractured, and her absence had been a quiet ache amid the chaos, texts piling up unanswered like unread letters from a ghost.

She cleared her throat, the sound sharp in the tiled space, and looked down at her feet, scuffing one heel against the floor before meeting my eyes with a steel expression that didn't waver. "Are you okay?" She glanced at the stalls, her voice low but steady, like she already knew the answer. She knew I was going to purge, but in my defense, I truly felt like vomiting after that exchange with Nathan, his velvet rasp still slithering in my ears like poison ivy creeping under my skin.

"I could hear Nathan all the way down the hall. I just wanted to check on you."

I raised an eyebrow, the motion pulling at the tension in my forehead. "What are you doing here?" I stepped closer and leaned against the sink, the porcelain cool against my palms, grounding me just enough to steady my voice. "Where have you been? I've been texting and calling you."

She was dressed in a black pantsuit with a white blouse underneath her jacket, the fabric crisp and tailored in a way that screamed authority, not the casual coffee-shop vibe I'd associated with her. Her long red hair was slicked back into a low, sleek ponytail, not a strand out of place, and the Lila I knew—the one who'd sworn off high heels after a bad date story involving a twisted ankle and too much tequila—stood there in two-inch pumps that clicked against the tile like punctuation marks in a sentence I didn't want to read. It was all wrong, like seeing a familiar painting hung upside down, the details skewed, but the essence mocking me.

Lila hesitated, her steel expression softening just a fraction, the corners of her mouth twitching like she was weighing words on a scale. She glanced at the door, as if ensuring we were alone, the hum of the vents above us the only other sound, recycling the same stale air that tasted faintly of dust and regret. "Alexis, there's something I need to tell you. Something I should have said a long time ago." She took a deep breath, her chest rising under the blouse, and when she spoke again, her voice was steady, but there was an undercurrent of apology, like she'd been carrying this weight for miles. "I'm not a student at the University. I never was. I'm an FBI agent—undercover. And I'm 30 years old, not your age. I was assigned to get close to you after the warehouse incident, to keep an eye on things, and gather intel if Nathan resurfaced. The barista gig, the 'friendship'... it was all part of the cover."

The words hit me like a slap from the wind on Bonnell, cold and stinging, leaving my cheeks flushed and my mind reeling. Lila—my lifeline in the library stacks, the one who'd coaxed smiles from me with lavender lattes and easy laughs, her auburn curls always smelling faintly of espresso and rain—had been a lie?

Thirty? The age gap suddenly explained the maturity in her eyes, the way she'd dodged questions about classes or dorm drama, her vine tattoo peeking from her wrist like a hidden badge.

Betrayal bloomed in my gut, hot and familiar, layering onto the pile of losses that never seemed to end—Benji's small hand going limp, Kaitlyn's scream cut short in a gurgle of blood, Zane's final wheeze echoing off the cliff like a broken rhyme.

How many more masks would people wear around me?

"You lied," I said, my voice flat but edged, the sink's edge digging into my back as I straightened, the bile in my throat turning to acid anger. "All this time, you were just... watching? Reporting back like I was some case file? After everything—Benji, the tower, the cradle—you let me think you were a friend?"

Lila's eyes didn't waver, but her posture softened, her heels shifting on the tile with a soft click that echoed in the small space. "I know it sounds bad, Alexis. It *is* bad. But it started as an assignment, yeah. Get close, monitor for Nathan's patterns, keep you safe without tipping our hand. But it became real. The lattes, the library huddles, the way you'd open up about Benji... that wasn't cover. You're not just a file to me. Not anymore." She paused, running a hand over her ponytail, the sleek strands catching the fluorescent light like polished copper. "That's why I'm here now. I convinced Fields to let you look at some of the evidence from Becca's clocktower death. We're trying to find his last captive—the one Zane gasped about before... before the end. The ladybug-wolf carved on that cloth? It's not just a symbol; it's a clue. And with your... intuition, your connection to the Moore stuff, you might see something we missed. Help us end this."

The confession hung in the air, heavy as the rain drumming on the roof outside, each drop a punctuation to her words. Convinced Fields? Evidence from Becca's death—the woman who'd worn stepmom smiles for a week of whispers and wrong turns, her throat popped in Nathan's tower twist, blood tacky on threads that still haunted my dreams.

The last captive? The frail shadow from the warehouse, assisting Nathan like a ghost in chains, her identity a void that pulled at me like the riptide of continual loss, the spiral dipping deeper with every name erased: Benji's innocence snuffed in sterile beeps, Kaitlyn's trust fractured in the cradle's crash, Zane's defiance guttering out in a pool of his own blood on limestone.

And now this—Lila, my anchor, unmasked as another FBI string, pulling me toward evidence that might unravel Nathan's final knot, the captive's crib waiting under East Sixth's oaks, where hangman's history whispered rhymes to the dead.

My hands trembled on the sink, the porcelain cool and unyielding, grounding me just enough to nod, the anger simmering but not boiling over—not yet. "Fine. Show me. But if this is another game, Lila—or whatever your name is—I'll make sure Fields knows how deep your 'real' went." She nodded, her heels clicking as she led me out, the bathroom door swinging shut behind us with a sigh, but the hook sank deeper—evidence from Becca's gore, the captive's shadow calling, and Nathan's verses still humming in my blood like a lullaby I couldn't shake. What if he was right? What if the wolf was already awake?

50

Alexis

As we turned the corner into the main corridor, the fluorescent lights cast long shadows that danced like ghosts on the linoleum. I spotted Asher leaning against the wall near the evidence room door, his arms crossed over his chest, the fabric of his Henley shirt stretched tight across shoulders, tensed with barely contained energy. He looked up as we approached, his eyes—those storm-gray depths I willingly drowned in—narrowing at the sight of Lila in her pantsuit, the heels clicking like a countdown on the floor. Tanner and Cooper hovered nearby, their expressions a mix of concern and suspicion. Tanner's lopsided grin was gone, replaced by a scowl that pulled at his stubble. Cooper's fingers tapped restlessly on his phone, as if he were already coding a plan.

Asher pushed off the wall, his boots gently scuffing, the sound muffled in the quiet hall, and stepped into our path, his gaze flicking from me to Lila with a question that hung heavy. "Lex? What's going on? White said something about evidence—why's she here?" He nodded at Lila, his voice low but edged, the protectiveness in it a warmth that cut through the chill seeping into my body.

I looked at Lila, her ponytail swinging slightly as she met his eyes without flinching, then shifted my gaze back to Asher, feeling the coil in my chest loosen just a bit at the sight of him—solid, steady, the anchor I'd relied on, his flannel rumpled from the day's chaos, sleeves rolled up to show forearms corded from late-night sketches and the weight of holding us all together. "She's FBI," I said quickly, the words tasting bitter on my tongue, like the bile I'd come here to purge. "Undercover. She's been... watching. Convinced Fields to let me see Becca's evidence. Might be a clue to the captive."

Asher's brows furrowed, a storm cloud gathering in his eyes, but he nodded, his hand brushing my arm in a lingering, warm, and reassuring touch that sparked a flicker through the numbness Nathan's games had left. "FBI? Shit, Lila—if that's your name. If you're helping, fine. But if this is another layer of bullshit..." He trailed off, his jaw tightening like Tanner's behind him, the unspoken threat hanging in the air like damp rain. Lila simply nodded curtly, her heels clicking as she pushed open the evidence room door, the lock beeping its approval with a high-pitched tone that grated on my nerves.

The evidence room was a sterile vault, with rows of metal shelves filled with boxes wrapped in plastic that crinkled like dry leaves under the junior agent's gloved hands as he retrieved an item—a cloth, a bloodied rag from the tower, now sealed in a clear bag that fogged slightly under the lights, the crimson stains dark and flaking like rust from a forgotten pipe. The agent—young, with acne scars dotting his cheeks and a notepad tucked under his arm—laid it on the steel table with a soft thunk, the surface cold under my fingers as I leaned in, the air in the room chilled and tinged with the faint, chemical smell of preservative sprays. Lila stood beside me, her pantsuit whispering when she shifted. Asher was on my other side, his breath warm against my shoulder. Tanner and Cooper crowded in, their boots scuffing the floor, the scent of rain-damp clothes mingling with the room's musty undertone.

The image was ladybug wings unfurling into wolf fangs, the lines crude but vicious, smeared in arterial script that had dried to a flaky brown, the fabric stiff with it, the coppery tang faint but unmistakable even through the plastic, like Becca's final accusation lingering in the fibers. But as I tilted the bag under the light, the fluorescents buzzing like a persistent headache, something caught my eye—the edge torn ragged, fibers frayed like they'd been ripped in haste, and there, half-hidden in the crease, additional writing in the same bloody scrawl, the top half of letters peeking like secrets half-buried: "The Wolf's Pet." The words hit me in the gut, cold and cutting—The Wolf, another rhyme, the one who'd hummed lullabies while popping weasels and rocking cradles to ruin.

"Look," I whispered, my finger tracing the air above the plastic, the chill of the room raising gooseflesh on my arms. "It's not just the symbol. There's more—torn off. 'The Wolf's Pet.' It is another rhyme. I remember it from the book: 'Wolf, Wolf' they shepherd cried. But no one came—Until the Wolf was real.'"

Asher leaned in closer, his shoulder brushing mine, solid and warm against the room's chill, his breath stirring my hair as he squinted, the faint stubble on his jaw rasping softly as he rubbed it. "You're right. Another rhyme. *The Boy Who Called Wolf.* Pet? The captive. She's leaving clues," he said, echoing my thoughts.

Tanner grabbed his phone, fingers flying over the screen with a series of taps that echoed in the quiet, Cooper nodding beside him, his hoodie zipped tight, the fabric whispering as he shifted. "Decipher time," Tanner said, voice low and edged, pulling up notes from all his research. "????" His eyes went wide. "Wait...could this be another alias like Rhyme Reaper or Black Sheep?"

We huddled around the table, the agent's notepad flipping pages with a rustle as he jotted, the plastic bag crinkling under our breaths, and the evidence room's vents wheezing cold air that carried the faint, musty scent of archived death. "The Wolf's Pet," Cooper muttered, his eyes narrowing behind glasses fogged from the chill. "Rhymes with... wet, set, bet. But Nathan's style—nursery twists. 'The Wolf had a pet'? No. Wait—Becca's tower was 'Pop Goes the Weasel.' She was there, helping him like Egor helped Frankenstein. This cloth was her clue, torn to hide, but she meant for us to find it. The warehouse woman. She's his 'pet.'

The realization struck me like a thorn in my chest, sharp and piercing—the captive, the fragile shadow helping Nathan in the warehouse, moved mechanically, trying to leave a clue: the cloth, a desperate plea smeared with her own blood, was stiff and sticky beneath the plastic's shine. Becca's death was the distraction, her body the bait to lure us out, but the true message was the captive's hidden cry, "The Wolf's Pet," with the top half torn to hide it, yet now serving as a map to her cage.

"She's helping us," I said, voice steady but laced with rage, my fury at Nathan's wolfish grin as the cradle fell, Kaitlyn and Zane's tangled ruin a scar on my soul. "We need to make Nathan talk. Now."

The coil in my chest unwound into action, and I marched back to the interrogation room, the hallway's linoleum slick under my boots from tracked rain. White tried to block me at the door, his bulk filling the frame like a wall, but I shoved past, the junior suit scrambling to his feet with a chair scrape that grated like nails on my nerves.

Nathan was still cuffed, but his eyes lit up at my return, that clown-like smile stretching wide, amusement glistening like dew on a blade. And there, beside him—Ronny, chains linking ankles to the floor with a soft clink, his green eyes—flecked with the same storm as mine—watching me with a mix of curiosity and something deeper. Why was he still here? The FBI is listening in, hoping Nathan slips under paternal pressure? Or something more twisted, Nathan's agenda pulling strings even in chains? The air thickened, heavy with the scent of unwashed regret and institutional soap, as I slammed my hands on the table, the steel cold under my palms.

"The captive," I demanded, voice a whipcrack that made the recorder jump. "Who is she? The cloth from the tower—The Wolf's Pet. She left clues. Where is she? Tell me, Nathan—or Ronny, you know, don't you?" My gaze shifted back and forth. "You both have so many secrets. Why is he really here? Why did he want you?"

Nathan's smile widened, his teeth bared in the lights' glare, but he leaned back, cuffs rattling applause. "Ah, ladybug. Back so soon? The wind called, and you flew. Flesh to flesh, the air thick with salt and secrets. The captive? She's running up the clock, humming the rhyme you know by heart. Hickory, dickory, dock—the mouse ran up the clock. Come again, and I'll whisper the grove's full stanza. Or she falls when the clock strikes one, and the bough breaks alone."

I turned to Ronny, the rage coiling tighter, my nails digging crescents into the table's surface. "Tell me. What does that mean? You know his games—you're part of this, aren't you? Ronny's mess, the Moore curse. Why are you here?"

Ronny shifted, his chains clinking like broken rhymes, his voice a husky rasp filtered through years of prison coughs, each word wheezing out like air from a punctured tire. "Ale xis... I don't know his full games." He laughs. "I'm beginning to believe I'm just another mannequin in his verses. The only thing that comes to mind is mice like to play and what better place to play is in a resort for the beasts." His eyes met mine, the green storm swirling, but I pushed, the desperation burning hot in my throat like bile I couldn't swallow.

"That's all? More twisting of words? You're his father—the man who sired this monster. Tell me where she is!"

Nathan chuckled, the sound low and wet, bubbling up like blood from a fresh wound, his head tilting to catch the light on the scar on his jaw, the puckered skin pulling tight. "Clever, Father. The mice are where other animals love to be. But the full verse? For her ears alone. Come on, sister. The clock's ticking, and the mouse will soon die."

The rhymes—always the damn rhymes, twisting everything into knots of nonsense and nightmare, the verses that had stolen Benji's breath, sealed Becca's throat, and rocked Kaitlyn and Zane to their bloody end. The spiral sank deeper, the constant loss crashing over me in waves that tasted of salt and regret. The nuns, the hospital, all the innocent people who have died at the hands of this psychopath, were tying me to this half-brother in ways that made my skin crawl.

Unhinged fury erupted then, a bonfire that scorched through the numbness, hotter than the warehouse blaze, and I lunged across the table, my fists flying like rusted hooks, slamming into Nathan's nose with a wet crunch that sprayed blood across the steel, warm droplets spattering my knuckles like rain turned venomous. He reeled, but I didn't stop, kicking at his chair with a boot that thudded against his shin, the impact vibrating up my leg like a rhyme's echo, my screams ripping free— "Enough with the rhymes, you bastard! You killed them all, your verses are poison, and I'll end you!" The junior suit scrambled back, his chair toppling with a clatter, notepad fluttered to the floor, then White burst in with two agents, their boots pounding the linoleum, hands grabbing my arms with grips like iron vices, pulling me off as I spat on Nathan's face, the glob landing wet on his cheek, mixing with the blood dripping from his nose in thick rivulets that pattered on the table like rain on tin.

Nathan laughed, blood bubbling from his lips in a froth that stained his teeth red, the sound maniacal and molten, swelling in the room like a symphony's crescendo. His eyes glistened with amusement even as the crimson trickled down his chin, warm and sticky against the coarse weave of his jumpsuit. "You've scarred me once, Ladybug," he rasped, with words gurgling through the blood, "that won't happen again. You're running out of time—the mouse will die. Tick tock."

The agents hauled me out, White's voice a gravelly growl in my ear— "Dammit, Alexis, you're done here"—but the hook sank deeper, Nathan's laugh echoing in my mind like a broken rhyme, the "mouse" a cryptic taunt that tugged at my intuition, the Moore curse whispering that the captive's clock was ticking, and somehow I'd have to silence it.

51
Nathan - The Wolf

The door hissed open again, casting a thin slice of hallway light across the floor—pale, sterile, surgical. It stretched toward me like a scalpel aiming for exposed flesh.

Not White this time. Not the trembling junior.

She stepped in.

Controlled. Measured. Balanced like a sharp blade.

A woman in a bureau jacket, dark hair pulled back so tightly it shaped her skull into a weapon. A badge shimmered against her hip like a cold, metallic sun. Boots were quiet on the tile. Shoulders squared with the kind of confidence that grows in secret places, in shadowed training rooms, in lives built from lies.

But I knew her.

I knew her face.

Not from case files. Not from surveillance. Not from anything in this decaying maze of federal rooms and recycled air.

I knew her from photographs. Newspaper clippings. Sports pages. Podiums framed in school colors.

Alexis, with her arm around Lila—both flushed with triumph, medals swinging at their throats like shiny little trophies.

Two girls who thought the world was simple enough to race on tracks and collect ribbons.

I drank in the sight of her. And I laughed—soft, dangerous, a pulse of something unhinged.

"Look at you," I murmured. "Trading in your track shoes for a gun. Trading in friendship for orders."

She didn't react. Her composure was like a wall built stone by stone. But I saw it: a flicker, a twitch at the corner of her mouth, and a betrayal in her eyelids—too fast for training to catch.

Perfect.

Another knife pressed into the spine of my ladybug.

Alexis trusted Lila. Held her secrets close. Bared her throat.

And all the while, Lila was an undercover agent. A plant. A watcher. A ghost woven into Alexis's life without her permission.

I felt joy coil warm and electric through me. One more thread snapping in the web of Alexis's fragile trust.

But then—a different heat flared.

My cheek. The left side. Still raw. Still burning. Still stinging from her fist crashing into my skin—Ladybug's fury unleashed with the force of a hammer and the tremor of old trauma.

She had hit me—beat me.

Not because of strength. Because of grief. Because of desperation. From the storm she bears in her ribs like a loaded gun, she doesn't know how to aim.

The skin there pulsed—hot, swollen, singing with pain.

Every pulse a love letter. Every burn a bond.

She hit me and left a mark.

That made her mine.

My breath hitched just a little when Lila moved further into the room, the light highlighting her cheekbones, her eyes, and the tilt of her mouth.

And suddenly—she wasn't Lila.

She blurred. Softened. Shifted.

She became my mother.

Not exactly. Not fully. But enough.

Enough to punch a hole through the armor I had perfected over years—the armor of riddles, rhymes, and calculated cruelty. The armor Alexis had dented. The armor my father had forged from bone and fear.

My mother's ghost hovered within Lila's silhouette, as her red hair escaped its tie, along the slope of her jaw, and in the softness beneath her eyes.

My lungs tightened.

The room shrank. Tilted. Warped.

Ronny moved—chained, pathetic, his ankles dragging melody behind him like a broken music box.

And the fuse lit.

Because Lila's resemblance wasn't just a ghost—it was a reminder.

Of the noose. Of her scream swallowed as it squeezed. Of Nicole's fingers digging into her arm. Of Ronny's voice—threat, command, verdict.

From that moment, the woman became weightless and then vanished into nothing.

Ronny pushed my mother to her death. Nicole helped. And the world kept spinning like it didn't notice.

I was happy I got rid of that whore.

And I will be getting rid of Ronny.

My face burned again—not from Alexis's strike this time, but from a memory searing through my marrow.

White sensed the change first, his eyes immediately locking onto me.

Lila instinctively reached for her holster.

Ronny sensed nothing until my stare turned to knives.

"You," I whispered. The room froze. "You shouldn't look like her."

Lila's throat moved as she tried to hide a swallow.

My voice cracked—not from sadness, but from rage so intense it tore at the edges of my calm.

"Take that face off," I hissed. "Take it off before I rip—"

White barked a warning, the junior agent stumbled, and Ronny flinched like a kicked stray.

But it was already too late.

Alexis's punches had cracked my mask. Lila's face had shattered it. Ronny's presence had ground it to dust.

My fingers twitched violently, chains slicing into already-torn skin. Blood welled warm. Comforting.

The rhyme rose like bile.

"Hickory..." My voice vibrated. The table shook. "Dickory..."

The chain snapped taut—metal slicing a fresh, wet line down my wrist.

"DOCK."

The recorder light blinked like a dying heartbeat. The vents moaned cold. The agents held their breath.

And I smiled—broken, blistered, bruised, and blazing with something feral.

Because this was evolution.

The boy who lost his mother. The son who lost love and learned violence. The predator was shaped by pain. The heir carved from choking screams.

The man Alexis struck—and awakened.

The man who would destroy the world to keep her near.

And when Lila's face flickered in my mind as my mother's—I knew it.

The rhyme had become a countdown.

52
Asher

The FBI medical wing didn't smell like a hospital. It smelled like fluorescent lights and recycled air—dry, metallic, too clean in a way that made my teeth ache. Stainless steel counters lined the walls, every surface reflecting the brightness overhead, casting harsh shadows that danced faintly with each flicker of the bulbs. The hum of the vents was constant, flat, oppressive, like a mechanical heartbeat pulsing through the sterile void. Doors slid open somewhere down the hallway, agents' voices bouncing off tile, sharp and rapid in the aftermath of the chaos she'd caused, their words fragmenting into echoes that lingered just long enough to unsettle the air.

And in the center of all that sterile order—stood the girl I loved, looking like she'd just walked out of a war.

"First aid kit," I snapped at the nearest agent.

He blinked, startled, then reached up to a wall-mounted cabinet with fumbling hands. The fluorescent lights flickered over his face as he shoved the kit at me, his fingers brushing mine in a clumsy haste. "She, uh—she might need a psych eval—"

"I've got her," I said, already turning away. "Go."

The agent backed out quickly, relief obvious in his shoulders as the door clicked shut behind him, the soft whoosh of the seal emphasizing the sudden isolation.

Now it was just us.

Alexis stood stiffly, like her bones weren't sure how to hold her up, her weight shifting uneasily from one foot to the other. Her hoodie was soaked at the collar from sweat, the fabric clinging to her arms in damp patches that darkened the material. Her hair—usually messy in that way that somehow made her look both feral and soft—was plastered to her temples, strands falling over her eyes in wild, sweat-matted curls. There was a faint sheen of sweat on her skin, catching the harsh overhead lights and making her glow with an unnatural, feverish luminescence.

But her eyes—her eyes were the part that twisted something deep inside me.

Wide. Dilated. Black swallowing the green.

A storm without a center.

She looked electric.

Dangerous.

Beautiful in a way that terrified me, like a live wire exposed and sparking in the rain.

Her chest rose and fell too fast, breaths shallow like she couldn't pull in enough air, each inhale ragged and uneven, as if the room's recycled oxygen wasn't enough to quench the fire raging inside her. Her lips were parted, bruised from where she must have bitten them, the faint imprint of teeth visible in the swollen flesh. Her cheeks were flushed a wild, feverish pink, and a single streak of blood—whose, I didn't know—ran from the base of her thumb halfway up her forearm, drying into a crusty line that cracked slightly with her movements.

"Baby," I said quietly, stepping in. "Come here."

I touched her elbow. Even through the hoodie fabric, I could feel the tremor beneath her skin—like she was vibrating apart, every muscle tight and quivering with residual energy.

"Sit," I whispered.

She let me guide her to the metal exam table, the cold surface creaking faintly under her weight. The legs of her jeans stuck to her skin, and I realized sweat had dampened them too, the denim clinging uncomfortably to her thighs. She wasn't collapsing, wasn't shaking in fear—no, this was different, a contained explosion simmering just beneath the surface.

She was trying not to fly apart.

Her knuckles—

Jesus.

Her knuckles were torn open. Deep, ugly splits. The skin shredded in jagged patterns that made my stomach twist, raw edges weeping tiny beads of blood. The bruising beneath was already blooming, dark purples and angry blues swirling like ink under skin, spreading outward in mottled patterns. One of her fingers was swelling—badly. The kind of swelling that screamed she hadn't just hit him.

She'd hammered him, unleashing a fury that left her own body as collateral.

Her fists rested in her lap, but her posture stayed coiled, shoulders tight, spine locked rigid like she was waiting for something—or holding back something that still clawed at the inside of her ribs, a primal urge not yet sated.

When I pulled a stool close and lifted her right hand to examine it, she sucked in a sharp breath, the sound slicing through the quiet hum of the room.

"Hurts?" I murmured.

"No."

Her voice was hoarse, thinned from shouting or crying—I couldn't tell which, but it carried the gravelly edge of someone who'd pushed their vocal cords to the limit.

Then she lifted her gaze to mine, and a faint, wild smile tugged at the corner of her mouth, a flicker of something untamed and exhilarating.

"It felt good."

Heat flooded my chest—fear, worry, and something else I didn't want to name, a dark admiration that mirrored her own rush.

Her lips twitched again, and the fluorescent lights caught the slightest sheen of tears in her eyes—not sadness, but adrenaline, the afterglow of a high that hadn't fully ebbed. Her face was flushed, freckles standing out starkly against her skin like scattered stars on a stormy canvas. A small cut near her cheekbone—probably from Nathan snapping his head back in the struggle—left a thin red line, a fresh scar in the making. Her mouth was swollen from clenching her jaw too hard, the muscles there still faintly twitching.

She looked like someone midway between panic and euphoria, teetering on the edge of both, her body a battlefield of conflicting impulses.

And she was shaking.

God, she was still shaking, fine tremors rippling through her frame like aftershocks from an earthquake.

"Lex," I said softly, "you're bleeding."

She looked down at her hands like she was seeing them for the first time. Her breath caught, a small hitch that betrayed the dawning reality. "Oh."

Her voice was small—confused. The high was wearing off, leaving behind the crash, a hollow exhaustion settling in like fog.

But not all of it.

She licked her lips, eyes flicking up again. "Ash... it felt good. Too good." She swallowed, the motion visible in her throat, her Adam's apple bobbing with the effort. "I wanted to hurt him."

I lifted her chin gently with my fingers, feeling the warmth of her skin against mine. "Look at me."

Her eyes snapped up instantly—like my voice was the first solid thing she'd been able to hear since she left that interrogation room, an anchor in the chaos.

"You're safe," I murmured. "I'm right here."

Her throat bobbed. Tears rimmed the edges of her eyes, not falling, just shimmering with the weight of everything she couldn't say out loud, a silent storm gathering.

I reached up, brushing a stray blood-dried strand of hair from her cheek. She leaned into my touch—barely—but enough for me to feel the tremble running through her, a subtle vibration that spoke of vulnerability beneath the ferocity.

"Let me fix your hands," I said softly.

She nodded, breath shaking, her exhale warm against my wrist.

As I cleaned her wounds, her legs swung slightly from the table—not in nervousness, but in exhaustion, a restless motion born from depleted energy. She was burnt out, running on fumes and adrenaline, half-collapsed but refusing to fall, her resilience a quiet force holding her together. Her skin smelled faintly of sweat and antiseptic, and there was a metallic tang in the air from her dried blood, mingling with the room's sterile scent to create something almost intimate in its rawness.

Each time the antiseptic stung, she inhaled sharply, but her eyes never left me, locked on with an intensity that pierced straight through.

There was trust in that stare.

And terror.

And something raw, something I hadn't seen in her before—the realization that part of her wanted the violence, craved the release it brought after years of pent-up torment.

"You're not him," I said quietly, as if reading the thought I saw flicker behind her eyes, the shadow of doubt creeping in.

"I don't know." Her voice cracked, fracturing on the words like brittle glass. "Ash, I... I liked it. I don't know what that means."

"It means you're human," I said. "A human who's been hunted, haunted, and broken open by the same monster for years."

She blinked hard. A tear slipped—just one—and slid down her cheek, leaving a clean line through the sweat and grime, tracing a path of quiet surrender.

Her face softened. Crumpled, almost, the hard edges giving way to something fragile and exposed.

When I wrapped her left hand, she exhaled through her nose, leaning forward until her forehead rested against my shoulder, the contact grounding us both. Her fingers curled into the fabric of my shirt, gripping lightly as if to steady herself.

"I didn't mean to lose it," she whispered, her words muffled against my collar.

"I know," I murmured, kissing the top of her head, inhaling the familiar scent of her shampoo mixed with the day's chaos. "You snapped because you were pushed. That's not the same thing."

She lingered there for several breaths, her entire body pressed against mine as if she was trying to borrow warmth or stability from me, our heartbeats aligning silently. When she finally pulled away, she wiped her face with the back of her newly bandaged hand, leaving a faint streak of residue.

And then, just like that, the fire lit again behind her eyes, a spark reigniting the embers.

"We need to figure out the riddle," she said. "Now."

Her voice was still shaky.

Her hands were battered.

Her hair was a mess, and her face was blotchy from tears and adrenaline.

But she was standing again.

Focused.

Dangerous in a way that made my chest ache with both fear and pride, a fierce protectiveness swelling alongside the awe.

"Yeah," I said. "We do."

I tossed the bloodied wipes into the trash and stood beside her, our shoulders brushing in silent solidarity.

She straightened her hoodie, wiped her nose, smoothed her hair back, even though it immediately fell forward again, with defiant strands framing her determined expression.

Then she threw her shoulders back.

Wounded or not—Alexis Harper was still there, her spirit unbroken, ready to chase the shadows again.

53

Alexis

It's totally natural to want to beat the shit out of someone who has wronged you, right?

I mean, I can't be the only one thinking that. I'm seriously questioning more and more if the FBI knows what the hell they're doing. Because why in the actual hell would they be okay with me continually talking to that bastard? To *Nathan*. My brother. God, I hate that word. Hated that connection. Hate that thin biological thread that ropes me to him like some sad cosmic joke.

I get it—technically, in some warped family tree sense, I am Nathan's sister. But if you took a normal family setting and asked me to identify what that felt like, I'd shrug. I had nothing to compare it to. The closest I could imagine was the relationship I had with Cooper and Tanner. The teasing. The loyalty. The stupid inside jokes. Knowing they'd always be the ones to pick me up and dust me off.

But this? This was not that. Nor would it ever be. This was the farthest thing from any kind of normal. Whatever "normal" even was—this sure as hell wasn't it.

Asher and I walked back to the waiting area. The hallway smelled faintly like bleach and coffee that had been roasted for twelve hours too long. Phones buzzed. Agents murmured into radios. Everything moved with a purpose except us.

Keith and Tami were in a deep conversation—heads bowed toward each other like they were trying to keep a secret from the world. The moment our footsteps echoed closer, both of them snapped their attention to us—eyes widening. Assessing. Worried.

"What's going on?" Asher's voice was low, cautious, shifting his gaze between his parents as he slowly sank into the seat across from them.

Keith ignored Asher completely—which was honestly impressive, fatherly blindness—and instead stared at my hand. The bandages wrapped around my knuckles were already tinged a faint pink, angry from where I'd split the skin across Nathan's mouth.

Then a slow, proud grin crept up Keith's face. "I bet that felt good."

I couldn't help smiling back as I sat next to Asher. "Yeah," I said, clearing my throat. "Who told you?"

"Oh, word travels fast when someone finally clocks the resident psychopath," Cooper announced as he sauntered in from the hallway, two vending machine sodas clutched in his hands like trophies. He tossed one to Tanner, who followed behind him holding a bag of pretzels like a supporting character in a snack-themed heist.

Tanner looked down at the pretzels. "He was crying when his Snickers got stuck," he informed us with the seriousness of a witness on the stand.

"I was *not* crying." Cooper cracked his soda open dramatically. "It was condensation."

"Condensation?" Tanner lifted a brow. "Bro, you screamed, 'You monster!' at a vending machine."

"It stole from me," Cooper defended. "That's a crime."

Keith shook his head and muttered something that sounded suspiciously like *my children are idiots.*

But it was exactly the stupid, familiar energy I needed after the chamber of horrors downstairs.

Asher nudged my knee lightly. "How is your hand feeling?"

"Like I punched someone," I snorted.

Asher huffed a laugh, but his eyes softened with worry.

We kept close—our knees touching—and that little contact was grounding. Every time I blinked, flashes of Nathan's smirk still pulsed through my brain. The way he seemed to enjoy every second I was in the room with him. Of toying with us. Of whispering things that were meant to unravel me.

But punching him had silenced him for a moment.

A moment of bliss.

"I'm sure it hurts," he murmured.

"His face is sharp," I said flatly.

"No," he corrected with a faint smile. "Your right hook is."

I stared at him. My chest tightened—not from fear, not from anger—from something softer and scarier. Asher took my injured hand in his and lightly touched his lips against the bandages. I flinched.

"Sorry," he whispered.

"You're forgiven," I whispered back.

His eyes lifted to meet mine. "You scared me down there."

"You and me both."

Tami offered me some ibuprofen from her purse. Asher reached for the offered bottle, then held it in his hands, twisting the childproof lid around. "Just... promise me you'll tell me if you start to lose control again. You don't have to hold everything inside."

I opened my mouth to argue—to defend myself with my usual sarcasm—but the words slipped out before I could stop them.

"It felt good, Ash." My voice cracked. "Too good."

His jaw clenched, but he didn't look away. "That doesn't make you like him."

"Are you sure?" I whispered. "Because sometimes... sometimes I don't recognize myself anymore."

He took my face in his hands—gentle, firm. "You're nothing like him. You're fighting for others. He destroys them."

That... helped. More than I wanted to admit.

He was about to kiss me when agents began swarming the waiting area like bees after someone kicked their hive. Screens lit up. Radios crackled. The room suddenly thrummed with adrenaline.

Keith stood immediately. "What's happening?"

Lila snapped a tablet at us. "We've located a property that matches Nathan's description—barn on a ranch outside Austin. We're mobilizing."

My heart lurched. Relief and panic collided inside me like two drunks running full-speed into each other.

"Is that where the captive is?" Tami asked.

"We're not certain," Lila replied. "But it's the strongest lead we've had."

"We need to go," I said, already stepping forward.

Lila blocked my path with one hand. "Absolutely not."

Cooper snorted. "Oh boy. Wrong answer."

"I'm serious," she snapped. "Alexis, you are not setting foot anywhere near that location."

"Why?" I shot back. "Because I might get the job done?"

"Because we are not risking you walking into a potential trap."

"You wouldn't even have this lead if it weren't for me," I argued, heat rising up my spine. "I know how he thinks—"

"Oh, do you?" Lila folded her arms. "Tell me, what does a serial killer think about while he's carving his latest victim? Do you understand that?"

The words hit me like a slap. Loud. Brutal.

Asher stepped in facing Lila, voice sharp. "Back off."

"No," I snapped, raising a hand to stop him. "It's fine." I took a breath. She was never my friend. Just another lie. "I'm not saying I'm an expert on torture. I'm saying I know Nathan's arrogance. He'd want to keep his prize somewhere close. Somewhere symbolic. Somewhere that mattered to him."

"But this barn doesn't—"

"It does," I interrupted. "You're thinking about maps. He's thinking about memories, rhymes."

Silence.

The agent's eyes narrowed. "You believe he chose a barn because…?"

"Because it fits what he was saying about animals, genius," Cooper chimed in.

Tanner added with a shrug, "Horses love barns."

"They're right," Tami said quietly.

Keith nodded. "He'd want to keep control in a space that was out of the city."

The agent swore under her breath.

"I'm going," I insisted.

"No," she shot back.

Asher touched my arm. "Alexis—"

"I *need* to do something," I said, voice shaking. "I need distance between him and me. Sitting here feels like drowning."

Keith stepped closer. "If you go, it won't be alone."

"I'm not leaving you unprotected," Asher said firmly. "We go together or not at all."

Lila looked between us, wrestling with the kind of decision that could end someone's career.

Finally, she exhaled. "Fine. But you follow orders. You stay behind tactical teams. No heroics. Nothing like the warehouse. Understood?"

"Define 'heroics,'" I muttered.

Tanner coughed. "She doesn't understand big words when she's emotionally compromised."

"Hey!" I glared at him.

He grinned. "There she is. The menace we know and love."

Asher squeezed my hand. I squeezed back.

For one fragile moment—it felt like hope existed.

There was a beat of calm — the fragile kind that feels like the world is holding its breath.

Then the doors to the waiting room exploded open.

A woman staggered inside like she'd slammed through the storm and dragged the lightning with her. Hair tangled. Face streaked with smeared mascara. Jacket half-on like she lost a fight with gravity on the way in.

Her scream didn't even sound human.

"I WANT TO SEE HIM!"

Every agent in the room jerked toward her. Hands hovered near guns. Chairs scraped. Conversations died mid-sentence.

Keith was on his feet instantly. Tami's heart practically launched out of her chest.

"Kate?" Tami breathed, voice cracking on the name.

Kate — her sister — the mother of Sadie. The only person whose grief looked uglier and louder than mine ever did.

She shoved past two agents who weren't fast enough. "WHERE IS HE? WHERE IS THE THING WHO KILLED MY BABY?"

Not *who.*
What.

A fresh stab of nausea twisted through me.

Three more agents rushed in behind her. Someone yelled for a medic. Someone else radioed for a security lockdown. One agent tried to calm her while another tried to block her from charging deeper into the building.

She saw me.
And the world... narrowed.
"You!" she screeched.

Asher stepped in front of me so fast I didn't even register the motion until his shoulders blocked my view.

But Kate kept coming. Her eyes were wild — too wide. Too bright. Everything about her was trembling except her voice. That was razor-sharp.

"You share his blood," she spat. "Do you ever look in the mirror and see *him* looking back at you?"

A ripple of gasps and radio chatter crackled through the room. Agents moved closer — too fast — and Kate screamed again, raw and jagged.

"LET ME SEE HIM! He doesn't get to sit in some cushy room playing GOD while my daughter rots in the ground!"

She lunged.

Every agent reacted. Guns half-drawn. Someone shouted, "Ma'am, STOP!" Another yelled, "Hands where we can see them!"

Tanner put his hands up like surrendering to chaos. "Hey, let's all just breathe—"

But Kate grabbed the stapler off the check-in desk and swung it at the nearest agent like it was a blade.

Cooper cursed. "Holy— That's office-supplies-assault!"

The agent caught her wrist, but she bit *him*. Actually, bit him. He yelped as she clawed like a trapped animal.

Two more agents piled on, trying to wrestle her down, but her grief was a freaking superpower. She thrashed, shrieking — the kind of sound that makes your bones think about running away.

Tami sobbed. "Kate, please! STOP! I told you not to come! This isn't the way!"

Kate's eyes shot back to me — wild, feral.

"He took MY BABY. Why does he get to LIVE? WHY DOES HE GET TO BREATHE?"

Her voice broke — shattering — rising. "WHY IS HE STILL SMILING DOWN THERE AND SHE'S NOT?!"

She collapsed to her knees mid-fight, her body shaking while agents still clung to her like she might explode.

One last scream ripped through her throat:

"I WANT HIS LIFE!"

Asher put an arm behind me, holding me back.

Because my whole body had surged forward—the instinct to shield her, or stop her, or silence her, I didn't even know which—but I felt myself ready to move.

Chaos.

Noise.

Too much.

Radios were overtalking each other.

Keith yelled at everyone to give her space.

Cooper told Tanner to "not pick up ANYTHING she drops."

An agent called for restraints.

Someone shouted, "Close those doors! NOW!"

Kate's grief shook the air like thunder—shaking me.

And then—a deeper panic cut through the frenzy:

"Go! We have movement at the barn!"

The room exploded into action.

Agents sprinted. Orders barked. Doors slammed. The barn. The captive. The clock running out.

Asher turned my face toward him, forcing eye contact — grounding me, dragging me back from the spiral.

"I told you," he said quietly, voice vibrating with urgency, "you're nothing like him."

And God help me... seeing Kate like that — seeing her drown — made me realize I was still swimming.

Barely.

But enough.

Kate sobbed as agents pulled her toward a side door, her screams turning into broken sounds of a woman with nothing left.

Tami reached helplessly toward her sister, then toward Asher, torn clean in half. Keith wrapped an arm around her shoulders, steadying her like he'd practiced for years.

The waiting room emptied around us, turning into controlled chaos. Everyone rushing to save someone, Kate, would never get back.

I wiped at my face and realized I was shaking — adrenaline, fear, rage — all tangled.

"Asher," I breathed, "we have to go. We have to find her. We cannot let there be another Sadie."

He squeezed my hand. Hard. Looked into my eyes. "Let's go!"

And for the first time all day, nobody argued with me.

54

The Captive

I couldn't remember when I'd drunk the last drop from the water bottles The Wolf left for me. Hours? Days? Time felt soft and wrong, like something he'd kneaded in his hands until it lost all shape. The walls around me reminded me of the Bandon warehouse, but worse—like its ghost had followed me here. The damp cold wasn't just in the concrete; it was inside me, burrowed deep.

And the water—God, the water—kept coming.

What had begun as a drip had swollen into a thin, relentless stream, crawling across the floor with quiet determination. I knew it was ridiculous to think it could kill me, but my mind wouldn't listen; it whispered that the cold would seep into my veins, freeze me from the inside out, hollow me like all the others. The more it spread, the more certain I became that the room wasn't filling with water—I was.

The Itsy Bitsy spider crawled up the water spot,
Down came the rain and washed the spider out....

55
Nathan - The Wolf

T ime was what I had here.

Waiting. Watching. Breathing in the inevitability of everything I'd sewn into the fabric of these moments.

People like to pretend patience is a virtue—something noble, something earned.

But patience, to me, was simply a knife: dull when held by the wrong hands, lethal when wielded by mine.

I never pretended to be a patient man, never claimed such a trait, yet here I sat—heart steady, blood crusting on my chin, the coppery tang still warm across my tongue—and I felt nothing but the hum of anticipation. Waiting wasn't suffering. It was savoring.

Because the reward always makes the waiting worth it.

And something was coming.

I *felt* it.

A pressure in the air, a shifting of the current, the kind of instinct most people ignore because they never learned to trust the animal inside themselves. I trusted mine. I fed it. I listened to it breathe.

Besides Alexis hitting me, everything was going exactly as planned.

Oh, sweet Ladybug.

Her hands on me... her fury... the sharp, beautiful clarity in her eyes as she finally broke that line she swore she'd never cross.

A match to gasoline.
A song played backward.
A secret was finally whispered aloud.

The EMT dabbing the wound above my eye kept glancing at me like he expected me to flinch or wince or curse. As if pain meant anything. As if it hadn't always been anything more than a conversation I controlled.

He muttered something about swelling, about bruising, about stitches. His voice was little more than static. I only registered the pressure of the disinfectant swab, the sting that should've hurt, but instead felt like a reminder—she *touched me with intent*. Finally.

Ronny lingered in the corner like a misplaced shadow. He hadn't said a word since Alexis was here. He was pale, jaw clenched tight, fingers flexing against his thighs. He didn't need to speak for me to understand him; silence was often louder, more honest.

He didn't want to be here.

Good.

It made this even sweeter.

Ronny thought he'd been dragged along because he was "involved." The poor man had no imagination. He didn't realize his presence was selected, curated, and placed like a chess piece exactly where I needed it.

He was here because I wanted to look him in the eye when the truth finally crawled into the light. I wanted to watch the recoil, the flicker of realization, that moment when a man understands he never had control — not for a second.

He hadn't noticed my grin yet.

Most people avoided looking directly at me when I smiled. Instinct, maybe. Or fear. Or that bone-deep understanding that a smile doesn't always mean kindness. Sometimes it means *I know something you don't*.

The EMT pressed gauze to my cheek and wanted me to hold it there. Then I realized I was chained. He paused just long enough to resemble a mannequin I positioned. Unlike a mannequin, his fingers trembled.

"I'm not going to bite," I murmured, though biting had never been off the table.

He swallowed hard, staring at the expanding purple bruise blooming across my jaw.

I felt nothing except a flicker of laughter under my ribs. Alexis really had put her whole soul behind those swings.

Her rage was magnificent.

It made her so much more alive.

"You uh... might have a mild concussion," the EMT said carefully, like he expected me to lash out.

"Mild," I echoed. "How disappointing."

Ronny shifted but didn't speak.

He still wouldn't look at me.

The EMT leaned closer, pressing another wipe into the cut. "Just hold still, okay? I need to get the bleeding under control."

Bleeding.

Such a dramatic word for something so trivial.

He didn't understand that this blood meant nothing compared to what was coming.

I tilted my head just enough to see Ronny clearly. The man was unraveling quietly, little threads pulling loose at the seams. He kept darting his eyes to the door, to the window, to my face, back to the floor. Somewhere in him he was hoping Alexis would return. Or the FBI would move him. Or I would disappear.

Cowardice looks the same on every man.

"Tell me," I said casually. "Do you think she meant it?"

Ronny blinked. "Meant what?"

"That hit." I smiled wider. "She didn't hold back. Not even a little. I could feel her bones shake."

"You're sick," he muttered, but it lacked conviction. His voice trembled at the edges, thin as wet paper.

"You would know."

The EMT cleared his throat, very much wishing to be anywhere but here. He stepped back, wiping his gloves on a towel. "Okay, the bleeding is slowing. I'll bring a butterfly closure in a moment."

Before he could move, the door swung open so hard the hinges shrieked.

Two agents stood there, faces hard and urgent.

"EMT, we need you in the lobby. Now," the taller one said. "There's a woman—completely hysterical." His eyes shifted to me.

The EMT blinked, startled. "Is she armed?"

"No," the agent said, "but she fought the uniforms at the door. She's screaming for someone—" He cleared his throat.

My heart opened like a blooming wound.

Did someone want me—need me?

Ronny's head snapped up. "What woman?"

The agents ignored him.

The EMT looked conflicted, glancing at my half-cleaned face, then back at the doorway. "I—uh—should I finish with him first?"

"No," the agent barked. "We need you now."

I didn't know who was out there.

The possibilities tasted divine.

Another sheep the wolf could kill?

My grin spread—slow and wide, stretching the cut, sending a thin trickle of blood down my lip.

"I'll be fine," I said, waving the EMT off. "Go. Help the lady."

Lady.

How generous a word.

Ronny's chains jerked and rattled so abruptly his chair scraped the floor. "Nathan—who is it? What did you do?"

I leaned back, savoring the pressure of the chair against my spine. The hum inside me sharpened.

"What did I do?" I repeated softly.

I let the question hang. Let Ronny feel it sink into the room like a temperature drop.

Then I smiled—the kind of smile that never reached the eyes.

"I finished what you started."

Even though I had no clue who it was, I enjoyed his discomfort.

Was he afraid it was someone he knew?

Interesting.

The footsteps in the hall told me everything I needed to know.

Not who—not yet—but *why*.

Someone out there wasn't being dragged in; they were *charging* in. Someone with purpose. Someone who'd decided this was the hill they'd die on.

Ronny heard it too. His shoulders stiffened, fingers tightening around the cuff chain like it could keep him grounded.

"What now?" he whispered.

I didn't answer.

Because anticipation tastes better when it's left to simmer.

The door slammed open. Agents spilled into the room first, bracing themselves as if trying to hold back a storm.

And then they brought her in.

Kate.

She didn't need to search or orient herself.

She wasn't confused or overwhelmed.

She *came here for me.*

Her breath came sharp, but not from surprise — from the rage she'd carried for three years. Her coat hung off one shoulder, hair wild, knuckles bloodied from whatever she'd hit on her way in.

She didn't bother looking at Ronny first. She didn't look at the agents.

Her eyes found me instantly.

She froze — not in shock, but in confirmation.

Of course, he's here.

Of cours,e I found him.

Ronny jolted. "Kate? Oh god — Kate, why would you come here?"

She didn't acknowledge him.

"You think I wouldn't?" she spat. "The second they told me he was finally in custody, I got in my car. I've waited three years for this moment."

The lead agent stepped between us. "Kate, listen. You're allowed to speak to him for one reason only: to help us locate the current missing victim. That's the only reason we're permitting this at all."

Kate shoved his arm aside like he weighed nothing. "Don't pretend you're in control of this. I'm here because you failed Sadie. You failed all of us. And now you need me."

Her voice cracked on Sadie's name — seventeen years old, Alexis's friend, Finn's cousin.

The girl I killed in the cave.

Ronny paled. "Kate... please don't do this."

She finally looked at him — a furious, grief-sharpened stare.

"You shut your mouth, Ronny. I loved her—." Her voice broke. "He destroyed everything."

Then her eyes snapped back at me.

"I came for you, Nathan."

Ah.

There it was.

Not fear.

Not hesitation.

Purpose.

I felt my smile slowly unfurl.

"Say it again," I murmured.

The agent slammed his hand on the table. "Moore, one more violation of protocol and you're gagged."

Kate didn't flinch.

"You took my daughter," she said, her voice trembling like a fault line. "You took a seventeen-year-old girl. You took her into that cave and left her like trash. And you *smiled* about it."

Ronny folded into himself, guilt strangling him.

Kate stayed rigid.

Controlled.

Focused.

"I came here to make sure justice was served."

I tilted my head. "And the other girl?"

The agents stiffened.

Kate's jaw tightened. "You know where she is. You know where the woman is. I'm not leaving this room until you give me something."

"Then what will you give me?" I asked, genuinely curious.

Her chin lifted, trembling but resolute.

"Closure," she whispered.

The room stilled.

"You don't deserve forgiveness. You don't deserve peace."

She took a shaky breath. "But if you tell me where she is—I'll disappear. I'll never speak of you again. I'll let you rot without haunting me."

Poor, deluded woman.

She thought she understood leverage.

My smile deepened. "Oh, Kate," I said softly, leaning forward so the chain pulled taut, "you didn't come here for closure."

Her eyes flashed.

"You came here because ..." I lowered my voice to a razor's edge. "...you finally found the courage to look your monster in the eyes."

The agent snapped, "Moore, STOP talking—Kate, SIT DOWN—"

But Kate didn't sit.

She stepped forward.

Just one step.

And suddenly every agent in the room braced for violence...

Again.

I smiled.

This was such an exciting day.

56

Alexis

Chaos erupted.

Not the kind you brace for. Not clean or cinematic. This was messy, loud, human chaos—voices overlapping, boots slamming concrete, hands grabbing gear too fast, radios crackling with urgency that felt contagious. Floodlights snapped on, bleaching the night into harsh white shapes, and the roar of helicopter blades ripped through the air like something tearing free from its restraints.

Cooper was arguing—hard. His voice tangled with Lila's and the agent's, rising and falling in sharp bursts I couldn't fully track. It sounded like lecturing colliding with swearing, rules fighting emotion. I caught pieces—*protocol, civilians, liability*—but none of it stuck.

My name did.

Every time it cut through the noise, my stomach clenched tighter.

"Fine!" the agent barked. "We can only take one. Alexis."

The ground felt unstable beneath my feet.

He looked straight at me, like this decision had been waiting for me all along.

I shook my head immediately. "I don't want to go," I said, too fast. "I can stay here. I'll wait. I don't need to—"

He crossed the space between us, lowering his voice, grounding it. "Alexis. You can stay back until it's clear. That's true. But if this is someone you know... you might help us. You might recognize something we won't."

The words slipped under my skin.

If this is someone you know.

My chest tightened, breath turning shallow. Faces flickered through my mind—friends, classmates, people I'd lost touch with. Names I didn't want to say out loud.

I grabbed Asher's hand like I was afraid I'd float away without it. "I'll go."

He pulled me into him instantly, arms crushing, desperate. Kissed me hard, uneven, like he was trying to anchor both of us.

"Go," he whispered. "Just... come back."

Cooper and Tanner hugged me next—fast, fierce, like they didn't trust themselves to linger.

"You got this," Cooper muttered.

I nodded. I didn't feel like I did.

It's go time.

The helicopter lifted, the world shrinking beneath us, and my body buzzed with adrenaline while my thoughts spun wildly, scraping against each other. My heart wouldn't slow. My palms were damp.

Was I lucky to be here?

No.

Luck didn't stalk people like me.

Chaos had always known my name.

The agents spoke through the headsets in fragments—coordinates, confirmations, something about property ownership. One phrase cut through the static and lodged in my chest.

Animal Oasis.

Nathan had said it like it was nothing. Like it was gentle. Like it was safe.

The farm appeared slowly out of the dark, illuminated in pieces as the helicopter descended. Fences stretched wide, enclosing land that looked peaceful at first glance. A large barn slumped off to one side, its paint peeling. The farm-house stood farther back, dark windows watching.

Too quiet.

We hit the ground hard. Dust and grass kicked up as agents poured out, weapons raised, voices sharp with command. I stayed back, my pulse pounding so loudly I was sure everyone could hear it.

"Barn first!"

The barn doors groaned open.

I stepped closer—and stopped cold.

Nathan's van sat inside like it had been waiting.

The mannequins were bad enough—lined up, scattered, posed in ways that twisted my stomach—but it was what surrounded them that made my skin crawl.

Dog crates. Large ones. Small ones.

Stacked. Rusted. Some bent slightly out of shape.

Chains hung from beams overhead, heavy links clinking softly as the air shifted. Some trailed down to the floor, others looped through metal rings bolted into the walls. There were scratches on the concrete—long, frantic gouges that didn't belong to animals.

Food bowls sat overturned in corners, dried residue crusted along the edges. A faint smell clung to the space—wet fur, metal, something sour underneath.

This wasn't a barn.

It was containment.

My throat burned. I tasted bile.

"This is sick," someone whispered.

I backed away, shaking, my breath coming too fast. I didn't want to imagine how long this place had been used. How many times someone—or something—had been locked inside those crates, listening.

The energy shifted behind me.

"Check the house!"

"Search the perimeter!"

The word hit me like a punch.

I followed without meaning to, legs moving on autopilot. Agents circled the farmhouse, flashlights sweeping low.

Then—

"I've got something!"

A metal hatch, half-hidden by dirt and straw.

My stomach dropped.

The hatch screamed as it was pulled open, rust scraping metal. The smell rolled out immediately—stagnant water, mold, rot.

"Oh my God…"

A flashlight plunged downward.

Water filled the cellar.

Not all the way—but enough. Enough to make my vision blur, knees weak.

"She's in there!"

Time fractured.

"She's face down!"

"Call paramedics—now!"

I didn't think.

I ran.

My boots slipped on wet grass, lungs burning, heart hammering so hard it hurt. Someone shouted my name, but I didn't stop.

They pulled her up, water cascading off her body in heavy sheets. Chains clinked faintly as someone moved nearby. The cellar swallowed the sound again.

Her hair clung to her face. Her clothes were soaked, heavy. Mud streaked her skin.

Paramedics surged forward, hands moving fast—checking airway, pulse, responsiveness.

"She's alive," someone said. "Barely."

My knees buckled.

"No," I whispered. "Please…"

They rolled her slightly.

Just enough.

Her face turned—and something inside me shattered completely.

The world didn't spin.
It stopped.

Her face was pale, bruised, familiar in a way that hollowed me out. Recognition slammed into my chest so hard it stole my breath.

I stepped forward, voice cracking as the truth ripped through me.

"I know her."

57

The Captive

The water burned like acid in my throat. I was ready to leave this cruel world behind. I had no strength left to fight. Without The Wolf, I was nothing. My only purpose was to serve him, and without him, life had no meaning.

As I began to sink into Hell—where I knew I belonged—muffled voices bled in and out of my awareness, warped by the water forcing its way down my throat as my body convulsed. Light fractured the surface above me, a thin beam slicing through the dark. Tiny spiders were dragged under beside me, their fragile bodies swallowed whole before drifting lifelessly upward.

The voices grew louder as my starved, weight-lost body betrayed me and rose from the icy depths. I fought it, kicking, clawing, trying to force myself back down, desperate to sink again. It didn't matter. I closed my eyes and begged my broken body to give in to the damage it had taken.

But the water in my lungs refused to let me go.

I rolled onto my side and coughed violently, fire ripping through me with every expulsion and every desperate breath.

Then a voice cut through the pain.

"I know her."

My eyes snapped open. I reached for her, fingers trembling, the ragged red ribbon still cinched tight around my wrist.

Was she real?

58

Alexis

There was so much to observe at this moment. Too much. My mind tried to catalog every detail the way it always had—methodical, detached—because if I let myself *feel* any of it, I knew I would shatter.

The way her yellow fingernails curled inward, twisted unnaturally against skin that had gone gray and slack. They looked like they no longer belonged to a living body, more like something unearthed than rescued. A dull red ribbon was tightly wrapped around her wrist, frayed and darkened with age, the fibers stiff as if they'd absorbed more than water over the years. And her fingers—God, her fingers—bent at those familiar, knotted angles I remembered from childhood. The same hands that had grabbed too hard. The same hands that had yanked, slapped, and shoved.

Her three fingers.

The missing ones screamed louder than anything else.

I stared at the stumps where her ring and pinky fingers should have been. It wasn't clean. It wasn't healed correctly. The bone jutted out at an obscene angle, jagged and pale, like it had tried to escape the flesh and failed. Skin clung to it in ragged layers, angry and inflamed, the way dirt clings stubbornly to a tree root ripped from the ground. Nathan hadn't amputated them properly. Of course, he hadn't. He never did anything clean.

The pumpkin.

The memory hit like a blow to the chest. The bloody pumpkin. The way it smiled when I saw it on her blood-soaked bed. Like it was *necessary*. He had taken her finger and turned it into a symbol. A warning. A promise.

My throat locked up.

I tried to speak, but it felt like I was drowning, like my lungs were filled with icy water and regret. "M-m-m—" My jaw trembled violently. I swallowed, my body refusing to cooperate. "Mom?"

The word tasted wrong. It always had.

This couldn't be happening. She was alive. She had been alive the whole time. Nathan lied—but that wasn't the shocking part. Nathan *always* lied. The shocking part was that everyone believed him. The police. The media. The town. When he said he'd disposed of her body in the ocean, when he said she was gone, erased, fed to the dark, they nodded and closed the case. A neat ending for something that had never been neat.

And all this time—three and a half years—she had been breathing somewhere.

Enduring.

Suffering.

Her eyelids fluttered weakly, lashes clumped together with salt and grime. They opened for half a second, unfocused, then slid shut again. No recognition. No reaction. Her hand slipped from where it had been loosely resting and hit the ground with a dull thud.

A paramedic shouted, "We're losing her!"

Everything fractured after that.

Hands everywhere. Voices overlapping. Someone barked orders while another counted compressions. CPR began, aggressive and desperate, ribs compressing beneath bruised skin. I stood frozen, unable to move, unable to breathe, my limbs heavy and useless like they didn't belong to me anymore.

I don't remember being pulled away, but suddenly I was being guided—no, dragged—toward an SUV. My feet moved without my permission. My body obeyed strangers better than it obeyed me. I watched from a distance as they loaded her onto a gurney. Tubes. Masks. Wires. She looked even smaller, strapped down, swallowed by medical equipment.

They must have stabilized her, because moments later she was rushed to the helicopter.

I stood outside the vehicle, numb, as dawn bled into the sky. Pink and soft and cruelly beautiful. The wind whipped my hair across my face as the helicopter blades began to spin, the sound deafening. I watched it rise slowly, carrying her away from me again.

Three and a half years.

That number repeated in my head like a broken record.

Three and a half years, Nathan kept her, caged her.

Alive.

Captive.

The realization hollowed me out. I couldn't comprehend it. Not fully. My brain refused to wrap itself around the idea that while I was grieving, while I was surviving, while I was trying to stitch myself back together, she had been locked away somewhere dark. Starved. Forgotten. Tortured. Left to rot in his care.

He hadn't killed her.

He'd kept her.

The thought made my skin crawl.

I imagined the conditions without trying to—and failed. I knew Nathan. I knew how he treated things he considered broken. He would have fed her just enough to keep her breathing. Water when he remembered. Food, when it amused him. Medical care? Never. Pain was part of the punishment. Neglect was the point.

He would have let infections fester. Bones heal wrong. Wounds stay open. He would have watched her deteriorate and called it justice.

And she survived it.

Why?

The question gnawed at me. Why keep her alive? Why not finish it? Nathan was meticulous when it came to his games. Purposeful. Nothing he did was random.

Then another realization crept in, colder than the water had been.

She had been alive this whole time... and she never tried to come back.

The guilt twisted instantly, sharp and cruel. What kind of thought was that? What kind of daughter thinks that? But the thought was already there, festering. She had survived captivity, abuse, starvation—yet she had never once reached out.

The memories began flooding in without warning.

Her voice—sharp and dismissive. Always irritated, tired, and angry. The way she'd look through me instead of at me. The way affection felt, conditional and transactional. Love was given only when I performed correctly—when I behaved and didn't inconvenience her.

The neglect had been subtle enough to hide behind excuses. She worked too much. She was stressed. She was overwhelmed. But neglect still starves, even when it wears a polite mask.

Then there was the abuse.

. The words she used—small, precise cuts meant to make me shrink. To remind me, I was unwanted by her. But wanted by men. Her men. A burden. Too much.

I had learned early how to disappear.

And now here she was, barely recognizable. The woman who had once towered over me was reduced to bones and gray skin. Her face—God, her face—had changed so drastically I almost couldn't recognize her. Cheeks hollowed out. Lips cracked and colorless. Hair was thin, tangled, and matted to her scalp. She looked older. Harder. Like captivity had stripped away whatever softness she'd once possessed.

Or maybe it had simply revealed what was always there.

I didn't know how to feel.

Relief tangled with resentment. Shock collided with rage. Pity fought disgust. Love—if that's what it was—curled weakly in the corner of my chest, uncertain and afraid to speak up.

She had been alive.

And I had mourned her.

I had buried her without a body. Had screamed into pillows. Had cried myself raw over the idea that she'd died alone and afraid. All the while, she *was* alone and afraid—but breathing. Enduring horrors I couldn't imagine.

The confusion was suffocating.

Memories kept crashing into me—unwanted, vivid, relentless. Her yelling. Her silence. The way she never defended me. The way she looked the other way when things went wrong. The way she told me to stop being dramatic. To stop crying. To toughen up.

And yet—she was still my mother.

The helicopter disappeared into the sky, leaving behind an unbearable quiet. The sunrise felt obscene. Like the world was celebrating something I didn't understand.

I stood there long after it was gone, staring at the empty space it had occupied, my mind unraveling thread by thread.

Nathan had taken so much from me.

But somehow, impossibly, he hadn't taken her life.

And that—more than anything—terrified me.

59
Alexis

Anger doesn't show up like it does in movies. It doesn't always slam doors or throw punches or scream itself hoarse.

Sometimes it's quieter.

Sometimes it's the way your brain starts counting—seconds, breaths, footsteps—because if you stop counting, you'll start feeling, and if you start feeling, you'll fall apart in a hospital hallway, with strangers watching like you're the next trauma story on their shift.

The hospital reeked of bleach and lingering panic—an odor that embeds itself into the walls and never entirely dissipates, no matter how often the floors are scrubbed until they shine.

"She's stable for now."

That was the phrase they kept giving me, as if it were supposed to be comforting.

Stable for now.

As if my mother were a weather pattern.

As if she weren't a barely alive body pulled from the water, with a jagged stump where her ring finger should've been.

The ribbon around her wrist was one of my old high school track ribbons.

She must remember.

Asher stood close enough that I could feel his heat without him touching me. He knew better than to crowd me or let me drift too far into my own head. Every so often, his hand brushed the small of my back, light and grounding, like a reminder: You're here. You're not drowning anymore.

Cooper paced. Not anxious pacing—Cooper doesn't do "anxious" like a normal person. His pacing was purposeful, as if he were searching the hallway for a target he could legally destroy. His jaw tightened every time a nurse passed, as if he wanted the world to be accountable for something it didn't even understand.

Tanner leaned against the wall with his arms crossed, watching me like I was a bomb he was trying to keep from detonating. He was quieter than usual, which told me he was doing math in his head—calculating what to say, what not to say, and how far I was from breaking.

Keith and Tami arrived together, but they didn't feel like they were.

Keith's face was pale, his eyes bloodshot, as if he'd been rubbing them raw. He looked like a man forced to remember parts of himself he'd rather keep buried. Tami's expression was harder—tight mouth, sharp eyes, posture like a blade.

And behind all of them, there was the unspoken truth none of us could ignore:

Nicole was alive.

My mother.

The woman the world had mourned.

The woman I had mourned even when I hated her.

The woman Nathan had kept for three and a half years, like a trophy he could put in a box and pull out whenever he wanted to watch someone bleed.

Tami was the first one to say it out loud.

"She's alive," she whispered, as if the words themselves might shatter if spoken at full volume.

I didn't answer. My throat had been too tight for hours. Like the hospital air was made of wire and every inhale cut me open.

Asher's hand slid into mine. He didn't squeeze. He didn't try to force comfort into me. He just held on—steady, quiet, real.

Cooper stopped pacing. "Where is she?" he asked, voice low, controlled.

"In surgery?" Tanner said, but it sounded like a question more than an answer. He looked at me. "Or ICU?"

"ICU," I managed. My voice sounded off, like it belonged to someone else. "They're—" I swallowed. "They're trying to stabilize her."

Stable for now.

Keith's eyes flicked away, as if he couldn't bear to picture what "stabilize" meant for someone who had been kept like that for years.

Tami took a step closer to me. Her gaze moved over my face, my damp hair, the faint bruising still rising on my throat from my fingertips clawing from stress. Then her eyes softened for half a second.

"You shouldn't have had to see her like that," she said.

I almost laughed, but it would've come out jagged. "I shouldn't have had to see a lot of things."

Her mouth tightened. She nodded once, as if she agreed but didn't want to admit it too loudly.

Keith's hands fidgeted at his sides, a nervous tell that reminded me of Luke. He didn't do that often. Keith was the steady one. The anchor. The man who could stare into darkness and not blink, forced to by his line of work.

But this—this wasn't an enemy outside us.

This was history crawling out of its grave.

Tami's gaze drifted to the far end of the hall, where a security guard stood by the double doors. "Are they letting anyone in?"

"No," Cooper said. "They're keeping her locked down."

I knew what he meant, but it still felt off. Locked down. Like she was evidence. Like she wasn't a person. Like she hadn't been a prisoner for years and wasn't now being guarded like a high-value asset.

I rubbed my wrist without realizing it, my fingers brushing phantom pressure where that ribbon had been on her.

Tanner shifted. "Alexis," he said carefully, "talk to us."

I stared at the floor. The tiles were patterned in a way that made my eyes want to follow the lines. Easy. Safe. Controlled.

"Talk about what?" I asked. "The fact that she's alive? The fact that she's been alive all this time while everyone believed she was dead? The fact that Nathan—"

My voice cracked when I said his name, and my hands balled into fists.

Asher tightened his grip on my fingers, just enough to remind me I wasn't alone.

Cooper's face darkened. "We're not letting him touch her again," he said, as if it were a vow carved in stone.

Tami let out a shaky breath. Then, quietly, she said, "I don't know how I'm supposed to feel."

None of us answered because if she said more, she might shatter.

I looked at her. Really looked. "How *are* you supposed to feel?"

Her eyes flashed, wet and furious. "She's your mother," she snapped. "And she—" She stopped, swallowing hard. Her voice dropped to something rougher. "She's Nicole."

There it was.

Not "your mom."

Nicole.

A name that carried years of baggage, even in the mouths of those outside her family.

Tami rubbed her arms as if she were cold. "Part of me wants her alive," she admitted. "Part of me wants her to... to be gone. Because then all of this could be over."

Keith's head dipped as if he understood too well. Then he looked up, his eyes haunted. "It's not going to be over," he murmured. "Not now."

My chest tightened. "Do you think I don't know that?"

Tanner stepped forward before my anger could find a new target. "Alexis, we're here for you," he said, voice firmer now. "Look at me."

I did, reluctantly. His eyes were steady.

"Name five things you can see," he said, sounding like Keith.

I stared at him like he'd lost his mind.

"Do it," Asher added softly, not pushing, just guiding.

I wanted to scream that I wasn't a child. That I didn't need tricks. That I needed Nathan's throat in my hands. But the truth was that my vision was tunneling, my lungs were forgetting how to work, and I wanted to purge.

So I did it.

"The... the blue sign," I said, voice thin. "The clock. The vending machine." My gaze snapped to Cooper. "Cooper's pacing." And then I saw it—Keith's wedding ring catching the fluorescent light. "Keith's ring."

Tami's face twitched at that, like the word ring had dragged her somewhere else.

"Good," Tanner said. "Four things you can feel."

"My... shoes." I swallowed. "The floor through them." I flexed my fingers in Asher's hand. "Your hand." My voice came out smaller. "My heartbeat."

Asher's thumb brushed my knuckles like a reward.

Cooper exhaled hard, frustration bleeding out of him. "We need to talk to Ronny," he said.

The name hit the air like a dropped plate.

Ronny.

Nathan's father.

My father.

The man with a face that looked like mine if you held it up to a mirror and squinted.

Tami's expression shifted. "How do you think he'll take the news?"

I cleared my throat. "I don't know," I said.

Keith's voice was quiet. "He loved her."

I felt my jaw tighten. "Did he, truly?"

Tanner's eyes flicked to me. "Alexis..."

"What?" I snapped. "He's caused this, whether he wants to be accountable or not."

Asher's grip tightened again—not restrictive, just steady. A tether.

Keith cleared his throat. "You're going to see Nathan and Ronny," he said. Not a question.

I stared at him. "Yes."

Tami's eyes widened. "Why would you—"

"Because I need to," I cut in. "Because he did this, they did this. Because they're still breathing, I'm done letting them dictate the story from inside a cage."

Cooper took a step closer to me. "We go with you."

I shook my head. "No."

Tanner's brows lifted. "Alexis—"

"I said no." My voice came out colder than I meant. "This is mine."

Asher didn't argue. He just asked, "Do you want me outside the door?"

My throat tightened again. I nodded once.

Tami studied me like she was trying to decide whether to slap me or hug me. With Tami, it could be either. "Don't let him get inside your head," she said finally, voice low.

I almost smiled. Almost.

"It's too late for that," I said. "He built a condo there years ago."

An agent escorted me through the tunnels under the hospital that led to FBI headquarters. Tanner walked on my other side like a shadow. Asher stayed back as we'd agreed, but I felt him even when he wasn't touching me.

When the door opened, the air inside changed. It smelled less like disinfectant and more like metal and sweat and something rotten you couldn't scrub out of a room, no matter how hard you tried.

Ronny had been moved out.

Nathan sat still, chained to his table, wrists cuffed, ankles secured. He looked too calm. Too put together. As if the world hadn't just cracked open.

His eyes lifted to mine, and his mouth curved slowly.

The smile.

It made my skin crawl.

"Alexis," he murmured. "You look... resurrected."

I didn't sit.

I stood across from him, my bruised hands clenched at my sides. "You kept her alive."

His eyes flickered—satisfaction, not surprise.

"Yes," he said. "I did."

My lungs forgot how to work for a second.

"You let us believe she was dead," I said, my voice trembling even as I tried to keep it sharp. "You let the world believe she was dead. You let me believe—"

"I let you grieve," he corrected, tone gentle like he was doing me a favor. "Grief builds character."

My body moved before my brain caught up. I surged forward, but Agent Fields' hand snapped out and stopped me, firm and quick. The agent shifted closer.

Nathan laughed—low and pleased.

"Still reactive," he said, his bruised eye twitched. "I always loved that about you."

I leaned forward as far as I could without losing control. "Why?"

His smile sharpened. "Because death would have been mercy," he said. "And mercy was never the point."

I swallowed, nauseated. "This wasn't about her."

Nathan's eyes glittered. "No," he said softly. "It wasn't."

My stomach dropped.

"It's about Ronny."

The name hung between us.

Nathan's mouth twitched like he'd been waiting for me to say it. "Oh," he purred. "You *are* learning."

The door behind me opened.

And suddenly the air felt heavier, like the room itself didn't want what was about to happen.

Ronny stepped in, chained and escorted by Lila and another agent.

He looked like he hadn't slept. His face was drawn, eyes rimmed red, the kind of exhaustion that doesn't come from lack of rest but from carrying something rotten in your chest for decades.

Behind him were Cooper and Keith standing next to Asher and Tanner. They gave me matching, tight smiles and Asher mouthed *'I love you'*.

Ronny's gaze landed on Nathan.

Nathan's grin widened like a wound reopening.

"Dad," he said, voice sweet. "Right on time."

Ronny didn't speak. His jaw flexed like he was grinding his teeth down to nothing.

Nathan leaned back, chains clinking softly. "Do you know how hard it is to keep a secret for three and a half years?"

Ronny's eyes narrowed as the agents secured him to a chair. "What are you talking about?"

Nathan looked at me, then back at Ronny. "Tell him," he said.

My throat constricted. I was reluctant to be the one. I didn't want to give Nathan the knife and assist him in aiming it. However, if Nathan brought it up, he would turn it into a performance. And we were his mannequins.

"She's alive," I said.

Ronny blinked. Once. Twice.

"What?" His voice cracked like something inside him snapped.

"My mother," I said. "Nicole. She's alive."

The color drained from his face so fast it made my skin prickle. His arms jerked against the chains, hands gripping the chair like he needed it to keep him grounded.

"That's not possible," he whispered. "He said—"

"I said many things," Nathan interrupted smoothly. "You believed the one that hurt you the most."

Ronny's eyes flashed as anger finally surfaced. "You killed her," he shouted. "You told us you—"

"I told you what you deserved," Nathan snapped, his tone cutting now. "Just like she did."

I watched Ronny's throat bob as he swallowed. "Where is she?"

Nathan's smile returned, calmer, satisfied. "Safe," he said. "For now."

My stomach rolled. The way he said it—like she was still his property.

"This is why you wanted me here," Ronny said slowly, voice hollowing out. "To watch me—"

Nathan leaned forward as far as the chains allowed. "To watch you realize," he said, "that you don't get to escape what you did."

Ronny's eyes narrowed. "What I did?"

Nathan's gaze sharpened into something colder than hate. "You remember what you did to my mother, your wife?" he asked.

The room went still.

Ronny flinched.

"Do you remember how she cried?" Nathan continued softly. "How she begged? How Nicole watched? How you stood there and did nothing?"

I felt my chest tighten. My heart wasn't beating right. It was stumbling.

Ronny's voice came out strained. "That's not—"

"You don't get to rewrite it," Nathan snapped. "You don't get absolution."

Lila and the other agent looked at one another.

Ronny's shoulders sagged. "I was stupid," he whispered. "I didn't know—"

"You knew enough," Nathan said. "Enough to think you could get away with it."

I tasted metal. I didn't know if it was memory or rage.

Nathan's mouth curved again, cruel and satisfied. "So I took something from you," he said. "I took the woman you loved. I kept her breathing long enough to matter."

Ronny's face crumpled, just slightly. "You used her."

Nathan's eyes glittered. "Yes," he said. "And I used you."

Then he turned his gaze to me like he was admiring his work.

"You were part of her," he said, almost casually. "That needed to be destroyed."

Tami's voice cut in from behind the door—she must've been just outside, listening, unable to stay away. "Nathan!" she snapped. "You did *what*?"

Nathan's smile widened at the sound of her anger, too. Like outrage was dessert.

Ronny jerked his head forward and puked into his lap, expelling the weight of a past he'd avoided naming.

And I—God help me—I felt nothing for him.

Not comfort. Not pity. Not even satisfaction.

Just the cold, sharp understanding that betrayal isn't always a stranger's knife.

Sometimes it's your own blood, handing it over.

Nathan's eyes stayed on Ronny, savoring every tremor. "This is the ultimate betrayal," he said softly, almost reverently. "You took my mother from me. So, I took the love of your life away. And you'll see her die."

Ronny's head lifted, eyes wet, voice hoarse. "Nicole didn't kill your mother."

Nathan's smile never left. "Didn't she?" he murmured. "I saw it. And your own neglect shaped me this way."

My stomach dropped through the floor.

Because that word—neglect—hit differently when the subject was Nicole.

Tami's voice outside the door sounded cracked now. "She's alive," she whispered again, but this time it didn't sound like hope. It sounded like fear.

I spoke quietly, as if I were trying to keep myself from exploding. "Nathan, why keep her alive? Why not end it?"

Nathan looked at me as if the question were childish.

"Because ending it would've been... simple," he said. "And I am not a simple man."

My voice was venomous. "You kept her suffering to punish Ronny."

Nathan's eyes flashed to Ronny. "Yes."

"And me," I added. "You did it to punish me too."

Nathan's gaze slid back to me. "You needed to learn," he said.

I felt my hands shaking and I gripped the table.

"Learn what?" I asked, voice low and dangerous.

Nathan's smile softened into something almost tender, which was somehow worse. "That monsters don't always come from the dark," he said. "Sometimes they raise you."

I went still.

Nicole's unkindness flashed through my mind—her sharp words, her cold eyes, the way her attention always felt like a spotlight I was failing under. Her neglect wasn't new. Her cruelty wasn't a surprise. But hearing Nathan say it like that—like he was validating it—made my stomach twist.

Tami burst into the doorway then, unable to stay outside. Keith caught her elbow like he was afraid she'd charge. Her eyes were wild.

"You kept her alive," she said, voice shaking. "You kept Nicole alive for—"

Nathan's grin widened. "Hello, Tami."

"Don't," she snapped. "Don't say my name like you know me."

Nathan tilted his head. "But I do know you," he said. "I know all of you. Keith's little secrets. Ronny's guilt. Tami's rage. Alexis's—" his gaze flicked to me "—need to be loved by people who don't know how."

Keith stiffened. "Leave him out of this," Tami snapped, but it was too late.

Nathan's eyes slid to Keith, predatory. "The affair," he murmured. "Years ago. Before Alexis was born."

Keith's face went blank—too controlled. Too practiced.

Tami's breath hitched like she'd been punched in the ribs. That old wound again. The one she pretended didn't still bleed.

Nathan smiled like he'd just flicked a bruise. "All of you keep pretending you're better than me," he said. "But you're not. You just hide your rot better."

Keith's voice was low, steady, and dangerous. "That has nothing to do with this."

Nathan's smile sharpened. "Everything has to do with everything," he said. "That's the point."

Tami's eyes glittered with tears she didn't let fall. "I wanted her alive," she whispered, voice breaking. "I did. I wanted you to be wrong."

Then her mouth hardened. "But I didn't want her alive like *that*."

Nathan's eyes brightened, pleased. "Mixed feelings," he murmured. "How human of you."

Cooper took a step forward, but the agents shifted.

Tanner's voice cut through, firm. "Alexis, breathe."

I realized I wasn't.

My lungs were locked. My vision was narrowing again. My body wanted to tip into the same cold dark the water had offered me.

Asher's voice came from the hall—steady, grounding, like a rope thrown into a pit. "Alexis. Look at me."

I turned my head just enough to see him through the open doorway. He didn't come in. He just held my gaze.

"Five things," he said quietly.

My throat bobbed. "The table," I forced out. "The cuffs. The light. Tanner's hand. Nathan's... mouth."

Nathan chuckled.

"Four things you can feel," Asher prompted.

"My... nails in my palms." I swallowed. "My heartbeat. The air. The floor."

"Good," Asher said softly. "Stay here with us."

With *us*.

Not with Nathan.

Not with the past.

Not with Nicole drowning in a hospital bed.

Ronny's voice cracked. "Where is she?"

Nathan turned back to him, satisfied again. "In the hospital," he said. "Being cared for by people who don't hate her."

Ronny flinched like he'd been slapped.

"Because I'm generous," Nathan added. "I wanted her to live long enough for you to see her."

My stomach lurched.

"This is the ultimate betrayal," I whispered, more to myself than anyone. "You kept her like a weapon."

Nathan's eyes met mine. "Yes," he said. "And it worked."

I felt something inside me go frighteningly quiet. Not numb. Not calm.

Focused.

Tanner sensed it. His hand moved closer to my elbow. "Alexis," he warned under his breath.

I didn't take my eyes off Nathan. "You think you won," I said.

Nathan's smile didn't falter. "I don't think," he replied softly. "I know."

I leaned forward, just enough. "You kept her alive to punish Ronny," I said, voice low. "You used me as collateral. You used her as a trophy. And you're sitting there like you're proud of it."

Nathan's gaze glittered. "I am proud," he said. "Because you're all finally looking at what you are."

Cooper's voice was a growl. "We're done here."

The agents moved in. Tanner guided me back a step. Keith caught Tami as she swayed, her face pale, eyes furious and shattered all at once. Ronny stayed frozen, staring at Nathan like the truth had finally burned through his skin.

As they stood Nathan up, chains rattling, he turned his head slightly toward me.

"Tell my pet I said hello," he murmured.

I didn't respond.

Because if I opened my mouth, I might say something that would turn me into him.

And the terrifying part?

At that moment, I understood why monsters are made.

Not because they're born wrong.

But because someone keeps shoving them into pain until pain is the only language left.

Outside the room, the hallway hit us like a slap of cold air.

Tami ripped her arm out of Keith's hold, pacing three steps before she spun back, eyes blazing. "He kept her alive for three and a half years," she said, her voice shaking. "Three and a half—"

Keith's voice was calm, but his face was strained. "I know."

Tami's laugh was ugly. "Do you? Because all I can think is—" She stopped, swallowing, eyes glassy. "What if she wakes up and she's still Nicole?"

No one answered.

Because we all knew what she meant.

Nicole being alive didn't automatically mean Nicole was *safe*. Or kind. Or changed. Nicole being alive meant the past wasn't past. It meant old wounds were going to reopen, and some of them would get infected.

Cooper stepped close to me, voice lowered. "Alexis, you don't have to do this alone."

I looked at him. "I've been doing it alone," I said softly. "My whole life."

Tanner's gaze softened, but he kept his voice practical. "We're going back to the ICU," he said. "We're getting updates. Then we're locking down every detail Nathan gave us, and we're making sure he never gets near her again."

Asher stepped in closer now, finally breaking the distance. His hand touched my shoulder, gentle but firm. "You did good," he murmured.

I almost laughed again. "Did I?"

He met my eyes. "You didn't drown in him," he said. "That's a win."

Keith cleared his throat. "Ronny," he said.

Ronny hadn't moved after the agents escorted him out of the room and had him stand against the wall. He looked like a man who'd been hollowed out and left standing.

"This was about you," Keith said quietly. Not cruel. Just the truth.

Ronny nodded once, barely.

"I know," he whispered.

Tami's eyes flashed. "You knew?"

Keith's jaw tightened—an old argument, a familiar fracture.

Nathan had done that too.

"Yes, I think I've always known something was to come from killing my wife, letting Nicole kill her. I didn't want to see, admit to my own son unraveling was because I had shaped him into this monster."

He'd thrown truth like a grenade and watched us scramble to pick up the pieces.

I stared down the tunnel toward the hospital, toward the woman who was my mother, whether I wanted her to be or not.

"She's alive," I whispered.

Asher's hand squeezed my shoulder once. "And you're here," he said. "You're still here."

I swallowed hard, forcing air into lungs that still wanted to lock.

Nathan wanted Ronny to watch.

He wanted Nicole's survival shoved into Ronny's face like punishment for sins that had never fully been confessed.

He wanted me to fracture.

He wanted Tami and Keith to bleed old pain again.

He wanted Asher, Cooper, and Tanner to feel helpless.

He wanted all of us to remember that he could still reach into our lives and twist.

And the worst part?

For one awful moment in that room, he did.

But not forever.

Not if I had anything to do with it.

I lifted my chin, feeling the anger settle into something steadier—something sharper than rage.

Resolve.

"Take me back to her," I said.

And this time, when we walked, we walked together.

60
Alexis

The ICU didn't feel like a place where people woke up. It felt like purgatory—plastic and salt, a sterile waiting room between dimensions where bodies negotiated with the universe in hisses and clicks. Here, life wasn't a right. It was a monitored privilege, rented by the hour and paid for in data. The air was scrubbed of anything human, leaving ozone and bleach to coat the back of my throat like powdered glass.

The ventilator sighed in a steady, synthetic rhythm. It vibrated in my teeth—a reminder that the air Nicole breathed wasn't hers. It was borrowed from a machine that didn't know her name.

Everything here was borrowed.

Monitors blinked jagged neon green. The machines were stable. The people weren't.

Nicole lay in the bed like something dredged from a shipwreck.

My mother. Alive.

But softened. Blurred. Her once beautiful ebony hair now a rats nest of black with gray. Her skin was translucent. Bruises bloomed across her arms in plum and yellow and green—stories still trapped inside her body. IV lines pierced her hands. Fluid dripped in a maddening rhythm. Liquid roots—trying to keep a fallen tree upright.

The machines didn't care who she'd been. To them, she was pressure. Voltage. Numbers.

I stood just inside the doorway, my shoes heavy. The floor felt tilted, like it wanted to slide me toward her. Asher stayed close behind me. He didn't touch me, but I felt his warmth at my back—the only warm thing in the building.

In the corner, Ronny sat shackled to a bolted chair.

And that was wrong.

He shouldn't have been here.

He should have been in a jail cell. Concrete walls. Steel door. No windows. No access to her. No access to me.

The metallic clink of his chains cut through the ventilator's rhythm every time he shifted. He smelled like intake—lye soap and old sweat and damp denim. His shoulders sagged like gravity had singled him out.

But chains didn't make him harmless.

They didn't make him forgiven.

They didn't make him trustworthy.

Why was he here?

To witness? To absolve himself? To watch the damage finish unfolding?

A ghost in chains was still a ghost.

The nurse spoke softly. "She's been in and out. Disorientation is expected. Trauma response. She may say things that don't make sense."

I thought of Nicole's voice from childhood—sharp, unyielding. *Don't be dramatic. Stand up straight.*

Then her eyelids fluttered.

The monitor snapped into frantic beeping. Her eyes flew open, pupils blown wide. Panic detonated. She fought the ventilator.

"No," she rasped.

Her gaze locked onto mine.

I waited for recognition.

Instead, terror.

"It's okay," I said, stepping forward. "Mom. You're safe. You're in the hospital."

She shook her head violently. "I'll be good. I won't fight. Just don't—don't take anything else. Please, Wolf—"

Wolf?

"It's me. Alexis. Your daughter."

Her eyes flicked to her left hand—to the blunt, missing stumps. She didn't scream with her throat. She screamed with something deeper.

Then her face hardened.

"It's your fault!"

She launched off the bed—yanking the tubes out of her arms and off her face—with feral strength I didn't think it was possible for her to have. We hit the floor. Her nails raked across my face. She tore at my hair. Pain burst white-hot behind my eyes.

"If you had just died, he would have loved me!" she shrieked. "You were always his favorite!"

Security bust through the door and yanked her off of me and strapped her to the bed.

Asher was at my side instantly. "We need a nurse!"

My fingers came away slick with blood and hair.

Nicole sagged against the restraints. "He kept me alive," she rasped. "Kept me useful."

"For what?" Cooper growled.

Her eyes locked on mine.

"You. His ladybug. I see it now. He said you understood the art. You had his blood. His eyes."

She knew.

"You lived. I didn't. You walked in the sun while I rotted in dirt. I hate you for it."

The words hurt more than the scratches.

Then her gaze drifted—until it landed on Ronny.

Recognition flared.

"You," she hissed.

Ronny slowly lifted his head. The chains echoed in the room.

"You didn't love him," she spat.

My stomach dropped.

She wasn't wrong.

Ronny shouldn't have let her convince him to kill his wife.

Ronny shouldn't have chosen her.

Ronny should have chosen Nathan. Me.

Instead, he was here. Shackled. Watching.

"Stop," he whispered.

Now he was quiet.

Now.

Nicole jerked her head toward me. "Look at her. Just like him."

"That's not true," I said, but it sounded thin.

"You lived. I didn't."

Then exhaustion hollowed her out.

"Your hair," she murmured suddenly. "You hated brushing it."

The memory cracked through me—lavender shampoo, sunlight on the kitchen table.

"I did."

"You cried," she whispered.

"I still do."

Her eyes filled. "In the dark, when I closed my eyes I saw your face, your green eyes. But I forgot who you were to me. You're real?" she asked faintly.

"I'm real."

Sedation pulled her under.

"I wasn't kind," she breathed.

"I know."

"I was cruel. I thought if I broke you first, he couldn't use you."

Silence thickened.

"I thought I was making you strong. Teaching you to disappear." A shallow breath. "But you can't disappear without losing yourself."

Tears slid down my face.

Her eyes opened once more—clear, cutting.

"You disappeared, Alexis. Right into him. You're his best work."

My grip on Asher tightened. "I survived him. I'm not his."

The light left her eyes. The ventilator resumed its steady, borrowed rhythm.

"She's sleeping," the nurse murmured.

No one moved.

Tami sobbed into Keith's shoulder. Cooper stared at the city lights. Tanner stood guard at the door.

Ronny bowed his head again, chains clinking softly.

He should have been in a cell.

Not here.

Not breathing the same air.

Not watching me bleed.

Asher wrapped his arms around me. Solid. Warm. Real. I buried my face in his chest.

I didn't fight it.

Because survival isn't healing. Being alive doesn't absolve what you did to stay that way. And family doesn't stop being a loaded gun just because the trigger finger is restrained.

Nicole slept.

Ronny remained.

And in the silence between the ventilator's breaths, the past stayed exactly where it had always been—

Close.

EPILOGUE

Alexis

The Cedar Crest Recovery Center didn't smell like the ICU's sterile bleach and ozone. It carried lavender-scented floor wax, stale bread, and the heavy, earthy weight of a Texas afternoon baking the limestone walls. It was a softer misery—the kind that didn't scream with monitors but whispered in the shuffle of rubber-soled slippers and the steady thunk of magnetic locks.

It had been months. Months of Austin sun trying to burn the gray nursery rhymes from my skin. Months of failing.

I walked the long, sun-drenched hallway, my boots echoing like gunshots against polished linoleum. Each window framed cedar trees and scorched grass—a brutal contrast to the Oregon nightmares that still snapped me awake at 3:00 a.m.

Asher waited in the lobby, perched on one of those stiff mid-century chairs designed to discourage comfort. He always offered to walk me back—to be the shield between me and the wreckage of my DNA. I always said no. This was a ghost I had to face alone.

My skin felt too tight. My heart battered my ribs. Every breath carried the phantom weight of the cellar, as if the oxygen itself were too heavy to lift.

Nicole sat in the sunroom, flooded with light yet somehow eclipsed. Wire mesh sliced the blue Hill Country sky into gray diamonds. A knitted shawl draped her shoulders despite the eighty-degree heat. She looked smaller than she had in the ICU—shrunken, as if trauma were acid slowly hollowing her from the inside out.

Her left hand rested in her lap, the gloved fingers ending in a blunt absence I could feel like a high-frequency ring in the room. The other hand stroked a black cat sitting on her lap. I was surprised they allowed her to have it, but they said it helped her stay calm.

The cat's name was Shadow, apparently one she had when Nathan hid inside an animal hospital.

Her expression was soft and she seemed miles away in her own thoughts.

"You came," she said. Her voice was thin and brittle.

"I said I would." I sat across from her. The plastic chair was cold against my back.

She leaned forward and handed me Shadow; she hissed then curled up on my lap. I pet her soft fur and understand why it brought her comfort.

She watched a lizard dart along the windowsill. "I dream about the concrete," she whispered. "Did I tell you? It wasn't just a floor, the Oregon-cold. The chains had teeth and tore at my skin. I couldn't move. I felt like nothing, but to him, I was his."

I let her speak. This was how she survived now—purging the poison one drop at a time.

"The Bandon warehouse," she continued, her eyes glazing over. "The ocean smell—salty, rotten. Nathan took care of me. Made sure I stayed alive. He loved me."

Her shawl slipped, revealing her protruding bones through her translucent skin.

"He took my fingers before leaving Ventura. Said I didn't need it to remember how to be a mother. Or a wife." Her mouth trembled. "The clippers were dull. The crunch of bone—he couldn't cut through. I still hear it when I snap a pencil. Then he drugged me. The needle was mercy. I prayed the dark would swallow me."

Bile burned my throat.

"The boat ride," she said faintly. "Waking to the world tilting. Pacific spray like needles. Diesel and salt. I'd see him at the rail, talking to himself. Or to me. I couldn't tell."

She looked at me then, eyes red-rimmed and raw.

"He beat me for killing his mother. Said every bruise was a debt. That Ronny and I made him into this. He wanted a white fence, Alexis. Not a hunting ground."

The room felt airless. She was remembering more each day. Just pieces.

"I heard voices in the warehouse," she whispered, leaning closer. "Nathan talking to people who weren't there. Or maybe they were. I screamed until my throat felt packed with glass. The concrete swallowed it. And when he breathed again, I wanted to save the lives he took. But I couldn't."

Kaitlyn. Trevor. Zane. Becca. William.

Benji.

Her hand found mine—papery, cold, twisted.

"Forgive me," she choked. "I brought predators into our house. I saw how they looked at you. I chose my own hunger over my daughter. I let the filth in."

I thought of years of silence. Of *don't be dramatic* echoing through hallways while I unraveled.

"You let him win long before the cellar, Nicole... Mom," I said quietly.

"I know."

She reached into a canvas bag and pulled out something wrapped in faded blue flannel.

"The FBI found this in the barn when they found me. I don't know why he kept it."

She unwrapped a small wooden music box—dark, water-stained, hinges crusted orange with rust. It looked like something unearthed.

"It belonged to his mother," she whispered. "He played it when the voices got loud. Said it made them quiet. That's why he whistled."

She turned the stiff crank.

The gears ground loudly in the still room.

Then the melody began—tinny, uneven, several notes missing. Limping. Predatory.

Hush, little baby, don't say a word...

The tune hung in the air like dust.

"He told me to give it to you," she said. "Said you'd remember. That it was the only thing you truly shared."

The melody looped, circling like a trap tightening.

Mama's gonna buy you a mockingbird...

I looked at the box. At my mother—broken, hollow, still carrying his messages from behind reinforced glass.

I didn't forgive her. I didn't feel closure. I felt the weight of survival.

I stood while the lullaby kept turning and put Shadow on her lap.

"Keep it, Nicole," I said. My voice was steady now. "I don't need a mockingbird. I already learned to sing for myself."

I walked out without looking back. Through magnetic locks. Past lavender and bread. Into the thick, honest heat of Austin.

Asher leaned against the truck, sunglasses on, solid in a world that had fractured. He read my face and said nothing. Just opened the door.

We pulled onto the highway. I looked in the visor mirror, at the faint scars on my face my mother inflicted, another reminder that I would never get rid of the pain. It would always be there, but I needed to find a way to heal—one way or another.

In the quiet hum of tires against asphalt, I could still hear it—the faint winding down of tinny notes in my head.

Hush.

The monster was caged. My mother was contained.

The song would never disappear.

But it didn't own my voice anymore.

Gratitude

First and always, to my husband, David.
You are the steady strength behind every late night and early morning. Thank you for believing in me when the words wouldn't come, for listening to plot spirals, and for reminding me why I began when the journey felt heavy. This dream is ours. I could not do this without your love and unwavering support.

To my children—
You are my why. Thank you for sharing your mom with imaginary worlds and fictional chaos. Your laughter and encouragement fuel more of these pages than you know. Every story carries a piece of you.

To my parents—
Thank you for teaching me resilience, hard work, and the courage to chase something bigger than fear. Your belief in me has shaped the foundation I stand on today.

This has been a wonderful journey—filled with growth and moments that once felt impossible. I'm endlessly grateful to walk it surrounded by people who lift me up and refuse to let me quit.

And finally, to those I've grown to love and now call friends—Tina S Transformation, J.D. Setzer, Jim Donohue, Danielle Lundquist, Dallin and Bri Johnson, Lori Whittle, Lisa Kilburn, Larke Gonzalez... the list continues to grow, which is one of my greatest blessings. Thank you for your support and for walking beside me.

I am so blessed.
— Kirsten Gale

About the author

Kirsten Gale is a psychological-thriller and dark-fiction author who writes emotionally raw stories exploring trauma, obsession, love, and survival. She became a published author in July 2025, but has been writing since high school, drawn to the darker edges of human nature and the truths people try to bury.

A mom of four, Kirsten balances family life with creativity, chaos, and an unfiltered sense of humor. Kirsten Gale writes dark, emotionally driven fiction that lingers long after the final page. Her stories dig into grief, buried secrets, and the thin line between survival and surrender. She's drawn to fractured characters and moments of quiet devastation—the kind that change people forever.

She is active in the indie author community, supporting and collaborating with fellow writers. Kirsten lives in Colorado, where stark landscapes and wide skies mirror the tension and contrast found in her work.

Learn more at www.authorkirstengale.com